The Last Prophecy
© 2006 Jennie Andrus

Hours before being murdered Maddy gives her last prophecy—her sister's death and salvation.

The MacElwain sisters had always been different. In search of a "normal" life, Lottie did her best to ignore her crazy sister, until Maddy predicts Lottie's death. Suddenly Maddy is dead and Lottie has a very short shelf life and, according to Maddy, she's going to need to find a moose if she wants to survive. Unfortunately, moose aren't too plentiful in downtown Toronto.

Not willing to trust her life to an animal, Lottie runs to the shores of Newfoundland, where danger, love and acceptance wait for her to fulfill the last prophecy of Mad Maddy MacElwain

Ritual Love
© *2006 Kate Davies*

A lost woman. A hunted man. On a night of forbidden rituals, the veil between past and present lifts—and their worlds will never be the same.

Scientist Moira Sinclair doesn't believe in magic. Or at least she hasn't since childhood. She's only come to Iona in remembrance of her long-deceased grandmother, the last person who encouraged her fanciful side. But now she's stumbled onto a secret druid ritual—and into another time.

Aedan Ap Crannog is furious to discover an outsider spying on their sacred, banned Samhain rites. With her strange garb and stranger mannerisms, Moira is unlike any woman he's ever known. But she could cause trouble for him and the people who follow him in the ancient ways. To prevent her from sounding the alarm, he takes her captive, hiding her in the labyrinth of caves along the far shore.

Despite their differences, sparks burn between them as brightly as the Samhain bonfire. Now captive and captor must find a way to bridge the centuries before the magic disappears with the dawn…

Babe in Woods
© 2006 Lorelei James

Animal attraction takes on a whole new meaning…

Manhattanite Lacy Buchanan is out to prove she's a tough cookie by signing up for a survivalist hiking trip in Wyoming's Bighorn Mountains. The last thing she expected was to get lost, forcing her to spend the rest of the hike alone with surly, too-sexy mountain man, Becker, who blames her entirely for their predicament. After Becker saves her from a rattlesnake, and gently calms her fears, Lacy feels lucky to be in his experienced hands.

But Sam Becker isn't really a hiking expert. He's strictly the moneyman in Back To Nature Guided Hiking Tours and a last minute, temporary fill-in guide. He can't believe his bad luck when his reluctant charge—a mouthy, but hot, blonde bombshell—pulverizes their only compass, destroying their chances of following the coordinates to base camp. Yet something about Lacy's trusting nature makes him want fulfill her idea he's her rugged hero.

As Sam and Lacy attempt to find a way out of the treacherous mountain passes, their natural instincts take them…farther away from civilized behavior and straight into the mating calls of the wild.

A Touch of Magic
© 2006 Cassandra Kane

A race against time to save a planet—will the price be too heavy to pay?

Captain Tirana Albasta leads the last scouting mission to mystery planet Samhain, which has already swallowed two previous missions and a starship full of New Wiccan colonists, Lalith's People.

Determined to keep the planet from UA Special Forces' harsh military control, Tirana finds much more than she expected. For the descendants of Lalith's People have split into two separate societies—the anti-magic Priests and the magical True People—and she has just been caught in the crossfire.

Complicating matters is her attraction to Loren, the broodingly handsome True People witch who ignites passions she has never before experienced, and who just might make leaving Samhain impossible in more ways than one…

A Warrior's Witch
© *2006 Mackenzie McKade*

Legacy bonds them—betrayal will test them—but, love and a little bit of magic will keep them together.

Gifted with both Berserka and Wicce heritage, Sabine wonders which legacy will determine her fate. A path of freedom and independence? Or will the Berserka curse tie her to one man, not of her choosing?

After his father's death, Conall returns to Scotland to take his rightful place as chieftain. Fate steps in and unleashes his hot-blooded lust on one obstinate woman resolved on defying destiny.

A forced marriage binds them. Desire and their animalistic nature draw them together. But someone is threatening to destroy the fiery love growing between them. Salt in the wine has everyone looking askew at Sabine, including her husband. A few more incidents set the clan on edge, but when a child is injured they demand justice.

When the clan demands Sabine's death, Conall must choose between family and the woman he loves.

Night Music
© 2006 Charlene Teglia

When death marked her, he offered her rebirth…

Meghan Davies has been living a dream as the bass player for the all-female hit rock band, The Sirens. But the dream becomes a nightmare with the discovery that cancer, undetected and now too far gone, heralds the end of everything.

Romney Kearns has been watching the sharp-tongued, flame haired woman from afar, wanting, but never approaching because he can offer her nothing but death.

When he discovers that death already has her marked, he sets out on All Hallow's Eve to seduce her, claim her, and make her willing to accept his dark offer. An alternative. Not life as she's known it, but a kind of rebirth. Eternity with him and immortality for her to make night music.

Beginnings:
A Samhain Anthology

Jennie Andrus
Kate Davies
Lorelei James
Cassandra Kane
Mackenzie McKade
Charlene Teglia

A Samhain Publishing, Ltd. publication.

Samhain Publishing, Ltd.
2932 Ross Clark Circle, #384
Dothan, AL 36301
www.samhainpublishing.com

First Samhain Publishing, Ltd. Print publication: November 2006

The Last Prophecy

Jennie Andrus

Dedication

For mum, fellow lover of all things moose.

And with thanks to Kim Knox and Pollyanna Williamson for the moose T-shirt ideas.

Chapter One

With trembling fingers, I picked up the portable phone and greeted the man who planned to kill me on Halloween. Despite the shaky hands, I wasn't freaking out. Much. I'd already known what was coming before the calls started up.

My crazy sister predicted it.

I cradled the phone against my face and listened to the rapid, gasping breaths. "Are you just about done?" I asked, my voice as bland and bored as I could make it while my heart raced out of control.

His breath rasped with excitement and a tremor of fear rippled over my body from head to toe. "What do you want, asshole?"

"You know what I want." The voice was cold, unnatural. Not human. Obviously some kind of electronic device made it seem that way but knowing that didn't make it any less creepy.

"You're crazy." Insulting a madman probably wasn't smart, but I'd figured out that sarcasm and sniping just rolled off him.

"I like your nightgown. Very—patriotic."

My heart leapt up to my throat as I looked down at the battered jersey I wore—Canadian Olympic hockey jersey. Oh God!

"Why can't you just leave me alone?" I cried, all trace of boredom vanishing from my voice. Could he really see me? Was it a bluff? My gaze darted to every cover, to the heavily curtained windows. I wanted to puke.

"You know I can't do that. I need you. I need your power."

"I don't have any fucking power! I've told you that."

"Don't lie to me, Lottie. I know things now, just like Maddy knew things because I took her power when I bathed in her blood. Just like I'll bathe in your blood. You can't escape from me. I'll always know how to find you now."

Nausea rolled in my stomach and tears trailed down my cheeks. "You're crazy." If he'd been there at that moment I'd have killed him, no regrets, for the glee in his voice when he spoke of her.

"You said that about your sister, too." He paused and I heard his breathing increase to harsh panting. "You will be mine, Lottie."

It was crazy of me to be packing a bag and booking a flight out of the province because of some nonsense my sister had spouted at me.

Normally I'm not a coward. I've been in my share of fights. How could I not with a baby sister who everyone referred to as "Mad" Maddy? Yeah, I figured she was a bit of a crackpot, but I wasn't going to let others call her that. That was my job and I broke quite a few noses in my youth to keep it my exclusive right.

And now, thanks to a madman, I'd never have the chance to tease her again. Tears threatened to spill free as I remembered our last night together.

Two weeks ago she'd dragged me out to dinner to meet the latest in a long string of freakazoid boyfriends. Trust me, most of them actually believed they were living in the world of *Buffy the Vampire Slayer*. But I went, and imagine my surprise to find Maddy with a guy who looked…normal. No black cape, no filed-down incisors, not a single extra hole in his face.

Will had looked like he'd stepped right out of the nearest office building. Seeing my sister with a guy whose hair was neatly trimmed, wearing a clean shirt and—oh my God!—tie, I honestly thought I'd gone into a coma. It had to be some kind of trick.

Through dinner Will spoke with surprising eloquence on a range of topics but not once did conversation turn to anything supernatural. He didn't invite me to join a "Spiritual Love Raising"—a.k.a. an orgy.

For the first time in my life I actually enjoyed an evening with my kooky sister.

Then she'd gone into psycho-mode and blew the whole thing by making one of her crazy-assed prophecies.

He will follow you in darkness with murder in his mind

On Halloween he will take his chance to steal your power

In searching for sanctuary, you will find love,

To save yourself, accept the moose and accept yourself.

The truth of it is I never doubted my sister had some kind of gift. She'd been right too many times. *A chicken will lead you to treasure,* she'd told our mother, and sure enough, mom had found her wedding ring under the fridge while picking up the frozen chicken that had fallen from the freezer. I wish I'd had the chance to say that to Maddy—I wish I'd told her, just once, that I believed in her.

I'd teased her almost all our lives, and not once had I given her my support. It wasn't that I never took her seriously, because I did. The problem had always been that her predictions were just so unbelievable. I tossed a sweater into my backpack and let the guilt burn in my stomach for every time I'd wished for a normal sister.

Then again, I wasn't exactly normal either, but it would take some pretty nasty torture to get me to admit it out loud.

If only Maddy had had a vision about herself, because that night, after we had dinner, she'd been murdered.

Will had dropped her off and gone home because he had an early morning meeting. Two hours later, a neighbor noticed Maddy's apartment door open and peeked in. Thank God for nosy neighbors. The police said it looked like a ritualistic sacrifice, then made comments about not being surprised. Maddy had tried to help them on a few cases, so they knew all about her—uniqueness.

When the calls began, I naturally called the police who, naturally speculated that perhaps craziness ran in the family. The cop who'd made the remark left my apartment with a broken nose and we danced around formal charges for a few days. After that there were mutters about mental hospitals and straitjackets so I figured it would be smarter to deal with the situation on my own.

No, I'm not normally a coward, but I was scared enough to run. Maddy said I had to accept a moose if I wanted to survive, and the chances of one running around Kensington Market, or anywhere in Toronto for that matter,

15

were pretty low. There were only three days to Halloween and I didn't want to take any chances. I was pretty happy living, thank you very much.

Besides, the whole nightgown thing freaked me out way past my breaking point.

My parents had owned a cottage in Newfoundland. When they died it came to Maddy and I and somehow we never got around putting it up for sale. It would be easier to go north, to Muskoka or something, but I wanted more distance. I'd always hated going east, not because I didn't like the place. Newfoundland is beautiful, the town itself charming and full of the friendly people. The problem lay in the town's name—Dildo, Newfoundland. I'd always wanted to be a normal kid; instead I was the kid with weird parents, a loony sister and a cottage in Dildo.

So, with mixed feelings, I packed some necessities, booked a flight and was just on my way out the door when the phone rang.

It was only five, not anywhere near dark yet. I doubted it could be *him*. Still, my heart thudded painfully at the sound.

"Hello?"

"Lottie? Hi. It's Will."

I groaned inwardly, but said, "Hi, Will. What's up?"

"I was wondering if you wanted to get together for drinks tonight."

I should have known. It had been two days since he'd called, wanting me to hold his hand while he cried into a martini. "I'm really sorry, but this isn't a good time. I—"

"Lottie, I really need to talk to someone." I gritted my teeth and resisted the urge to bang my head against the wall. "I miss her, you know? Maddy was everything to me and I just don't think I can go on without her."

I wish I could say I'm the kind of person who could tell him to bugger off. He'd known her a few weeks and I'd known her my whole life. He wanted pity from me when I'd just lost the last of my family? Instead, I fell back on a lifetime of not rocking the boat, and said, "Will, I know you cared for my sister, but she wouldn't want you to do this to yourself."

"Please, Lottie, just one drink?"

My eyes rolled back in annoyance. "I'm on my way to the airport. I'm running late as it is. I'm really sorry."

He laughed, a barking, forced kind of laugh. "The airport? Please tell me you aren't taking Maddy's prediction seriously. I mean, I loved your sister, but you can't possibly believe someone is going to kill you on Halloween."

"Of course not," I lied.

"Then where are you going?"

I hesitated. "Just away for some quiet. I need some time to mourn my sister." At least that was the truth.

"Oh, of course." His tone changed, became distant and cold. "Well, okay then, maybe we can get together when you get back."

"Definitely. We can have lunch." I hung up the phone and rolled my eyes. Dear God, who knew a man could be so much like a nagging mother? Sheesh. If there were a choice between a strong and competent vampire wannabe and Will, I'd take the vamp any day.

I took one last look around my apartment and stepped out, locking the door behind me. Prophecy or no prophecy, I'd find a way to get out of this situation, with or without the moose. And the man my sister had predicted? Well, I decided to reserve judgment on that for now.

Chapter Two

By the time the plane landed in St. John's, my eyes were gritty and sore. At some point I must have fallen asleep, because there was a crusty kind of feeling on my cheek where I'd drooled on myself.

Despite all that, I felt great. It's an unbelievable feeling to know you can walk somewhere without feeling you're about to get a knife in the back.

With a bounce in my step I found the car rental kiosk and flirted with the gray-haired man behind the counter. After signing away most of the remaining credit on my Visa, I bought a map and a bag of necessities (chips, pop and a paperback novel) and headed out to pick up my vehicle.

Cool fall air blew around me when I stepped out the doors into the night. I drew in a deep breath and imagined I could taste the tang of the sea over the airport smells of oil and tarmac. The blue, knee-length sweater I wore billowed in the breeze. I stood there just outside the door, simply breathing, for a good ten minutes.

It wasn't until I was in the dimly lit parkade that I felt the hairs on the back of my neck rise. I stopped, spun around and saw nothing but the shadows cast by parked sedans and minivans.

"You're being stupid," I whispered to myself. There was no way he could have followed me here. I hadn't told anyone where I was going, mostly because there wasn't anyone to tell. My parents had died in a car crash two years ago. All the friends I'd had at the hospital were the kind of friends you talked to at work, but didn't invite out for drinks after shift. Hell, I doubted any of them even noticed I'd quit two weeks ago. Being a trauma nurse didn't offer much time to contemplate the whereabouts of your co-workers.

Still the feeling would not go away. My skin itched. *Probably a janitor*, I told myself, and forced my legs to keep moving.

I found my car, a putrid green hatchback that made me question the wisdom of asking for the cheapest car on the lot. With a wince I unlocked the door and threw my lumpy backpack into the backseat. Green was so not my color.

The airport was about ten kilometers from St. John's, but I wasn't heading into the city anyway. The cottage was in a small town on the southern coast, about an hour and a half away. Actually it wasn't a cottage at all, in the way we think of them in Ontario. It wasn't on a lake, or any waterfront for that matter, just a small house with a view of the ocean (if you squinted through the trees while standing on the roof) that my parents had bought because real estate was so cheap there.

Two weeks of restless sleep, followed by a late flight, didn't exactly make me into the most competent of drivers. After forty-five minutes, I'd hit the shoulder about ten times and spilled half my pop in my lap. I was crashing, long past the point where a cup of coffee would help—even if there were any Tim Horton's out in the middle of nowhere. The car didn't come equipped with a radio of course, so I made do by sticking my head out the window like a golden retriever.

By the time I hit the outskirts of Dildo, I was holding one eye open with my left hand and driving with my right. Even snickering about the name of my destination wasn't helping me stay awake, which is really saying something. I know it's immature of me. Dildos are the pegs used to brace oars to a dory for rowing, but I was too tired to be thinking like an adult.

Maddy would be giggling right now. She'd always thought it was cool that we had a cottage here, and she told *everybody* all about it every chance she got. The only thing that kept our vacations here from falling into the realms of hell was that we were never here long enough for people to realize what a screwed up family we were.

As my eyes started to blur with exhaustion, I made a pact with whichever deity would listen—let me survive until November first and I'd never make another crack about Dildo again.

And that was when the moose stepped onto the highway.

"Son of a—" I swerved the car, aiming for the ditch. It would be just my luck to kill the damned moose that I was supposed to accept if I wanted to live. I'm pretty sure I was still giggling about how absurd that thought was, when I hit the tree and slipped into unconsciousness.

Chapter Three

Warm callus-roughened hands slipped up my body. The smell of forest and warm spices drifted across my face. My skin tingled and I arched my back, hungry for more. Large fingers skimmed the lower curve of one breast, slid higher to cup me.

When those hands tweaked my nipples I realized I wasn't dreaming.

Warm brown eyes peered down at me and I shrieked, then drew back and popped the guy in the nose.

"Bugger me!" The man stumbled back, raising his hands to his face, and I realized he was huge. Not obese, but one of those tall and burly guys who could give the hulk a run for his money.

I scrambled up, realized I'd been laying on what could possible be the ugliest couch in the known universe, and looked around for the door.

"What the hell d'ya do that for?"

"You were feeling me up!"

"I was checking for injuries. There's blood on your shirt."

I looked down and winced. A large stain spread across the white shirt and the inside of my sweater—my favorite sweater. My head snapped back up. "And you thought you'd pinch my nipples to see if they squirted?"

In the odd light cast from three hideous lamps, I watched his cheeks turn red, and he sighed dramatically—melodramatically. "It was an accident. You've got great breasts by the way." The boyish grin that split his face was so unexpected I couldn't help but giggle. Okay, so there was a slim chance this guy was my stalker, but I wouldn't have bet money on it. He was too boyishly charming, despite being in his late twenties. I'd always thought stalkers were supposed to be nondescript, though I have to admit I'm not an expert. This was my first experience with one.

"What's your name?" I asked.

"Perry Sullivan. I pulled you from your car and brought you to my home."

I looked around the room and cringed. It was like some sort of bad hippie flashback—orange shag carpet and brown and orange paisley wallpaper for God's sake.

"No offense, but this room is beyond ugly." The minute the words were out I slapped my hand to my mouth. "Shit, I'm sorry. I don't know what's wrong with me."

He laughed. "Don't be sorry. Everyone in town tells me the same thing. I'm told I'm perverse and lack taste, but I prefer to think I'm unique."

Unique? He was a huge bear of a man dressed in black jeans and a white T-shirt bearing the slogan "Of Moose and Men". His hair was a little too long, his chin had more than a five o'clock shadow but less than a beard and he was standing barefoot in a house that looked like a drug-induced hallucination. Unique would be a good description. I would have said comfortably eccentric and sexy as hell. Not out loud though. I'd already made one blunder.

"Well, thanks for getting me out of the car. How bad was the damage?"

"You'll need a new radiator, and the front end is a little crunched, but it could have been worse." His eyes dropped to the drying blood on my shirt. "Are you sure you aren't hurt?"

The truth was, I probably had been bleeding. I said before that I wasn't exactly normal, and this was the reason why. I heal freakishly fast and I can heal other people, too. When I worked in the ER I used the gift to help people who, by rights, should have died. Just a touch, just enough to keep them alive so the doctors could succeed. I'd always been careful about it, never doing more than necessary so people didn't ask questions.

Normally I could bluff my way out of situations like this, but Perry, Mr. Good Samaritan had already felt me up and knew I didn't have any visible injuries. I bit my lip. "Um, I had a bloody nose just before I crashed."

I'm a horrible liar, and when I panic it gets even worse. That whopper sounded pathetically obvious, almost cartoonishly obvious. If I'd had a nosebleed, there'd be dried blood on my face and my hands. I snuck a quick look and saw nothing on my fingers but a slight brown streak from the pop I'd spilled earlier.

His eyebrows rose. I waited for him to say something but he just shrugged and stuffed his hands into his pockets. "Well, then." He rocked back

21

on his heels. "Is there someone you'd like to call? I'm guessing you're visiting out here? If you tell me it's a man, you'll break my heart." He winked at me, and grinned crookedly, reminding me of Harrison Ford.

I rolled my eyes, but couldn't stop the surge of warmth from swirling in my stomach at his playful flirting. "I'm heading to my parents' cottage. It's on Chime Street."

Perry laughed. "Well then, darlin', it looks like we're neighbors."

"Neighbors?"

"Yep, there's only one house on this street owned by tourists and it's right next door." He looked pretty pleased about the news. "Which sister are you? I bet you're the crazy one right?"

Lovely. A glimmer of memory ticked my brain and I groaned. Perry Sullivan, object of my youthful fantasies until Maddy had stepped in and done her psychic act. Only two people out here knew about Maddy's visions. Figured I'd find one of them right away. Like an elastic band that had been slowly stretching for weeks, my temper finally reached the breaking point.

"No, that was my sister, and she wasn't crazy, she was different. I'd think you, of all people would appreciate that Mr. Unique. Now if you don't mind, I have to go get some sleep so I can find the damned moose that's supposed to save my life!"

He just stared at me for a minute, his left eyebrow raised and his mouth slack, before he shook his head. "Oh right, well, my mistake then. You're obviously not crazy at all."

The sarcasm in his voice was like a bucket of cold water dumped over my head. I hated it when I lost it like that. It had been a long time since I'd lost my temper, but I suppose I deserved to let off a little steam. I dropped heavily onto the couch behind me and sighed.

"Sorry. Maybe I am going a little nuts. I've had a crappy couple weeks."

"It's Lottie right? Want to talk about it?"

Did I? I looked up into Perry's soft brown eyes and felt the strangest urge to jump into his arms and tell him all my problems.

"My sister was killed two weeks ago."

He cursed and I saw his cheeks turn pink beneath the dark stubble. "I'm sorry. I shouldn't have said what I did."

"It's okay. You couldn't have known. Besides, it's not like I haven't heard worse."

"I remember when she told my father she'd had a vision about me driving Lisa Mullens out to that hotel in St. Johns. Blew all my well-made plans and I never even got out of town."

I frowned. "I remember that. Your dad got really mad. Weren't you twenty-two or something?" I'd always found that weird. My parents had been pretty lenient when it came to sex so Maddy and I had thought it strange that our neighbor's father showed up to ream him for getting it on with a girl. Obviously things were vastly different in Newfoundland.

"Something like that."

"You could have just told your dad to mind his own business."

His eyebrows drew together in a frown. "I could have, but he was right. It was stupid and dangerous."

My confusion must have shown, because he shrugged and looked away. "According to your sister, I would have gotten Lisa pregnant if we'd gone."

Okay, that made a bit more sense. Still, it was weird for his father to go all ape-shit over it when he couldn't possibly have known Maddy really could predict the future like that. The man had been out of his mind with anger and I could recall him making threats that involved the use of a sharp knife against his son's privates.

"How did your sister die?" His voice was soft and inviting. Tears pricked my eyes and I had to bite my lip to keep them from spilling out.

"I—I don't think I can talk about it." Something told me if I told him one thing my mouth would just keep on spilling the details of the last two weeks. My head pounded. I knew there were things I should probably do, like call the rental agency and report that I'd crashed the car, but I was too tired to think. All I wanted was a bed. Everything else could wait until tomorrow.

Chapter Four

It hadn't occurred to me there would be no power in the house. My parents had hired a woman to come in and clean before our trips out, but I hadn't thought to do the same. Thick cobwebs reflected the glow of Perry's flashlight. I also hadn't thought to call the electric company to have the power turned back on.

No power, no water, no heat. Lovely.

What furniture there was looked dull with layers of dust. The thought of cleaning all this brought a hard lump to my stomach. Thank God my mother hadn't been into knick-knacks and dust collectors. The furniture had all come from garage sales so it was an eclectic collection of old-lady cast-offs and cottage-style pine.

I shuddered and tossed my bag onto the couch, raising a cloud of dust into the gloomy light cast by Perry's flashlight.

"You sure you want to stay here? I have a king-size bed you could share."

I rolled my eyes and stepped forward, determined to ignore the swirl of heat his words sent through my stomach. "Do you always come on to women like this?"

"Only the pretty ones. Seriously, you can't stay here tonight, it's gross."

That was certainly true, but I wasn't going to hop into bed with a stranger to avoid dust bunnies. I had enough on my mind without tossing in an affair with a sexy neighbor. *But Maddy did say you'd find love.* I snorted at the nagging little voice. *Love doesn't mean getting busy with the first guy who makes a pass.*

And now I was talking to myself. Lovely.

"I'll be fine. It's not as bad as camping."

He sighed and handed me the flashlight. "I'll come check on you in the morning. I'll call about getting your power hooked up too, and pick you up some groceries."

"You don't have to do that."

He tipped my chin up with one finger and grinned crookedly. "It's all part of the rescue package."

"And what do you normally charge for hero services?" Whoa! Was that my voice sounding all breathless and soft? Was I flirting?

"That's negotiable. We'll discuss terms when you're not ready to collapse onto the floor."

He leaned down and pressed his lips softly to mine. While I was still struggling to catch my breath, he turned and left. I thought I heard him curse as he let himself out the door, but I couldn't be sure. I was too busy trying not to collapse onto the floor.

At first I didn't know where I was, or why I was waking up in the middle of the night. The dregs of a dream drifted away, leaving me with tingly skin and a longing for a slightly scruffy man with eyes like melted chocolate. Weird.

Then I breathed in the stale scent of the linens under me, sneezed violently and it all came back.

I was in Newfoundland.

With a groan, I rolled over and pressed the light on my watch. It took me a minute to realize I'd slept straight through the day and into the following night.

It was the night before Halloween. Well technically it was early Halloween morning here, but back in Ontario it was still just a bit before D-day.

My heart thumped rapidly against my ribs. For the first time I wondered what the heck I'd been thinking. Running away wasn't going to solve my problems. Sure maybe the killer wouldn't find me in time for Halloween. Did that mean he'd give up? No. The minute I returned to Toronto he'd be after me again.

All I'd done was delay the inevitable.

But Maddy was never wrong. If she said he'd get me on Halloween, he'd get me on Halloween. Had I given myself a year's respite or was I deluding myself about being safe here? My head was starting to spin with possibilities, consequences and outcomes, which, when I forced myself to push it aside, didn't make sense. None of her predictions had ever been complicated. It was just "this is going to happen" then it happened.

I was probably over-thinking the whole thing.

I crawled out from the dingy blanket and ran my fingers through my hair. Gross. The amount of dust collected there made each strand feel about an inch thick. I could feel my pores clogging up and there was that strange tickly feeling on my back like I had spiders skittering around under my shirt.

To my surprise, the bathroom light came on when I flicked the switch. With a mental note to thank Perry when I saw him again, I turned on the shower and watched, fascinated, as the avocado green tub swirled with brown. More than dirt washed down the drain. Little bugs scrambled for safety, but in the end lost the war against the battering water. I felt a little guilty about it. I had no problem with bugs as long as they weren't in my house. I'm one of those people who usually scoops up spiders and takes them outside rather than squishing them with a magazine.

Half an hour later I was clean, still dripping wet and wandering around the house naked because I'd realized too late there would be no clean towels.

True to his word, Perry had come in while I'd slept and stocked the fridge. His choices offered an interesting insight to the man. Yogurt, fresh fruit and no-fat milk. Yeesh. There were eggs, the omega-3 kind that were more expensive but promised added health benefits, a bag of baby carrots, some broccoli and green peppers. A white brick-like thing caught my eye. Tofu? Dear God, my big burly neighbor was a vegetarian? Worse, there was not a single bite of chocolate to be found.

Well, nobody was perfect.

A floorboard creaked softly and I froze, my naked butt still hanging out of the refrigerator, and beautifully backlit by the little light that hadn't worked last time we'd been here.

"Perry?" I whispered.

No answer.

Letting the door shut quietly I moved to the front door. Locked. How had Perry gotten in with the food?

Another creak, unmistakably a footstep this time. Blood pounded in my ears. The stalker had found me.

I ran.

The screen door flew open with a screech of stiff hinges and banged against the wooden frame like a gunshot in the night. The old deck boards bounced beneath my feet as I thundered across them. At the base of the steps I skidded to a halt.

Under the light of a half-moon, I saw it standing on the lawn. Silver light played over its body, making the massive rack shine like ebony. Overgrown grass caressed its gangly legs.

Holy crap it was big! I mean I know people call them the giants of the forest, but until you're only feet away from one, you just don't appreciate how true that statement really is. Up until now I'd been sure that expecting a moose to save me was foolish. Now, seeing one up close, I could imagine the oddly beautiful creature doing anything. Like Superman and Lassie all rolled into one.

Well if it was suppose to protect me, it could start now. I sprinted across the lawn and ducked behind its bulk. Maybe ducking wasn't necessary since it was tall enough to hide a pro basketball player, but I was going on instinct. Hugging to its side I drew in ragged breaths and waited for my heart rate to slow.

A spicy scent drifted through the cloud of panic fogging my brain. Huh. I'd always thought moose would smell musty, like stagnant water and rotting leaves.

Now, maybe sprinting towards a moose in the dark while completely naked wasn't the smartest thing I'd ever done. In hindsight I'd have to say it ranked up there with some of my dumbest ideas, but I trusted my sister. If she was watching this from wherever it is you go when you die, I hoped she took it as a sign that I really did respect her visions. Then again she was probably laughing her halo off.

The moose regarded me with appalled shock, as if it didn't know what to make of this pale creature clinging to his side. Craning his neck further, he pressed his round nose against my shoulder and I had the feeling I was being sniffed. When its nose brushed against my breast I nudged it away. When that nose went a little further south I gave it an annoyed slap.

"Mind your manners."

With a snort, the animal blew warm, misty breath over my stomach and then moved off into the trees towards Perry's house.

"Well that's just great," I muttered. What the heck was I supposed to do now? Stand out here naked or go back into the house and confront a psycho killer? Not the best options. And darn it, why didn't I pack a bathrobe? At least I wouldn't be out here naked and freezing my—

"Are you out of your flippin' mind?"

Turning, I saw Perry stomping out of the forest. I groaned and considered trying to hide in the tall grass, but I'd never been a coward. I crossed my arms under my breasts and turned to greet my neighbor. "Hi, how's it going?" I called cheerfully, hoping my voice sounded casual, like I walked around naked in the moonlight on a regular basis. I watched Perry's face contort as he worked through his anger and shock. Actually it would have been funny if I hadn't been about to die of embarrassment.

"Don't you know that moose are dangerous animals? How could you just run up to one like that?"

I winced. "I um, have a way with animals."

He threw his hands up into the air. "And everyone thought your sister was crazy! You got a death wish, lady?"

Now would be the perfect time to explain that I was actually trying to get myself out of a death sentence, but I didn't know if he'd believe me. At this exact moment I didn't think my credibility was too high.

I was starting to shiver, and was feeling pretty foolish now that I had time to think about what I'd done. Having someone else point out my stupidity didn't help.

He hesitated a second then shrugged out of his flannel shirt and helped me into it. His hands were warm against my arms. Amused, I watched his hands tremble as he tried to do up the buttons. Finally he looked up at me and ground out something that sounded like "Bugger it" before he kissed me.

His arms drew me in tight and I realized just how strong this man was. Desire licked through my stomach, my breasts began to tingle and I felt a singe of something shoot straight to my loins. I finally understood what real hunger was.

It was like drowning, or jumping out of a plane. It was like nothing I'd ever experienced in my life. The daring dreams from my youth had nothing on the reality of this man's lips on mine.

His hands slipped inside the half-buttoned shirt, hot as flames on my chilled flesh, and just that simple touch on my waist made everything in my body flip over. He didn't push, didn't demand anything, but that simple kiss felt like a branding, a claiming. Dear God!

After a few minutes he shuddered and carefully set me away from him. He drew in a ragged breath and ran his fingers through his hair. My gaze was drawn to his shirt where a moose in a tuxedo stood with a martini in one hoof while pointing a gun with the other. Along the bottom of the graphic it read "The Moose Who Loved Me".

Something clicked in my brain. Maybe I wasn't supposed to trust an actual moose. This was the second shirt I'd seen Perry wear that showed a moose on it. Could Maddy's prediction have been less literal than usual? If that was true then I'd done something very, very stupid tonight.

"I'm sorry. I shouldn't have attacked you like that. I don't know what it is about you, Lottie."

"Maybe you have a thing for crazy women," I commented, still reeling from the combined shock of Perry's kiss and the realization that he may be the key to my survival.

"I don't think you're crazy. You scared the hell out of me and I didn't deal with it very well." As he spoke he dropped his forehead gently against mine and closed his eyes. My heart melted. I loved that forehead-to-forehead thing.

"Oh, I'd have to argue with you there." I grinned.

An animal-like growl came from his throat and he closed the distance between us again, but to my disappointment, he simply pulled me into his arms. "Christ, I need to get a grip before I throw you to the ground and have my way with you a dozen times."

"That doesn't sound so bad," I squeaked against his chest. His laugh rumbled out, making both our bodies tremble.

"You're a fine one, Lottie MacElwain, but it's too dangerous. Go inside and put on some clothes."

"I can't go inside. There's someone in there."

His head came up. "What?"

"You don't think I ran out here naked on purpose did you? I got out of the shower and heard footsteps."

His eyes hardened, grew more intense. "Stay behind me."

29

A little confused about the sudden change in him, I followed, though I didn't expect we'd find anything. Half the town could have tromped into the house bearing welcome-to-the-neighborhood casseroles and I wouldn't have noticed. The intruder would be long gone.

There was nobody in the house. Surprise! We searched every room and found nothing but dust and cobwebs.

"Could have been a mouse," he suggested when we were back in the kitchen scrambling eggs and making toast for a very early breakfast. We'd had to scrub the counters and wash all the dishes. Thankfully, Perry had included dish soap in his grocery shopping.

"It wasn't a mouse," I grumped, slopping milk into the bowl of eggs. "Maybe it was you. How'd you get in here with the food, anyway?"

His head whipped around so fast I heard a soft snap. "I wasn't sneaking around in your house, and I picked the lock when I came with the groceries. You might want to replace the knob. It was pathetically easy to get in here."

I hadn't really thought it was him. He'd have made more noise, as big as he was. "What were you doing wandering around outside in the middle of the night?"

"Couldn't sleep."

The conversation paused for a moment while Perry cooked the eggs and I buttered toast.

"It could have been kids. I've caught a few of them sneaking in here at nights. It'd be easy for them to get in with that lock," he commented, waving the spatula towards the door.

Great, teenagers had been using my parents' cottage as a love shack. "Maybe."

I bit my lip. Should I tell him about the stalker? If I was right about Perry being the "moose" in Maddy's prophecy, it could be important.

I couldn't do it. He already thought I was a few sandwiches short of a picnic and I didn't want to scare him away. Stupid pride. I could almost hear Maddy giving me grief over it—or maybe I just read too many romance novels. The heroine always ends up in trouble when she hides things from the hero.

A few minutes later we were sitting at the newly scrubbed table, drinking coffee and looking at each other through lowered lashes.

While I ate I ran through the words of Maddy's prophecy in my mind. I'd run to sanctuary—check. I'd nearly been killed by a moose on the highway, and then been foolish enough to run towards one, but at least I'd found a moose. I'd found a guy who turned my legs to jelly with one kiss so I was probably well on my way to fulfilling that love bit. Actually, watching the muscles bunch under Perry's T-shirt had me well on my way to sweeping everything off the table and—scratch that. Time to think about sex when all this stalker mess was cleared up.

Maybe coming to Newfoundland hadn't been a mistake.

"Do you have plans for tonight?" Perry's question drew me from my musing. I remembered it was Halloween. Did I have plans?

"No, not really."

"There's a party at the hall. Some folks will be in costume, but it's not required."

I hesitated. Could I go to a party when there was a maniac out to kill me? Did I really want to sit in this house and wait for him to get me?

"Sure, that sounds like fun."

"Great. I'd pick you up, but I'm supposed to be there to set up."

"That's okay, it's not too far to walk." He must have heard the tremor in my voice because his eyes swung to mine and I could see he had questions. The warmth left his eyes and for a second his expression grew hard. I held my breath and waited, knowing if he asked outright I'd tell him everything.

Fortunately, or maybe unfortunately, he remained silent.

Chapter Five

I spent the day scrubbing and washing. Part of me wondered why the heck I bothered when I could be dead by midnight anyway.

The chipper, optimistic side shoved that part of me out of the way and chose to concentrate on happier thoughts—like Perry Sullivan.

I knew nothing about the man other than he seemed to be a health-food junkie, had appalling taste in decor and seemed to rejoice in his status as "weird". As someone who'd spent her whole life trying to be as normal as possible, this fact should have set off alarm bells. Instead it felt comforting. He might possibly be the only man who would accept my own freakish secret.

And the guy was seriously hot and could kiss my pants off.

Dusk was closing in, casting long shadows across my lawn. I shuddered. The hair on the back of my neck prickled. Somewhere, in those deepening shadows, a maniac waited.

I no longer had any doubts that he'd followed me east. Maddy had never been wrong. He was here and, sometime in the next few hours, he'd make his move. I didn't know if I'd made a mistake, not telling Perry everything. Trusting a guy I'd only known for a few days (I couldn't count the times Maddy and I watched him mowing his lawn when we'd been teenagers) wasn't easy and trusting in a wild animal was even harder. Why couldn't Maddy have made things simple, just once?

Why hadn't she seen her own death? Maybe she had. Maybe she'd just not been able to see a way out for herself the way she had for me.

The only thing to do was let things play out, and pray that I hadn't bungled my only hope of surviving.

With that depressing thought ringing in my head, I grabbed my purse and headed for the door. The night air chilled the panic-sweat on my forehead.

Children in costumes were beginning to haunt the streets. From every front step, glowing eyes watched from orange faces. I'd never been good at carving pumpkins, and in the city it wasn't the same anyway, so I hadn't bothered in years. Now I wished I had a few to carve up.

Maddy had always made the best pumpkins. When we were kids, half the neighborhood would come to our house just to see what she'd done. Mine had always looked like the victim of a horrible car crash, but our parents had insisted we each do at least one.

It wasn't far to the hall, but the distance seemed impossible when every few seconds I swore I heard footsteps behind me. Each time I turned to look over my shoulder I saw only a darkening street, and pint-sized ghosts, firemen and princesses.

When I reached the end of Chime, I had two options—take the long and well-lit way down a populated street or duck down the alley behind the pub and get there in half the time.

I've seen enough horror movies to know you never go down a dark alley alone when there's a killer on the loose. The thing was, that alley was pretty short, and there were a lot of people on the other end of it. How bad could it be?

My mind made up, I ducked off the sidewalk and behind the dumpster. The air smelled of stale beer and grease, reminding me of my own days as a waitress during college. It's amazing how the smell of frying food can cling to hair, skin and clothes. If only perfume lasted that long.

A loud clang behind me jerked my heart up to my throat. I spun around and saw the dumpster blocking the back of the lane.

Well crud. I turned and ran harder than I've ever run in my entire life. My high-school gym teacher would have been proud. When I burst out onto the well-lit street I stopped and looked around. I'd more than half-expected this end of the alley to be blocked as well, so I was shocked to find myself surrounded by giggling ghosts, firemen and princesses all of whom were pointing at the scaredy-cat grownup.

Nothing like the taunting of adolescents to send your ego plummeting.

With my dignity in tatters, I walked away, letting their laughter fade into the distance.

33

Fiddle music drifted out the doors of the hall, a large wooden building used for everything from weddings to poker night. I grinned and quickened my step. The lights were dim and the air sharp with the scents of cinnamon and burning candles. Only a few people stood in the room and of those, only three were in costume. A shepherdess, a leprechaun and a moose.

I laughed. Even if his size hadn't given him away, I'd have known it was Perry behind that fake fur. I don't know why, but somehow I knew it was so like him to dress up. Back home you hardly ever saw a grown man get into the Halloween spirit, unless you counted some of Maddy's ex-boyfriends, but to them, every day was Halloween. I wondered if any of them would be dressed in normal clothes tonight, leaving off their black leather pants and silk capes.

The moose had spotted me and I could feel the goofy grin on my face as he headed my way.

"Nice costume."

His laugh was muffled, but I could see his eyes twinkling through the moose's mouth. "How'd you know it was me?"

"Lucky guess." A shriek pierced the air and I jumped. My heart thudded erratically as I looked behind me.

"Just one of the trick or treaters." Perry's gaze held mine for several long seconds. "Are you going to tell me what's wrong?"

"I don't know what you mean." Another pathetically obvious lie.

"You're hiding something, and you're scared."

"I had a bit of a scare on the way here. Just some kids playing tricks. It's nothing."

Again he studied me, and it was impossible to read his expression in the shadows of the stuffed moose nose. When he leaned forward and whispered, "After the party we'll talk," I knew he didn't believe me. Not that I blamed him. I was a really rotten liar. What's more, for those seconds when his gaze had bored into mine, he'd again seemed like a completely different person than the playful charmer I knew. It reminded me of something, I just couldn't figure out what.

A short man with fake vampire teeth came up and slapped Perry lightly on the back. "Thith the girl you menthoned?"

Perry sighed and turned to the man. "Take out the teeth, Minkey. You're spitting all over the place."

The man grinned and spit the plastic teeth into his hand. He looked to be in his forties, with thinning blond hair and mischievous blue eyes. Other than the teeth he wore jeans and a flannel shirt. Either the teeth were the extent of his costume or he was portraying a very different kind of vampire than you normally read about.

"Sorry about that. I think they're meant for kids. Been a bitch to keep them in place. Now, is this little lady the one who plowed that really ugly car into a tree?"

I sighed. "Yeah, that's me. It's a rental. On the other hand, I managed to miss the moose so it could have been worse."

Minkey's eyes popped, and he cast a curious glance up at Perry.

"Uh, right, could have been worse." He looked distinctly uncomfortable and clicked the plastic teeth together. "Glad to hear it was a rental, otherwise I'd have wondered if you had horrible taste like the big guy here. Nobody in their right mind would buy a car that color," Minkey joked. "I'll have it right as rain in a few days, don't you worry."

"Minkey's the best mechanic in the county," Perry added.

It occurred to me that I'd forgotten to deal with the car thing. I frowned. "I should have called the rental agency about the accident, shouldn't I have? Don't they usually deal with stuff like this?"

"Already done. Don't worry."

I looked at Perry and blinked. "You called them?"

"Well sure he did. As first officer on the scene, it's his job to take care of details."

First officer? "You're a cop?" A chill ran down my spine that had nothing to do with the breeze blowing in the door. Cops were dangerous.

"Well shit, Perry. You didn't tell her what you do for a living?"

"It hasn't come up. Would you excuse us, Mink?" Without waiting for an answer, Perry guided me away to the bar. A lump had formed in my throat.

Perry was a cop. The thought kept bouncing around in my brain like a pinball. I'd told him Maddy had been killed. I knew it would be easy for him to get information about the case from the police in Toronto, and if he had talked to the metro police, had they told him I was crazy? Hell, if he'd talked to the right cop he'd have heard more than that. Technically I'd assaulted an

35

officer, though in my defense he'd been a jerk. The charges had been dropped, but still.

He shoved a beer into my hands and studied me through the mouth hole in his mask. "You got a problem with the police I should know about?"

"Of course not." My response was a little too quick and forceful. His eyes narrowed.

"Look, Lottie, I know something's up. Tonight we'll talk and you're going to tell me everything."

I nodded and took a sip of my beer to avoid meeting his eyes. Maybe I should have told him earlier. Trust the moose. As he led me away to meet the other partygoers, I wondered if maybe I'd screwed up, and if that were true, I wouldn't be around to tell Perry anything.

Chapter Six

In the next hour the room swelled with people. A long table had appeared near the bar, and with each new guest more treats were added until it threatened to collapse under the weight. I'd met more people than I could keep track of, and I'd noted more than one woman giving me dirty looks because Perry hadn't left my side once.

I wasn't sure what to make of Perry tonight. One minute he was looking at me as if he'd like to toss me over his shoulder and carry me off to his cave, and the next he looked at me with something resembling regret.

Maybe he hadn't looked into the events in Ontario. I had the feeling he thought I was on the run from the law, instead of some imaginary stalker, which is what he'd have been told if he'd called Toronto. It wasn't so much anything he said, just a feeling that he was struggling with something.

"And who is this young lady?" An older man stepped up beside us. My first impression was of a bear, but he lacked the predatory features one would associate with that animal. The man was huge, and I realized he must be Perry's father. I vaguely recognized him from the past and he hadn't changed much—a stern-looking man with close-cut brown hair just graying at the temples.

"Lottie, this is my dad, Dave Sullivan. Dad, this is Lottie MacElwain. I'm sure you remember her and her family. They own the cottage next door to me and spent summers here a while back."

The man's eyebrows rose. "Is that so?" His brown eyes settled on my face for a long minute then shifted to study his son's. "Perhaps she'd give us a minute to talk. I've a question to ask of you."

I nodded and watched them walk away to the bar. Bodies drifted in and out of my field of view, keeping me from seeing what was going on. I shrugged and turned to look around the room. Somehow I'd forgotten how friendly and welcoming people were here.

As I watched a group of balding men do a jig I let my mind wander. Maddy would have loved this. A lump formed in my throat at the thought of never seeing her again. There are always regrets when someone dies. I wish I'd spent more time, wish I'd told them, wish I'd repaid that money—the list went on.

I'd been near enough grieving families at work to know how it worked, and to know that when the loved one was taken from them violently, purposefully, the need for revenge and justice overwhelmed grief until those responsible were punished.

In my own panic I'd never gotten to that stage, but now, watching these happy people celebrating, it struck me how much that bastard had stolen from her, and from me.

Cold fury washed over me, and in its wake came the need to act. As soon as Perry returned I'd tell him everything, and together we'd see this murdering prick strung up by his balls.

My determination slipped when Perry rejoined me. His face was grim, his eyes bright with anger. His hand enveloped mine in a grip so firm and possessive I nearly jerked free from shock.

"What's wrong?" I asked.

"Nothing, just an argument with my father."

I frowned. I didn't want to be nosy and ask what they'd argued about, nor did I want to rush right into my own confession, thereby saying his problems were insignificant next to mine. Technically it was true. Raving lunatic versus meddling father. No real contest there. Still, I couldn't just say that.

So I waited, deciding I'd give him a few minutes to cool down before I dumped all my troubles at his feet.

"Not long now, Lottie." The voice was a whisper, barely audible.

I jumped and frowned up into Perry's face. "What did you say?"

"I didn't say anything." I realized Perry had been talking to someone whose name I couldn't remember. Twisting my lips in confusion I looked over my shoulder. Nobody stood close enough to have whispered in my ear.

Great, now I was hearing voices.

A few minutes later I felt warm breath on my neck and a soft voice say "You will be mine, Lottie."

I spun around, jerking out of Perry's one-armed embrace. There was nobody there.

I squealed as hands clamped onto my shoulders. "What's wrong?" Perry asked, turning me around and tilting my chin up with one finger.

My heart, which had taken a trip down to my feet, thundered back into its customary place. "Um, nothing. Claustrophobic. I think I need some air."

I don't think he believed me, but I didn't care. *He* was here, somewhere in this room, and all I knew was that I had to get out.

Without a word, Perry guided me through the crowd towards the door. My shoulder blades itched and all the hair on my body stood on end.

"Oh good, there you are, Perry!" Minkey sprinted over to block our way. "Marcus went and got himself snookered again. He's threatening to beat Lenny with a candy apple if Lenny won't give him back his keys. Oh, and Lester said some fax came through for you from Toronto"

Perry cursed. "I'll take care of it." He looked down at me and frowned, then kissed me on the forehead and said, "I'll be out in five." He turned and followed the mechanic back into the mob.

Alone, I stood on the threshold trying to decide what to do. If I stayed inside there was a good chance the stalker wouldn't make a move because of the crowd, but if I could get away, maybe hide somewhere, then when Perry came out we could talk. If the fax was about me, I really didn't want to be standing beside him when he read about me being a nut job.

Hiding sounded good.

The streets were deserted. Trick or treating was done for another year and tomorrow there would be hundreds of kids with stomachaches, unless they had parents like mine. Every year my sister and I had to take all our candy down to the women's shelter. We were never allowed sweets, which could explain why I pretty much lived on junk as an adult.

A Kit-Kat would really calm my nerves right now.

Unfortunately there were no kids around to steal candy from so I kept walking, deciding that if I could get a good hiding spot where I could watch the door, I'd be able to see the stalker come out and *BAM!* I'd have him.

I chose a rusty Ford pickup parked across the street and hunkered down in the shadows under the lowered tailgate to wait. A young couple came out of the hall, holding hands and giggling over a shared secret. Probably going off to have their own private party. I squelched the spurt of envy and kept my eyes on the door.

Ten minutes later my butt tingled and my legs ached. Nobody else had come out. I wondered if Perry was still dealing with the drunk guy or if some other crisis had come up. Maybe he'd decided not to bother with me after reading that fax.

Crud, I'd really messed this up.

"Happy Halloween, Lottie." The voice was cold and flat. Every drop of blood in my body plummeted to my toes as I scrambled to my feet.

In the shadows, only a foot behind where I'd crouched, stood my sister's killer. He wore all black, from his boots to the hood on his billowing cloak. The hood hid his face, all but a sliver of pale cheek.

He looked like death.

I should have run. I should have kicked him in the balls. Instead I stood there, frozen with fear, like a deer caught in the headlights of an oncoming car.

He moved, one pale hand appearing from the folds of the cloak, breaking the spell. I spun around and slammed into the lowered tailgate of the pickup.

A strong arm wrapped around my waist, and cold fingers closed over my mouth. I tried to scream, tried to bite, but he only tightened his grip around me, driving the air from my lungs.

Dropping like a stone did no good since he dragged me away just as easily. The guy wasn't big but he was strong.

"You're so predictable, Lottie. You did exactly what your sister said, running away like that. You didn't think you could escape me did you?"

I didn't answer since his hand was still clamped over my mouth. He dragged me towards the trees, and I had to close my eyes when low hanging branches slapped against my cheeks.

He tripped, whether over his cloak or something on the ground I didn't know. I landed hard on the ground and scrambled to my feet, desperate to get away. I tried to scream but no sound came out.

A hand clamped down on my shoulder and at the same time I stumbled over a root or a rock. With my arms flailing wildly I fell forward and bashed my head on a tree.

As blackness overtook me I had enough time to realize I was completely and utterly screwed.

Chapter Seven

I awoke to the sound of cold, eerie laughter. I was tied to something flat like a table or a rock. Shivers wracked my body and I realized I was naked. Frantic, I jerked at my bindings but there was no give. A moan escaped my throat and I heard the crunch of footsteps on dead leaves.

He loomed over me, his face in shadow with only a halo of moonlight circling his head.

Still, I recognized him.

"Will?"

"Surprise."

Tell me about it. Will was my stalker? Will had murdered Maddy, mutilating her body and bathing in her blood? It was like imagining Barney or Bullwinkle as killers.

"Why?" I realized I really wanted to know. More than that I had to know. What made this guy, who had average-Joe written all over him, into a psycho?

"Power. Did you know Maddy was so careful to keep up the appearance that she was normal around me? Ironic, isn't it, that she handed me the proof of her power to save you, when I'd just about given her up as a fraud? If she'd stayed quiet, she'd be alive and you wouldn't be here."

My mom would have said it was destiny, but I wasn't about to argue with him about it.

"Will, you can't honestly believe you can steal power. It's insane."

"Oh but it's not. My mother was a powerful witch, but to her disappointment I showed no signs of having her gifts. I learned quite by accident that my abilities lay elsewhere. I can have every power, every magical skill. That is my magic."

"But you have to kill to get it."

He shrugged. "I enjoyed your sister. She was a wild thing in the sack and she didn't beg or plead when she died. She was strong and the power she fed me was like nothing I've ever felt before."

Great. Maddy had been brave and strong during her murder. No way was I going to break down and turn into a blubbering baby.

"But it was always you I wanted, Lottie. Your ability to regenerate will make me all but invincible. Of course I'll need to test the limitations of this power—on you naturally." An unholy gleam lit his eyes and I knew then that more than stealing my powers, what Will wanted was the chance to torture someone who could heal within seconds, someone who would enable him to prolong his fun.

The knife he pulled from somewhere in the cloak caught the moonlight, flashing silver fire in my eyes.

The hell with that.

The instant the blade pierced my flesh, a sharp stab to the kidney, I screamed. The second bite of steel sliced across my upper thigh, and blood sprayed over my stomach and legs.

Will stepped back and waited, his face alight with glee.

Slowly the pain eased as the wounds closed themselves. It would take a few hours for the pink scars to disappear, but I was in no danger from the wounds.

That didn't mean I was going to keep letting him cut me.

I screamed. "Perry!" A swift jab of the knife pierced a lung, cutting off my plea for help. Blood clogged my throat, left me gagging and choking.

"Scream for me again, Lottie." Will's face was close to mine, his breath harsh against my cheek. His gaze bore into mine and I knew he was enjoying the gleam of panic in my eyes.

I spat in his face, watched the spittle and blood spatter on his pale cheeks. He reared back, snarling and swiping at his face.

"You shouldn't have done that." Clutching the knife high over his head he sneered and brought it down, once to shoulder, stomach, groin.

Panic gripped me. I couldn't survive this, couldn't have this many wounds and regenerate them all. Again and again the blade sank into my flesh.

Black spots flicked before my eyes. My body felt light, like it was floating.

"Perry!" I called again, knowing my voice was weak. There was no way he could hear me, but I knew I had to trust him to find me. Somehow.

Something crashed to my right. The ground shook.

My vision wavered, both from waning energy and the splatter of blood in my eyes. I blinked, determined to remain conscious. The gleam of silver flashed, like a dozen knives coming from the shadows.

Will screamed and I saw his body fly through the air, hovering over mine before he was flung away. A sickening crunch split the night, the wet popping of bone breaking.

"Hell and damnation, Perry, leave some for the rest of us." I recognized the voice, and when Minkey emerged from the shadows I wanted to cry with relief. Perry had come.

Tears glinted in my eyes but I blinked them back, desperately looking for him.

Instead I saw a moose. His massive chest heaved, steam puffed from his nostrils with each ragged breath. His rack glistened with blood.

Trust the moose. Christ.

"Here now, little lady, don't try and move." It was Perry's father. I realized then that the clearing was full of people but still I couldn't find Perry. What if he hadn't come? But Minkey had spoken to him. Adrenaline and blood loss were making me dizzy, confused. Where was Perry?

"Get me loose. I have to find him. I have to explain."

Dave frowned. "You need to lie still until the ambulance gets here."

"Christ, she's never going to survive this." Minkey swore and I heard others mutter in agreement.

"You have to cut me loose."

"Perry, you have to get a hold of yourself and tell her to lie still."

Why couldn't I find him? He was here, so why couldn't I see him?

"Jumpin' Jesus on a pogo stick! Will you look at that."

Suddenly a dozen men were crossing themselves. Dave stared at my body with rapt fascination. "What in the name of God is going on?" The question came out on a gasp of horrified breath.

"I'm a freak okay? Can you untie me now?" See, only extreme torture would get me to reveal my secret. Besides, now that my body was replacing the lost blood, my strength was returning. The last thing I wanted was to be lying here, naked, while a bunch of men ogled me like I was some sort of circus sideshow exhibit. Within seconds I was free and helped up by Minkey and Perry's dad. Someone slipped a jacket over my shoulders.

"Where's Perry?"

Nobody answered, instead they spent a good minute looking at each other, stuffing their hands in their pockets and I swear one of them started to innocently whistle. I'd have laughed if the situation weren't so serious.

The moose stepped forward, pushing through the circle of men around me. Dave stepped in front of me to block its path, but the moose simply nudged him out of the way with one swipe of its head.

"Don't do it," he warned.

Before I could ask whom he was talking to, the air around the moose shimmered and the massive animal was gone. In its place stood a man dressed in fake fur.

"Perry?" I asked. Then I fainted.

Chapter Eight

I woke to the sound of two men arguing. Someone was a meddling old fool and someone was an irresponsible idiot.

I opened my eyes and frowned at the tall ceiling filled with orange and black balloons.

"You might want to wake up and join this conversation."

I sat up and realized I was in the hall, on a really uncomfortable couch. Minkey sat on the armrest, and it was him who had whispered in my ear.

"What's going on?" My voice drew Perry and his father's gaze. In an instant Perry was there, pulling me tight against his chest.

"Are you sure you're all right?" he asked a minute later when he finally released me enough to look me over.

"I'm fine." I realized half the town was still there. Mortified, I looked down at myself, suddenly remembering that I'd been naked, and saw I was wearing Perry's moose costume.

Then I remembered what I'd seen. My gaze flew to his and he winced. A few coughs broke the awkward silence.

I looked away and bit my lip, trying to think of something to say. "So I guess we're both a little different, eh?"

He grinned but I could see the wariness in his eyes. "Are you okay with that?"

Was I? I realized with a start that it didn't bother me at all. I thought about how hard I'd worked to have a normal life, away from strange powers. Was that really what I wanted? Maybe it had more to do with being accepted.

The reason I'd resented Maddy wasn't because she was different, but because nobody accepted her for it, and by default, they treated me the same way.

The truth was I missed the bizarre existence I'd had as a kid. Weird, I know. Most people move out and miss their mother's cooking; I missed being able to be myself around people who didn't judge me. Huh. Who'd have thought?

"I guess normal is pretty boring. I'm okay with it if you are."

His grin grew and I was pulled back into his arms again. He bent his head and I stretched up to receive his kiss only to be dragged away before our lips could touch.

"No! I refuse to allow this. It's too dangerous." Mr. Sullivan's eyes were dark with rage. His grip dug into my upper arms and would have left bruises on anyone else. What was with this guy and his screwed-up views of relationships?

"Sir, he's kissed me before and I survived it just fine." Apparently that was the wrong thing to say. Dave's shoulders snapped back, his eyes narrowed dangerously and he looked like he might jump on his son and throttle the hell out of him.

"Dad, that's enough."

"I won't let you go through what I did with your mother."

"She's not going to die," Perry insisted, pulling me back against his side. I moved to stand partially behind him to avoid being tugged around. I'd had enough of that for one night.

"Of course I'm not. Why would you say that?"

"Because every one of our people who've taken fully human mates has watched his woman die in childbirth," Dave yelled.

Ouch. I wanted to tell him he was jumping way ahead of himself, but obviously this was a touchy subject. "Mr. Sullivan, I don't think that's going to be a problem."

"Christ, Dave, the girl was stabbed about thirty times tonight and she's right as rain. If she can survive that, she can handle birthin' one of you moose men," Minkey commented.

"Dad, I know you feel the line should end, but I've never agreed with you."

Minkey nodded. "Never did agree with you keeping the boy from having a family."

Okay, this was getting out of hand. "Mr. Sullivan, I'm sure you remember my sister and her—special gift. She foresaw this, and my sister is never wrong."

His eyebrows rose all the way up to his hairline. "And what did you sister foresee?"

I looked up at Perry and wondered if I should have kept my mouth shut. I bit my lip and sighed. I'd made the mistake of not telling him the truth before. I wouldn't make that mistake again.

"She predicted the attempted murder and that I'd need to trust a moose if I was to survive. She said that in searching for sanctuary I'd find love."

I looked up again, saw the look of amusement on Perry's face. Honestly I didn't know if I loved him yet, but I was willing to take the chance.

"I put a stop to your sister's prophecy before. I can do it again."

"No you didn't, Dad."

Dave blinked. "What the hell does that mean?"

Everyone was watching Perry now. "It means I did get Lisa pregnant. You may have stopped us going to St. John's but that didn't keep us from being together. She had a miscarriage a few weeks later."

Dave's jaw dropped, and before he could resume his rant, Perry gathered me against his side, turned, and led me through the silent crowd and out into the night.

In the distance the horizon had begun to bloom with the coming dawn. It was over.

"So you're really okay with this?" he asked. "I should warn you, when I lose my temper I can't control it. Once I lost it in the squad car and ended up shifting. Moose don't fit in a car too well."

I laughed. God it felt good to be able to do that. I wondered then if Maddy was watching. I could almost see her laughing at the trouble she'd caused. With a smile, I hoped she was, and I hoped she knew how thankful I was that I'd been able to fulfill her final prophecy.

About the Author

To learn more about Jennie, please visit http://jennieandrus.com. Send an email to Jennie at jennie@jennieandrus.com or join her Yahoo! group to join in the fun with other readers as well as Jennie http://groups.yahoo.com/group/authorbox or http://groups.yahoo.com/group/daughters_of_circe

Look for these titles

Now Available
Dragon's Birth by Jennie Andrus

Coming Soon
Moving Atlantis by Jennie Andrus

Ritual Love

Kate Davies

Dedication

To Mom. For always believing in me, for sharing the magic of Iona, for being my friend and my biggest fan. I love you.

Now go practice your piano.

Chapter One

Damn.

Moira Sinclair scratched a line through the last listing in her guidebook. There wasn't a single room available on the entire freaking island.

The proprietor had been apologetic, but firm. The entire village had been booked for weeks, she'd said. It was just poor luck that Moira had come to Iona today.

Poor luck. Moira snorted as she let herself out through the gate and started walking towards the village. More like a comedy of errors.

The first mistake was listening to that damn backpacker in Loch Lomond. "The place is full of B and B's," he'd drawled in his laidback Australian accent. "Just knock on a few doors and you'll be right as rain, mate."

Ri-i-i-ight.

She never should have come to Iona. It was a stupid, foolish, ridiculous idea, and there was no reason for her to be here.

Her grandmother was dead. Long dead, so long ago Moira barely remembered her. Hadn't her parents always complained about Gran filling her head with foolishness? Look where those fairy tales had brought her.

To an insignificant island on the other side of the world, on a cold, nasty, October night, with nowhere to stay.

Not just October, though. If it was just a day in October, finding a place to stay would have been a snap. But tonight was Halloween—also known as Samhain, an ancient Celtic holiday. And Iona, apparently, was a big draw.

Who knew that neo-druids would have booked the island solid, weeks in advance?

Not Moira.

Out across the harbor, a whistle blew. Moira looked up, her lips pursing as she realized the last ferry for Mull had just pulled away from the docks. Her stubborn insistence on finding a room had made her miss the last opportunity to get back to civilization.

She should have gotten on the ferry as soon as she realized her mistake. Spending time on an island Gran had loved in her youth wasn't going to bring her any closer to the woman.

Disheartened, she trudged down the main road toward the harbor. Maybe, if she were lucky, there'd be someone with a boat willing to take her back to Mull.

Gran may have loved this island, but to Moira it was no more than a pile of rocks on a bare patch of land.

Magic didn't exist. And neither did her grandmother. Not anymore.

"Hey!"

Turning at the sound, she saw a gangly, stringy-haired guy in a black polyester cape standing on the beach next to a pile of wood. "You here for the ceremony?"

"What ceremony?"

"The Samhain ceremony, of course." He stretched out a hand. "Lughaidh Saidear."

"Excuse me?"

"Lughaidh," he repeated. "You can call me Luke."

"Nice to meet you, Luke," she said, resisting the urge to roll her eyes.

He leaned forward. "Actually, Luke's my real name," he confided, as if she hadn't already figured that out. "But we're using our Druid names for Samhain. For realism's sake."

Realism. Moira smiled politely and tugged her hand out of his grasp. "Big night, huh?"

"The biggest of the year. We're having a bonfire and performing a true-to-life reenactment of sacred Druid rituals. You're welcome to join us."

54

She'd rather poke her eyes out with a sharp stick. "No, thanks," she said. She cast about for a reasonable-sounding excuse. "I'm going to check out the rest of the island. Scientific inquiry, that sort of thing."

"Oh, you're a scientist?" His face fell. "Huh."

People tended to have one of two reactions to the fact that she was a scientist. They either assumed she was too brilliant to bother mixing with "real" people, or they decided she must be boring and predictable. Either way, it was a conversation killer.

Hell. According to her parents, she wasn't a real scientist, anyway. Cultural anthropology wasn't a pure enough science to suit them.

She shook off the bad memory. She was through trying to please them. Or anyone else besides herself.

"Yeah," she said. "Maybe I'll see you around."

With a wave, she walked away from Luke, the harbor, and the little town clinging to the eastern edge of Iona.

She followed the paved road to the edge of the village. Before her lay uninhabited Iona, which took up far more space than the village and monastery.

The warmth and light of the village faded behind her as she trudged up the tallest hill on Iona at a whopping three hundred feet in elevation. From her vantage point she could see the bare landscape, sweeping down to the rocky beaches on the far west side of the island.

Even at twilight, the moon was bright enough for her to be able to pick her way down the rough and tumble rocks. Waves lapped at the deserted coastline, playing tag with her feet as she walked the beach. Though geology wasn't her field of study, she hadn't been kidding when she told Luke she was interested in studying Iona. But it wasn't science-related, as she'd implied. What she really wanted, the reason she'd made this crazy pilgrimage in the first place, was to connect to her grandmother again.

Gran had been dead for almost fifteen years now, passing away in her sleep when Moira was only nine. It had been the worst day of her life, and the end of the only soft place she'd ever had.

Her scientist parents had been supremely uninterested in their only offspring, surfacing only when their research grants ran out. They'd been happy to leave her to Gran during school holidays. Free from the stifling restrictions of boarding school, Moira had blossomed under the care of her sweet, slightly dotty Scottish grandmother.

She'd loved everything about Gran's farmhouse, from the old-fashioned steel-cut oatmeal at breakfast to the hours spent puttering around in the garden. Most of all, though, she loved the stories.

She hadn't thought of those stories in years, not after her parents had sat her down for a very serious, thoroughly terrifying lecture. If Gran kept filling her head with nonsense, they threatened, she'd just have to stay at school during breaks instead of going home.

And because home *was* at Gran's place, not school, and certainly not the sterile apartment her parents kept for their infrequent stops between research trips, she'd kept her mouth shut from that point on.

Once Gran had died, though, the stories died with her.

At least Moira had thought so, up until last year. She'd finished her Masters in Cultural Anthropology and suddenly found herself at loose ends. No close friends, no plan for the future, no family ties to speak of—and all she'd been able to think of was coming to Iona.

She crossed her arms over her chest as the wind picked up. The weather had shifted while she was distracted by old memories, a thick fog now swirling around her legs.

She'd left the rocky beach behind, though she could hear the waves clearly enough to identify the coastline to her left. Theoretically, that meant the village had to be somewhere to her right.

Swallowing down a rush of nerves, Moira began picking her way through the fog. Keeping the sound of the waves to her back, she navigated the twists and turns of the rugged landscape, hoping she'd run into civilization soon.

It was a tiny rock of an island. How in the world could someone get lost on it?

Moira trudged across the deserted fields, the fog so thick she could barely see her own toes. Suddenly, something caught at her boot, sending her stumbling onto one knee. Swearing under her breath, she inspected the damage.

Deciding that her jeans had taken the brunt of the fall, Moira stood, brushing off the dirt and leaves. A tall ash tree stood a foot or so away, insubstantial in the swirling fog.

Trust her to find the one tree on the whole damn island, and then trip over it.

Moira squinted through the fog at a flicker of light. Apparently, the village was closer than she'd thought.

The faint red glow grew steadily brighter as she approached. She could hear low, indistinct voices as well. There was a peculiar cadence to their words, an ebb and flow that made her breath catch in her throat. She was too far away to understand what they were saying, but it was clear that this was more than just chanting around a campfire.

Luke had struck her as a poser—someone who played at being a Druid just to be different. He must not have been representative of the rest of the group. Even without seeing them, she could tell the people around that fire were deadly serious.

A twig snapped beneath her foot and she froze, suddenly hesitant to intrude on their religious rite. More trees she hadn't noticed before rose up through the fog, creating a natural barrier between her and the bonfire. Slipping behind one, a thick-trunked elm, she peered at the group gathered around the fire.

The bonfire was huge, with a fragrant smoke that curled and mingled with the thick fog. The flames crackled and snapped, sparks dancing through the trees.

Moira looked around. Trees ringed the open area where the fire burned. There was no beach, no sign of the little town. Somehow, she'd gotten lost— and in the process, stumbled on a completely different group.

"Tonight!"

The deep, resonant voice snapped her attention back to the fire. Even from her hiding place, she could identify the owner of that voice. He stood apart from the other celebrants, his body still. An almost palpable aura of power wrapped around him, as naturally as the cloak that covered him from shoulder to ankle.

He was the leader—in position, in bearing, in sheer physical presence. And Moira was drawn to him just as strongly as the celebrants gathered around him.

Creeping forward, she kept the trees between her and the gathering. If only she could get close enough to truly see them—to see *him*...

"Tonight, the veil is lifted," he intoned, the red glow of the fire catching on the planes and angles of his face. "And though there are those who would banish us from hallowed ground, we dinna bow to their god. We will not abandon *our* gods, not on this day, when the veil is thin and the dead walk among us. We will welcome the turning of the season in this, our sacred grove."

"Earth!" A bearded man sprinkled dirt in a circle around the fire.

"Water!" A pitcher was used to dash water in the four directions, the fire popping and hissing.

"Air!" A different celebrant took a tree branch, making sweeping motions that stirred the fog and sent the smoke of the fire spiraling into the trees.

"Fire!" The leader stepped forward again, casting a handful of something directly into the bonfire. The flames roared upward, lighting the grove and startling a gasp out of Moira.

She shouldn't be here. This was too private, too intimate, to be watched in secret. She crouched down and began to scoot backwards, intending to slip away and find her way back to the village somehow. These men deserved to go through their ceremony without her prying eyes despoiling it.

Suddenly her foot bumped into something solid. Shifting a little, she moved again—and shrieked when a hand clamped down on her shoulder.

The blood drained from her face as rough hands hauled her unceremoniously to her feet.

"Laird Aedan!" A forceful shove sent her sprawling forward, landing with a grunt in the dirt on the edge of the clearing. "We have no need for a calf now. This spy will make a much better sacrifice."

Chapter Two

Sacrifice?

These neo-pagans were taking their role-playing a bit too far, if you asked her.

Moira spat out a mouthful of dirt. "Look, I'm sorry," she started, but a swift kick to the ribs stunned her into silence.

"No slave of Columba will defile our rites with his lies," snarled the man who'd discovered her. "Laird Aedan, how shall we dispose of him?"

Moira scrambled to a sitting position, not quite confident enough with this crowd to stand, at least not yet. "I'm sorry I ruined your celebration tonight. But come on. 'Defile the rites?' Can't you just drop the period accuracy and talk like normal people?"

A malevolent silence met her comment. Moira imagined that even the wind stopped shushing through the trees. Then the man she'd identified as the leader stepped forward and spoke.

"Brave words, from a spy and a slave," he said, stalking around the fire to stand in front of her. "Ye have spirit, I give ye that, lad."

"I guess I should take that as a compliment," she muttered. Moira looked up at Aedan. From her vantage point on the ground, it was a long way up. The man topped her five-feet-seven-inches easily.

His hair, a rich golden brown, was pulled back from his face with a leather thong. His face set in harsh lines, his forbidding expression heightened by the stark light of the fire.

She swallowed and looked away, a flutter of something dark and delicious settling deep inside her. She struggled to find something coherent to say. Finally, she blurted out, "Happy Halloween."

God, she was an idiot.

"I dinna understand one word in five this boy utters," grumbled a large, bearded man standing off to the side. "Can ye make sense of his comments, Laird Aedan?"

"Nay," Aedan said with a grim smile. "We must do the best we can, given the circumstances."

"What circumstances?" Moira threw her hands in the air, then pulled them back protectively when half a dozen glowering men surged forward. "What the hell are you talking about?"

The one they called Aedan flicked a brief glance at her before turning back to his men. "Check the grove and outlying areas. We shall see if he is alone, or part of a larger group."

To her astonishment, two of the men stepped forward and grabbed her by the elbows, hauling her upright until she stood between them. She tried to tug her arms out of their grip, but they held fast.

Crap. This was getting out of control.

What had started as an embarrassing incident had turned into something far more sinister. These "Society for Creative Anachronism" rejects just weren't letting go of their characters. And she had no idea what to do about it.

"Naught but the one, me laird," reported Keir, returned from his search through the grove.

Aedan nodded once, staring hard at the intruder. Behind them, the bonfire cracked and hissed, a reminder of the incomplete ritual. A pang of regret pierced him, but he set it aside for more serious matters.

A spy in their midst could spell the death of him—and of his men.

Two of his men held the stranger in a punishing grip, one to each arm. The stranger had struggled briefly, but subsided soon enough. Aedan did not doubt that those arms would sprout bruises afore long.

The spy glared at him, but said naught. And if Aedan did not miss his mark, there was a touch of fear in those eyes.

Good. He needed every weapon at his disposal in this battle. The element of fear was a powerful weapon, indeed.

One of the men jostled the intruder, who stumbled before pulling upright. "Look, I said I was sorry," he said again, in his high clear voice.

Aedan frowned at the reminder of just how green this lad was. The first time he had spoken, it had taken all of Aedan's skill to mask his surprise. Why, the lad's voice had not changed yet. Had Columba truly sent a mere child to search out followers of the ancient rites?

Christians. In all his years, he would never understand them.

"It wasn't deliberate," the boy said, the words almost tripping over one another in their haste to escape his mouth. "I got lost in the fog. I know you neo-pagans take this seriously, so I'll just go and let you commune with whatever you're communing with. Okay?" He tugged once again at his captors' grip, but they held fast.

Aedan narrowed his eyes. It did no good to let the lad chatter away when every second word was nonsense.

"Can't you just let me go? Please?"

Aedan shook his head. "And let ye run back to Columba with tales of our forbidden rites? Nay, that I canna do."

"Who?"

Keir stepped forward with a forbidding glare. "Do ye deny that Columba sent ye?"

"I don't even know who you're talking about," the lad said.

At the blatant falsehood, Aedan crossed his arms over his chest. "Bind him," he said with a nod to his men.

One of the men took both of the captive's arms and tugged them behind his back, holding them fast. Another man brought out a length of rope and began to wind it around his wrists.

"What the hell?" The spy struggled in earnest now, twisting against his much stronger opponents. The strange garment he wore pulled taut against his chest, and…

61

Aedan stepped forward, eyes narrowed, as he looked at the captive more closely.

"Halt!"

At the sound of his voice, all movement ceased. Even their intruder froze.

"I see I have been mistaken." He took another step forward. "I thought ye were naught but a green lad."

"Wh-what?"

With one hand, he traced the intruder from the shoulder down, his palm skimming over the swell of her breasts, the indent of her waist, the luscious curve of her hip.

In dress and manner, she portrayed a man. But in truth, she was a woman born.

"How dare you?" The lass gave him a heated glare that rivaled the Samhain fire. "Who do you think you are?"

He straightened, a smile fighting to break free. She had spirit, this one did. "I am Aedan ap Crannog," he said. "Laird of Ormaig. And the knowledge that ye are a woman changes all."

He heard a murmur of disbelief from his men, but it faded to the background as he locked eyes with the woman in front of him.

"Who might ye be, lass?" He searched her face. "And why are ye abroad at night disguised as a lad?"

Because she's heard tell of the other ancient rites," said Keir with a low chuckle. "As a good Christian woman, she would wish to protect her virtue."

"Fool! Those are Beltane rites, not Samhain rites," jeered another.

"And how would an intruder know the difference?"

"The gods wouldna mind them being performed on this night, I dinna think."

"And are ye offering yerself for the rites?"

Aedan stepped between them with a glare directed at both. The two bickering fools faded back into the crowd. He could not have staked his claim more clearly if he had shouted *mine*.

Though why he sought to claim a woman who did not follow the old ways, he could not explain.

He looked back at the stranger. Her face was stormy, furrows marring the clear line of her forehead. He clenched his hand into a fist, still feeling the imprint of her curves against his palm.

"I'm not in disguise, you morons," she snapped. "You'd think you had never seen jeans and a zip-up sweatshirt before."

What in the world was she talking about?

"I mean, I know you guys all live in your parents' basements, but this is ridiculous."

Aedan crossed his arms over his chest. "I have told ye my name. Who might ye be?"

She pursed her lips, eyes narrowed. "Moira."

Aedan nodded once. "And ye still deny that Columba sent ye?"

"Who the hell is Columba?"

"Brave words for a liar," shouted one of the men.

"Mayhap she does have a point," said Aedan thoughtfully. "None of us here are welcome on this island. She may wish to conceal her presence from Columba as well."

"Then she is not a spy?"

Aedan looked at Moira, his eyes unblinking, though his words were for his men. "Ah, I didna say that."

"I'm not," she insisted.

"So ye say." Perhaps if it had just been the two of them…but he could not risk his men. He turned away from her. "'Tis not safe to release her now."

"So we hold her until the dawning?"

"What other choice have we?"

"She is fair enough, Laird Aedan," said Keir. "Mayhap ye should perform the ancient rites with her. 'Twould fill the hours to the dawn quite nicely. I vow the gods would not look askance."

His groin tightened. An image of the two of them, naked in the glow of the Samhain fire, coming together in the ancient ritual, teased the edge of his consciousness.

"Nay." He skimmed a knuckle down the side of her face. She shivered again. "Both parties must be willing for the ritual to honor the gods."

Orin spat on the ground, close to Moira's feet. "I say we use her for the ancient sacrifice instead."

There was a low murmur, but Aedan stopped that idea with a harsh look. "Nay."

Chastened, Orin stepped back.

Though Aedan's voice remained low, it carried no less weight. "No harm shall come to the lass."

"Thank God for that." Her voice shook. "Now could you please just let me go?"

"Unbind her." He gestured at the man who still held her.

As the bonds loosened, she shook her hands free. "Thank you," she said. "I promise, I won't tell anyone about your—what the hell are you doing?"

He looked up from her wrists, which he had caught up in front of her. He looped the rope around her wrists and bound them securely. "What does it appear that I am doing?"

"You asshole! You said I wouldn't be harmed!"

"And so it shall be," he said calmly. "But I canna let ye go, either."

"Why bother untying me if all you're going to do is tie me up again?"

"'Tis more comfortable to be bound in front." Satisfied, he wrapped one hand around the bond between her wrists. "'Tis time. Come."

"Like I have a choice," she muttered.

Aedan signaled to his men. They set to work removing the signs of their presence. He watched with bitterness as two of them doused the Samhain fire, using dirt to bury the wood and ashes.

Despite all the planning, all the effort, they had failed.

He had failed.

A heaviness settled on him, the weight of fighting to protect the ancient ways in a changing world. Even on this sacred night, they could not escape the encroachment of these newcomers. The cradle of the Druids no longer belonged to the old ways.

Jaw clenched tight, he turned away from the destruction of the fire, only to be confronted by the sight of his unwanted prisoner.

Logic dictated that now she was bound, she was no longer a threat.

But the hint of compassion in her face told him she saw more than he wanted her to see, and he realized with a shock that she did, indeed, threaten him.

He would not have true peace of mind until she was far, far away from him.

Sucking in one last smoke-scented breath, he turned to his men. "We must away," he said. Refusing to look at the sacred grove again, he took hold of the stranger by her bonds and led the group toward the distant shore.

Chapter Three

Moira struggled to stay upright as Aedan marched her along the uneven landscape. "Sorry," she muttered as she tripped on a rock, then rolled her eyes. What kind of an idiot apologized to her kidnapper for slowing him down?

And what kind of an idiot felt sorry for him, too?

She'd watched him as the evidence of the ritual was systematically taken down. The regret on his face touched an answering pang inside of her. She knew what it was like to have something—or someone—special taken away.

So she'd felt badly for him. Which made no sense, considering he'd tied her up and was dragging her all over the godforsaken island.

"Come." Aedan tugged her forward, catching her arm as she stumbled again, this time over a tree root. "Time is not on our side."

Moira glared at him. "Don't presume to talk about us as an *us*, buddy."

In response, he ignored her. Which was pretty much par for the course.

She tried to pay attention to where they were going, but the fog was so thick—and the landscape so unfamiliar—that she wouldn't recognize the way back even if she had an opportunity to escape.

"Almost there," he murmured, not bothering to look back at her.

Moira glanced around. The other men had faded into the thick fog, and though she could hear mutterings and the tromp of footsteps, Aedan was the only one she could see.

He looked to the left, then the right, finally choosing a path Moira couldn't even begin to see. His fingers looped casually through the ropes binding her hands together, urging her forward with that unspoken authority that suffused his every movement.

He adjusted his grip on the ropes, taking a little of the pressure off. She flexed her hands, trying to get the blood flowing.

"Are ye all right?" Aedan finally glanced back at her. "I regret the need to bind ye, but…"

"Bullshit." Moira pulled back. He automatically tightened his grip on the ropes, his hand sliding between hers. "You don't regret it at all."

He shrugged. "Aye. I never regret that which is a necessity."

"And tying me up is a necessity how?"

He heaved a sigh that telegraphed his annoyance. "If ye are free to move about, ye are free to tell Columba of our presence. I will not jeopardize my men."

"Is there any chance you could drop the bad Robin Hood dialogue and talk normally?"

Even through the fog she could see the furrows on his brow. "Ye must be verra far from home, lass. I dinna understand more than a handful of the words ye say, though they sound like my own tongue."

Yeah, I know how you feel.

"It stands to reason, as ye are so ignorant of the island and its inhabitants."

"I am not ignorant," she hissed. "I'm a tourist. Couldn't you please let me go?"

He paused for a moment, then shook his head. "I canna take that chance."

Her shoulders slumped. "Well, it was worth a try," she mumbled.

"Aye." He flashed a grin at her over his shoulder before turning back again.

Whoa.

He was packing some serious wattage there. For some insane reason her heart did a slow backflip and her breath caught in her throat.

67

What the hell was wrong with her?

She stumbled again, this time over a slick, lichen-covered rock. Cursing under her breath, she glanced up. They were standing at the shoreline.

Somehow, while she'd been busy arguing with herself over the appropriateness of being attracted to the man who'd kidnapped her, they'd arrived at one of the beaches on the uninhabited side of the island.

"This is the place."

"Oh, you have got to be kidding me." Moira squinted through the pea-soup fog at the rugged cliff rising up from the rock-strewn beach. The men who'd accompanied the two of them on their march through the midnight darkness scaled the cliff with jaw-dropping ease, clambering quickly up the rough surface. One by one they disappeared into the caves scattered across the cliff face.

Moira bit her lip. "Please tell me you don't expect me to do that."

"Of course not." Before she could let out a sigh of relief, Aedan hefted her over his shoulder. "Ye might try to escape."

"You pig!" Her head jounced against his back, making sparks dance in front of her eyes. Her bound hands could do little more than pound ineffectually at whatever part of his body she could reach. Her feet did more damage, drumming against his powerful legs and, once, connecting with a much more sensitive part of his body. "Put me down!"

"If ye unman me," he said, "we both will fall."

She stopped immediately. Holding herself still, she squeezed her eyes shut. "Oh, God, I'm going to die."

He ignored her, his attention apparently focused on finding hand-holds. His shoulder muscles bunched under her waist as he reached for an outcropping. He pulled them both up another couple of feet, Moira slipping precariously as he moved.

Her heels scraped against the cliff face as Aedan shifted again. At least the fog prevented her from seeing just how high up they were.

And then she gave a shriek as she tumbled backwards, landing with a thud on a flat rock surface. What light had been visible through the fog was cut off abruptly. Groaning, she rolled to the side, only to come up against a solid barrier. "Where the hell are we?"

Aedan pulled himself over the lip of the entrance, stretching out next to her. "Our safe place 'til dawn," he muttered. "And I'd thank ye to be silent for a wee moment."

"Oh, you'd just love that, wouldn't you?" Moira tugged her bound hands, swearing under her breath to find them just as tightly wrapped as ever. "So what happens at dawn?"

Aedan heaved a sigh, evidently recognizing that he wasn't going to get his requested silence. He drew himself up to a seated position. "At dawn, we retrieve our skiffs and return across the waters before we are discovered by Columba."

"I'll be so sorry to see you go," she said with barely disguised sarcasm. "We've had such a lovely time."

"And why would ye be thinking I would let ye stay?"

She actually felt her heart skip a beat. "What are you talking about?"

"If ye remain, ye could yet betray us," he said. "We will take ye with us, of course."

"Oh, my God."

"Once we have escaped Columba's influence, we will return ye to yer people," he continued.

"My people?"

He ignored her. "Besides, ye are as unwelcome here as are we."

"What are you talking about?"

He turned toward her. "Are ye daft, or just stubborn? How can it be that ye are here, and yet still so ignorant of the island?"

Temper flared, rushing a wave of heat to her cheeks. "Just because I didn't memorize the guidebook doesn't mean I know nothing about Iona."

"How is it I have to explain everything to ye?"

"If you would just bother to make sense, we wouldn't have an issue, Mr. Thinks-He's-a-Druid-Priest."

The silence that followed her snippy comment was full of barely repressed fury.

69

Feeling ashamed, Moira backtracked. "I apologize. That was uncalled for. Your religious beliefs are none of my business, and…"

"I would have given much to continue my studies with the Druids long enough to claim that title," Aedan said softly. "Yer people have made that impossible now."

"My people again. Who do you think are my people?"

"The followers of Columba."

"You keep saying that name like I should know who you're talking about."

He laughed, a short humorless bark that echoed in the small enclosure. "I thought all Christians knew of Columba."

"Why do you assume I'm a Christian?"

Aedan reached out and tapped one of her earrings, setting the tiny Celtic cross swinging. "If not, why wear their sacred symbol?"

Her face warmed at the featherlight touch. "It's just an earring."

"Nay, I think not."

"Really." She swallowed, wishing her voice didn't sound quite so breathless. "I bought them at the gift shop this afternoon."

She still didn't understand why. One minute she'd been half-listening to the tour guide, and the next she was standing in front of a jewelry display. She'd been drawn to the delicate earrings immediately. Fifteen minutes later, she was fastening them onto her lobes as she walked out the door.

Probably because they reminded her of Gran.

Slowly she realized Aedan was staring at her, a puzzled frown marring his brow. "What is a gift shop?"

She rolled her eyes. "Tell you what," she said. "I'll tell you what a gift shop is if you tell me who Columba is."

"The man who brought Christians to Iona and claimed our sacred island for his own."

"Are you talking about Saint Columba? The guy who founded the abbey?"

"Aye."

She snorted. "Maybe you could explain to me how I could tattle on you to someone who's been dead for fifteen centuries."

"Now ye are the one who makes no sense. He is building his kirk on the far side of the island even now."

Moira started to laugh, but stopped abruptly. "You truly believe that, don't you?"

"'Tis not a matter of belief. I tell only the truth."

She sighed. "Can't you give up this charade for one minute?"

"I dinna ken what ye mean."

Her eyes had adjusted now, and even in the twilight darkness of the cave she could see the expression on his face. It was a combination of skepticism and indulgence that chafed on her last nerve.

"Look," she snapped, "I've been more than considerate. I've let you play your medieval faire games. I'm even a little impressed at your ability to stay in character way longer than any normal person. Frankly, though, it's getting old. Come back to the twenty-first century, okay?"

"The what?"

"Oh, my God!" She kicked at the floor of the cave in frustration. "Would you quit pretending that we're in the dark ages here?"

He shook his head, clearly baffled. "What are ye talking about?"

She counted to ten. "Answer me one question."

"Aye."

"What year is it?"

"By the Christian calendar, or in the ancient way?"

She glared at him.

"Very well. According to the Christian calendar, we are living in the year of yer lord Jesu Christe, 592."

"Yeah. Like I said. You're well on your way to delusional, fella."

To her surprise, Aedan didn't take offense. Instead, his expression turned thoughtful. "And what year do ye believe it to be?"

Moira rolled her eyes. "2006, of course."

71

"Ah. Now I ken." He turned and looked toward the entrance of the cave. "I have heard tell of passage through the veil between life and afterlife, but not across time."

"What are you talking about?"

He leaned back against the cave wall. "Ye have slipped from yer time and entered mine."

Chapter Four

Her jaw dropped. "What?"

"Samhain," he said.

"What about it?"

"'Tis the time when the veil between the worlds of the living and the dead is lifted. And if the dead can walk among the living, why could a living soul not travel across time, as well?" He shoved a hand through his hair. "It explains much. Yer strange clothing, yer words, yer mannerisms."

"Setting aside the fact that I could say the same thing about you, it's impossible."

"Why?"

"Time travel doesn't exist."

"Are ye so blinded to the world beyond yer ken, ye canna consider the possibility?"

"Of course I canna—can't—consider it. I'm a scientist, for God's sake!"

"And what would that be?"

Moira blew out a frustrated breath. "Someone who believes in facts and reality, who researches and predicts and accepts the natural world as it is, not someone who indulges in fantasy or wishful thinking."

"And ye know all of the world as it is?"

"No, but…"

He raised an eyebrow. "Can ye devise another explanation?"

"Well, no, but…"

"But ye are unwilling to consider this explanation, at least for tonight."

She crossed her arms over her chest. "Fine. Explain it."

"Gladly." Aedan stretched his legs out in front of him. "First, ye are right ignorant of life today." He lifted a hand. "Not to say ye are a fool, just— unschooled."

Unschooled? After two advanced degrees?

"Ye know naught about Columba, nor the struggle between his people and ours. Ye talk of things I know nothing about. Ye believe me to be something I am not, and I know naught of what you are."

"How do I know you aren't just pretending?"

He leaned toward her until their faces were mere inches apart. "I dinna lie, and I dinna pretend. Can you say the same?"

"Of course!"

His expression darkened. "Then I dinna understand why ye keep denying the truth, and yet call me the liar."

She glared at him. "Okay, not a liar, but not grounded in reality, either."

"Reality." He snorted. "Ye deny reality."

"*I* deny reality? *You* think I've traveled fifteen centuries back in time!"

"And why could this not happen?"

"Because the only way that it could happen is magic, and magic doesn't exist!"

He regarded her with something uncomfortably close to pity. "It must be a sad, empty time ye live in."

She opened her mouth, but clamped it shut again. How could she argue with him when she'd come to Iona because of that very reason? Once Gran was gone from her life, the magic had disappeared, too.

It didn't mean she believed his fairy-tale explanation for what had happened tonight. But he was right.

Her life was sad. And empty. But she couldn't bring herself to tell him so.

Instead, she closed her eyes. At least she didn't have to look at his too-perceptive, too-attractive face.

74

Why did he have to be so gorgeous, when he'd obviously been dropped on his head as a child?

Because face it, the man was about as close to perfection as she'd ever seen. She squinted one eye open, inspecting him surreptitiously in the dimness of the cave. His light brown hair was just past shoulder-length, tied back with a leather thong at the base of his neck. Rich brown eyes, the color of bittersweet chocolate, gazed out at the darkness beyond the cave. A fierce strength suffused his face, reminding her of a bird of prey.

The rest of him was just as impressive. A bronze torc circled his neck. Broad, strong shoulders strained against the rough woolen cape fastened across his chest. Underneath, he wore a tunic of the same indeterminate color over leggings that hugged his powerful thighs.

"And do ye like what ye see?"

Her gaze flew upwards in time to see the smug look on his face. "I wasn't…" But of course, she had been, so she just clamped her mouth shut and glared at him.

In response, he laughed softly and settled back against the wall of the cave opposite her, his long, muscular legs pressing against hers. Moira tried to shift, but in the cramped confines of the cave she didn't have anywhere to move. Instead, the friction of their legs rubbing against each other sent an unwelcome shock of sexual awareness through her.

No, dammit. She did *not* want this man.

Well, she didn't want to want him, anyway.

"We have many hours until the dawning," he said. "Ye may sleep if ye wish."

Yeah, right. The last thing she wanted to do was fall asleep with a man who'd kidnapped her. "I'm fine."

He shook his head. "Ye are a stubborn one, aren't ye?"

"Me?" She threw up her hands, which she'd forgotten were tied together until they smacked her in the forehead. Swearing, she let them drop back into her lap.

Immediately, Aedan was up and at her side. "Are ye hurt, lass?" He ran his fingertips over her forehead, searching for a bruise or lump. "That was quite a wallop."

"Stop," she insisted, but it came out as more of a plea than a command. The breathless quality of her voice made her blush.

His hand stilled, and he looked into her eyes. She could see his Adam's apple bob. "If it is what you wish," he said, withdrawing his hand slowly.

As soon as his touch was gone, Moira was struck with a pang of regret.

Maybe *she* was the one who had been dropped on the head as a child.

"I do regret the need to bind ye." He crossed his arms over his chest as if to keep himself from touching her again.

She held his gaze as she lifted her arms, holding her wrists out in mute appeal.

"Nay, I canna."

"What do you think I'm going to do? Fly out of here?" She dropped them back into her lap with a huff of frustration. "God, you are the most stubborn, pigheaded, obnoxious…"

"High praise indeed, from ye." He quirked a brow. "For I am sure that you are familiar with those qualities in yerself."

"Is that some fancy way of saying 'it takes one to know one'?" She rolled her eyes. "I don't know why I even bother."

There was a long silence. Then Aedan said softly, "Perhaps because talking makes the hours of darkness easier to bear."

A shiver danced down her spine. Hadn't Gran said almost the same thing more times than she could count, when nightmares drove Moira from her bed? They'd sat at the scarred wooden table in the farmhouse kitchen, drinking hot chocolate and talking.

"What is it, lass?" He leaned forward and placed a hand on her knee. "Is something disturbing ye?"

"I'm fine." She shifted, dislodging his hand, and he pulled back. She wasn't about to tell him how his touch sparked a flame that traveled through her entire body.

Was it some kind of sexual Stockholm syndrome, or what? And why, dear Lord, why did it have to happen to her?

"I'm fine," she said again. "In fact, I'm a little tired." She faked a huge yawn that mostly served to prove to herself that she never would have made it as an actress. "Good night."

Then she scooted as far away from him as possible, given the confines of the cave, and rolled over to pretend to sleep.

Chapter Five

The lass was not asleep.

Aedan shook his head, gazing at the odd, prickly woman he'd managed to acquire on this most unusual of Samhain eves.

She was fair to look at, that was true; her form was lithe and curved in all the right places. Though why she covered herself in such odd, formless clothing was a mystery.

As was why she had passed through the veil to his time. She was here for a reason, of that he had no doubt. The trouble was deciphering what reason that might be. And then convincing her of that.

She shifted a little, one arm resting across her eyes. He shook his head and bit his lip against a smile. There was something compelling about the lass, even in her stubborn refusal to face the truth.

Outside, the surf crashed against the shore. The tide was turning; they were on the far side of night. 'Twould not be long before dawn arrived, and with it, new problems.

He could not return her to her people, 'twas now clear to see. She had no people in this time; beyond these shores there was nowhere for her to go.

Nor could he leave her behind. He would not deliver her to his enemy. He shuddered at the thought of this woman in the hands of those who looked on magic as evil.

But how could he keep her with him, either?

His ways were as foreign to her as hers were to him.

'Twas a puzzle with no solution.

Frustrated, he took out his dagger and began to sharpen the edge. With naught else to do until morn, a mindless chore would keep him occupied.

For several minutes, the only sound in the cave was the rhythmic stroke of blade on strop. Then a muted gasp drew Aedan's attention.

Moira was watching him with unblinking eyes. Every muscle in her body was tense; he could see it in the set of her jaw, the fine trembling in her hands.

"Are ye all right, lass?" He leaned forward, reaching out a hand to her, but stopped abruptly when she shrank back against the wall of the cave. Her gaze shifted down to his hand, then back up again, and he realized with a start that he was still holding the dagger.

With an oath, he cast it away, barely noticing when it fell against the opposite wall of the cave with a clatter.

"Did ye think I meant to harm ye?"

She said nothing, but the tension in her body was answer enough.

Moving slowly, he said, "I swore I would not hurt ye, lass."

She looked across the dark gloom of the cave to the spot where his blade had landed.

"Ye must believe me."

Though he did not know why it mattered. It should be of no consequence whether she saw him as a monster or a man.

Even as he thought the words, he knew them for a lie.

She swallowed once, convulsively, then whispered, "It looks so real."

For a moment, he was puzzled. Catching her meaning, he nodded. "Aye, 'tis."

"What were you doing?"

"Working the blade." Hands held out in front of him to show he was no threat, he moved so he was sitting next to her against the rough cave wall. "Naught sinister, I promise ye."

"Okay." She shifted, too, so they were close but not touching.

No matter. He could feel the heat of her despite the lack of contact.

Her voice was low. "Do you truly believe we are from different times?"

"Aye."

She was silent for a moment, looking away toward the entrance to the cave. "There are some things…"

"What things?"

She glanced at him. "You. The way you dress, the way you talk, the absolute period accuracy in everything you do. I find it hard to believe anyone could stay in character that long."

Aedan didn't quite follow, but he nodded anyway.

"Though that doesn't necessarily mean I'm the time-traveler. You could have jumped forward."

"'Twould mean all my men came forward, too."

"Oh. Good point." She pondered that, her gaze focused inward. "And then there's the whole tree thing."

Now he was truly lost. "What do ye mean?"

"There are no trees on Iona."

The words pierced him through the heart. "None?"

"Oh, a few, here and there, but nothing like the grove you were celebrating in."

Something of his emotions must have shown on his face, because she hurried to add, "At least, that's what the guidebook said. I could be wrong."

But he knew, in his bones, she told the truth. Running a hand through his hair, he said, "'Tis of no consequence. Time circles on, and all changes."

She shifted. Her leg brushed against his, sending a bolt of heat through him. "I know it bothers you," she whispered. "I'm sorry."

How could this woman, a stranger, see into his soul?

Uncomfortable, he muttered, "'Tis nothing, lass," and thankfully she let it go.

"Anyway, what I'm trying to say is that I'm not totally denying the possibility anymore."

He laid a hand on her shoulder. "It must be hard for ye to grasp, if such a thing is considered impossible in yer time."

"I just don't understand why."

Aedan brushed a strand of hair away from her face, tucking it behind her ear. "Why, what?"

Almost imperceptibly, she leaned into his touch, and he felt like shouting with fierce pleasure.

"Why did this happen?"

"For some reason the gods have brought us together. It is the way of Samhain."

"But what reason could there possibly be?"

"The gods have not shown us yet. We must be patient."

She laughed. "Patience is not one of my strong suits."

"I had noticed that."

"Hey." She bumped her shoulder against his. "You're not supposed to agree with me."

"My apologies." He slanted a glance at her. "I will be certain not to agree with ye again."

She burst out laughing. "When did you get a sense of humor?"

"There has not been much to laugh about tonight."

She sobered then. "True."

He turned so he was facing her directly. "Have ye any other questions, lass?"

"How long?"

"What do you mean?"

"How long will I be here?"

"That, lass, I dinna ken." He pulled himself upright and returned to the edge of the cave, gazing down at the thick fog blanketing the ground beneath them. It made it impossible for him to see any intruders, but it also kept him and his men from being discovered as well.

A blessing and a curse in one.

Turning, he asked her, "When did ye find yerself in my time?"

81

Moira shrugged. "Sometime after dark, I think. I left the village at dusk, and wandered around for a while before stumbling on your group. The fog made it difficult to see where I was going."

He looked outside again. "Perhaps that is the key."

She narrowed her eyes, puzzled. "The key to what?"

"I canna believe I didna think of it afore." He paced over to where she was sitting, talking more to himself than to her. "Aye, it looks like a veil, in some ways."

"Aedan, if you don't tell me what in the hell you're talking about, I may have to hurt you."

"Come." He leaned down and grasped her elbow, lifting her up. Leading her to the edge of the cave, he said, "'Tis the fog, you see."

"No. I don't see."

He waved a hand at the mist below. "Ye walked through the veil of fog to the past. It stands to reason that ye would be able to walk back in the same way."

"Really?" She leaned over. "Right now?"

"I think not." He steadied her with a hand on her arm. "The magic is strongest at the point between night and day. Ye passed through as day turned to night; ye must try again when night turns to day."

He refused to think on why the idea of her going back through the veil disturbed him.

"And you think it will work?"

He looked at her earnest, hopeful face. "I think 'tis the best chance ye have, yes."

He would not lie and say he was certain, for the ways of the gods were beyond his ken. But he could not take that hope away from her, either.

"So, how long do we have until morning?"

The night sky was still black as pitch, though the stars twinkled in the distance. "A few hours at least."

"Great! We have a few hours for my favorite activity."

His groin tightened at the thought of using those hours in the pursuit of pleasure. "And what would that be?"

The smile that lit her face touched an answering chord inside him. "Research."

"I dinna recognize that word."

"It's part of that science thing I was telling you about. I want to learn everything I can in whatever time I've got here."

He could think of many more enjoyable ways to pass the time until the dawning, especially with a lass as fair as his reluctant prisoner. But he could not disappoint her. "What is it ye wish to know?"

Chapter Six

He was a treasure trove.

Moira itched for a notepad and paper, or her laptop. She didn't want to lose a single thought, even one piece of information on life in this time period.

Too bad she'd never be able to use it. No one in their right mind would believe her.

Hell, she hardly believed it herself.

But talking with Aedan had gone a long way to convincing her.

She was trained in anthropology, a student of cultural mores and practices. And she could not deny the depth of his knowledge, nor the evidence in front of her own eyes.

Even more fascinating than the technical information, though, was the man himself.

As the conversation ranged from topic to topic, he became more enthusiastic, more animated. The dour, forbidding man who had taken her prisoner disappeared, replaced by a gently humorous, thoughtful man.

He worried about the people under his leadership. He struggled with the changes happening so quickly in his world. Genuinely curious, he had as many questions about her time as she had about his.

She respected him. More than that, she liked him.

And on a primal level she hadn't even been aware existed before tonight, she wanted him.

She wanted him more than she'd ever wanted a man. And in a few short hours, she would never see him again.

Shaken, she leaned back against the wall and closed her eyes.

"I apologize, lass. I dinna mean to bore ye."

"Stop it." She squinted one eye open. "You haven't been even close to boring."

"The hour is late." He turned her by her shoulders so she faced away from him. "Ye are unused to this uncomfortable setting. Here, let me soothe you."

He began rubbing her shoulders and neck, alleviating the stress in the muscles with deep, rhythmic strokes. She bit back a moan as his strong fingers found each cord of tightness, each sore spot. Part of her felt like she could melt into a puddle right there on the cave floor.

Another part was far from soothed. Tendrils of heat spiraled through her, setting each nerve ending ablaze. Her heartbeat accelerated and her breathing turned shallow.

She tilted her head back, resting against his broad shoulder. His hands stilled for a moment. "Are ye all right, lass?"

Never better. Moira nodded once, her cheek brushing against the rough fabric of his cloak. She breathed in his woodsy scent, so uniquely him, and she swallowed hard.

She'd been alone for so long, holding herself separate in a world where she was surrounded by people. Tonight, she finally felt connected to another human being, for the first time since she was a child.

Maybe this was why she'd ended up here.

When Samhain ended, she would be alone again, back in her own time.

But she wasn't alone now.

She squared her shoulders. "Tell me."

"Tell you what?"

"About the sacred rites. Between a man and a woman."

His hands stilled. "What did ye wish to know?"

"Everything." She turned around, so close their knees were touching. "On second thought, don't tell me."

Leaning in, she whispered in his ear, "Show me."

She was going to be the death of him.

Never in a thousand lifetimes had he anticipated the passing to be so pleasurable.

He leaned back, the better to look her in the eye. "What are ye saying, lass?"

Even in the dim light of the cave, he could see color flood her face. "I think you know."

"Why?"

She bit her lip. "I—I'm very attracted to you, Aedan. And this may be our only chance…" Her voice trailed off.

He had considered that fact, wanting to seek pleasure with her before the dawning. But never had he thought she would invoke the sacred union.

"But do ye know, truly, what the sacred rites mean?" He shifted so they were no longer in contact, though his very blood shouted in protest.

He had known that touching her was playing with fire. But he had been unable to resist the temptation.

Now, she was tempting him beyond his endurance. His body burned for her; the words she spoke turned him hard as stone. But he could not take her in the ancient rites without knowing for sure that she understood the significance.

"'Tis more than just a tumble, lass," he said. "'Tis the union of male and female, the sun and the earth. It celebrates the connection of the god and goddess."

She nodded, her eyes wide.

"As said before, both parties must be willing. To do otherwise is to dishonor the ritual."

"I'm willing." She swallowed. "Are—are you?"

"Aye." He took her hands, still bound, and brought them to his lap. He watched her eyes widen as she traced the length and breadth of him, her fingers exploring him through the rough fabric of his trews. "Most willing."

86

He watched her closely, waiting to see a flicker of doubt, of uncertainty. Naught remained but her desire.

"Maybe that's why I'm here," she whispered. "One ritual was taken away from you. I can offer another. I *want* to offer another."

He nodded once. "Then I choose ye, Moira of a distant time, to be my partner in the ancient rites."

In that moment, everything changed.

For the first time, he had called her by name.

Moira felt her breath hitch in her throat. The air fairly crackled around them as he stood and held out a hand.

She stood as well, and leaned against the rough wall of the cave, anxious and excited. To her surprise, he knelt down again. With deft economy of movement, he removed first one shoe, then the other, leaving her in stocking feet.

It didn't matter. Even standing on the cold stone of the cave floor, Moira burned.

And as he stood slowly, stroking fingertips up her legs, over her hips, circling her breasts, she knew she had walked into the flames without hesitation.

With the pad of one thumb, he traced her lower lip. Moira's mouth opened on a breathless sigh, her eyes fluttering closed as he moved in.

The first kiss was no more than the brush of a butterfly wing, a whisper of sensation that sent a jolt of longing all the way to her toes. Even though her eyes were closed, she felt it when he stilled. The knowledge that he was affected just as strongly was a rush of feminine power.

"So *bonnie*," he murmured, and descended for another kiss.

This time, there was no gentleness, no soft exploration. His firm, unyielding mouth moved over hers in an unmistakable act of possession. His tongue stroked along the seam of her mouth, and she opened willingly, welcoming him inside.

He teased and tasted, his tongue dancing with hers, and she held back a moan.

Suddenly, he pulled back, his dark eyes gleaming in the dim interior of the cave.

"Nay," he said. "Dinna swallow yer cries. It pleases the gods for us to take our pleasure freely."

He licked his lips, drawing her gaze to his mouth. Moira's thighs clenched.

Eyes focused intently on hers, he reached forward and cupped her breast, rubbing his thumb over the beaded nipple. Even through her sweatshirt, Moira could feel the gentle touch, and the answering tug deep in her belly. She hummed with pleasure, and the smile that flashed across Aedan's face was fierce and proud.

"Aye." He stroked once more. "Just like that."

His mouth crushed against hers again, moving with even more urgency. With each kiss, his hand trailed lower, stopping to rest on the curve of her stomach. She squirmed a little, and he smiled against her lips. He moved lower still, teasing under the hem of her sweatshirt until he touched bare skin.

They both groaned at the contact. Moira writhed with each featherlight touch, a trail of fire following his calloused fingertips. "Aye, lass," he whispered. His lips feathered kisses along the column of her neck, finally ending as he reached the neckline of her shirt.

He lifted his head, reaching out to smooth her hair. "Are ye sure? Is this truly what you wish?"

Outside, the tide rolled against the shore in a muted rhythm. Inside, their labored breathing mingled with the rapid beating of her heart. She lifted her bound hands to the front of his cloak, grabbed two fistfuls of fabric, and pulled him closer for a searing kiss.

His hips ground against hers, pressing her back into the rough wall of the cave. Her hands, caught between their bodies, kept a distance between them that almost made her weep with longing.

Aedan must have felt it, too, because he broke the kiss with a muttered oath. Taking her hands in his, he lifted them by the rope and pressed them above her head. He stroked a hand down her arm, tantalizingly close to the curve of her breast, across her stomach, then back up the opposite arm. He rested his hand on the knot between her wrists. "Keep yer hands aloft."

Stomach quivering, she acquiesced.

He stepped forward again, and this time there were no barriers between them. His hard, muscled form molded to her softer curves, the thick length of his erection pulsing against her thigh. Without conscious thought, she wrapped one leg around him, holding him close.

He groaned into her mouth, tilting his hips against hers. The heat of his body enveloped her, his scent intoxicating.

They stood that way for long moments, bodies entwined, mouths voracious in their hunger. Then he stepped back, breathing harshly. He unfastened his cloak with a brevity of motion that took her breath away. Shaking it out with one flick of the wrist, he laid it on the floor of the cave. Lifting her in his arms, he laid her gently on the thick wool fabric.

With the cloak gone, Moira could see Aedan's physique more clearly. A pale tunic covered him from shoulders to thighs, his muscular arms bare. A knotwork tattoo circled his left bicep. Close-fitting leggings hugged his thighs. He knelt over her, his muscular thighs bracketing hers. Again, he hooked one finger around the ropes, lifting her hands until they were stretched out fully above her head.

He crossed his arms over his chest and pondered her zip-front sweatshirt.

He stared so intently, and for such an extended period of time, she thought she'd go mad with the waiting. "You take the little pull thingy," she started, but he pressed one finger to her lips, silencing her.

"Let me explore."

Well, when he put it like that…

He traced one finger down the length of the zipper, sending fire skittering along her nerve endings and setting her entire body ablaze. He flicked the zipper pull, the clink of metal on metal sounding unusually loud in the close confines of the cave. Through the darkness, she could see the gleam of his even white teeth.

"I do believe I have unwrapped the mystery," he murmured, taking the zipper pull between thumb and forefinger and lowering it, inch by excruciating inch, until the sweatshirt opened. One hand, wide and hot, splayed possessively on her quivering stomach. "Exquisite."

Moira sucked in a breath as he spread the thick fabric apart, revealing her torso. His brows knit together in a frown as his gaze fell on her breasts.

"Uh, not the reaction a woman hopes for," Moira said with an embarrassed laugh.

He looked up at her and shook his head, a smile tugging at the corners of his lips. "'Tis the binding that puzzles me. Why do ye cover yerself in this way?"

She glanced down. "Oh, the bra."

"Is that what it is called?" He wrinkled his nose. "I dinna think I like it."

Reaching out, he traced the outline of her white lace bra, fingertips stroking the hypersensitive skin. Her nipples beaded painfully tight.

"Although perhaps it has some charm."

Moira shuddered under his touch, arching her back to silently offer her aching breasts to his waiting hands.

He didn't disappoint. With masterful strokes he teased and tormented until she was tossing her head and whimpering. The delicate roughness of the lace gently chafed her nipples. Again and again his thumbs strummed across them, the rhythmic motion calling forth an answering cadence deep inside.

His eyes, dark and promising, watched her intently. "Does that please ye?"

Mutely, she nodded, then sucked in a breath as he caught one nipple between thumb and forefinger and tugged.

"Enough." He pushed the straps down. "I must see all of ye."

"The clasp—in front..." she panted, moving her hands to indicate the closure.

In response, he caught her wrists. "Not yet," he said. With a quick glance, he found what he was looking for. Sitting back, he moved her closer to the cave wall. He pushed the sleeves of her sweatshirt up until they pooled at the edge of the rope binding her wrists. Holding the fabric in one hand, he lifted her arms back over her head.

In a flash, she understood why. An outcropping of stone extended from the base of the cave wall. Her bonds, caught over the edge of the stone, held fast.

A rush of moisture dampened her thighs. Biting her lip, she flexed her fingers around the cool stone.

"Just like that, my sweet," he murmured. "Let it anchor ye."

In a matter of seconds, he'd broken the front clasp of her bra apart. Moira couldn't bring herself to care. Not when strong fingers were skimming it open, leaving trails of flame along her overheated skin.

They both groaned at the sensation. "Beautiful," he murmured, then leaned over to draw a nipple into his mouth.

Moira tossed her head back and forth, Aedan's cloak protecting her from the rough cave floor. Her fingers dug into the rock, holding herself steady beneath his ministrations.

Her hips arched upward, aching for more contact. Lifting his head, he moved to the other breast, then trailed kisses down her stomach to the top edge of her jeans.

Aedan was a quick study. This time, the zipper was no match for his clever fingers, and he skimmed her jeans and panties off in one swift motion. He sat back, his muscled thighs bracketing hers, and looked his fill.

Moira felt her breathing accelerate, her skin burn with a heated flush. She felt open, exposed, vulnerable.

And more excited than she could have believed possible.

Drawing a finger through the tangle of curls at the apex of her thighs, he gathered the moisture that flowed from her. He withdrew his hand and slowly raised it to his lips. "Ah, Moira," he groaned. He moved back, giving himself full access to her. "I canna wait any longer to taste ye."

And taste her he did, with long, lazy strokes of his tongue that sent her arching off the cloak. He pressed her legs wider, opening her to his sensual assault. Little mewling cries she barely recognized as coming from her own throat echoed off the walls of the cave. The only thing grounding her was the stone holding her bound hands.

He pressed one finger inside her and she gasped, little contractions starting to flutter around him. "So close," he murmured, withdrawing it inch by inch until she could have wept. "Wait for me, sweet."

It was only a moment before he had removed his clothing, yet Moira burned for his return. Her hands clenched her stone anchor, a rhythmic pattern that echoed between her legs.

The last barrier of clothing removed, Aedan stood before her, gloriously naked. Muscled and bronzed, his body showed every sign of a life of physical

91

labor and hard work. A dusting of hair covered his chest, arrowing down his abdomen, drawing her eye downward.

He was fully, proudly erect, his penis jutting out from the nest of curls between his legs. A drop of moisture on the head was barely visible in the dim light of the cave. Moira gripped the stone, wanting to touch him, but holding herself back.

The flare of desire in his eyes told her he recognized her struggle. He knelt between her legs, lifting her hips for his entry.

"I take ye, Moira, in the ancient rites," he murmured against her mouth, and in the same moment he pressed inside her.

They both groaned as he filled her. He slid forward, slow and steady, until he was seated in her to the hilt. Arms braced on either side of her shoulders, he began to move.

Moira tilted her hips upward as he surged into her again and again, each thrust building the fire inside to a roaring blaze. Her nipples rasped against his chest, the roughness of his hair beading them even tighter.

Her fingers ached to cling to him, to stroke down his back to the firm buttocks thrusting between her thighs. She wanted to fist her hands in his sweat-dampened hair, hold his head steady for her kiss.

Instead, she wrapped her legs around his waist, holding onto him in the only way she could. Skin to skin, heartbeat to heartbeat, she touched him with her body and soul as the fire of their passion burned.

Heat gathered between her legs, the sweet friction of his thrusts bringing her to the edge. He was close, too, if the tension in his muscles was any indication. Suddenly, he reached to the side and grabbed his dagger.

"Aedan?" Her heart stuttered for a moment. He stretched his arm above both their heads and sliced through the bonds holding her hands together.

Tossing the blade away, he tugged her arms free of the severed rope and knotted sweatshirt. "I would have ye complete the rites a free woman," he said, taking up their rhythm again.

It was enough to tumble her over the precipice, shuddering, convulsing, as he pumped into her. Her hands, free now, touched him everywhere, stroking his shoulders, his back, grabbing his buttocks to pull him closer. She sobbed her release, clinging to him with every ounce of strength left in her.

Moments later, he followed her into the flames, surging into her with a hoarse shout. Then he collapsed, panting, atop her.

Sudden tears pricked the backs of her eyelids, but she blinked them away.

He was right. This had been more than just a tumble. And she had no idea how she was ever going to walk away from him now.

Chapter Seven

Gods, but she was beautiful, naked and panting beneath him. He rolled to the side, taking his weight off of her. Her hair, snarled and damp from their exertion, spread out across the pale wool of his cloak.

He toyed with one of the curls, winding it around his finger. Draping it over her naked breast, he traced a gentle path along the creamy skin to circle the tight berry of her nipple.

Moira groaned. "You're a wicked one, Aedan ap Crannog." Her fingers stroked down his back, playing over the muscles damp with sweat. "But I find I have a taste for wicked now."

He lifted up on one elbow and looked down on her love-sated face. A face that, even after their short time together, he was going to miss so very, very much.

A glance outside confirmed what he knew deep in his bones. "The dawn is coming," he said heavily. "It is time."

They dressed in silence. Moira stole quick glances at Aedan as he fastened his tunic over the rangy, sleek muscles of his upper body. Her stomach swooped and dove on a wave of longing. She could still feel him pressed against her, pulsing deep inside her body. For the first time in forever she'd felt comfortable in her own skin, as if she wasn't alone in the world anymore.

"We have no time to lose," he said in the low, rich voice that sent shivers down her spine. "Are ye ready, lass?"

Lass. She winced inwardly. Moments ago, she'd been Moira to him. "As ready as I'll ever be," she answered.

"I will descend from the cave first." He strapped his dagger back under his cloak. "Place yer hands and feet where I do, and ye will be perfectly safe."

"I trust you," she said.

With a sharp glance, he nodded. Then he strode to the edge of the cave and began to climb down.

"Come, lass," he called up in a hoarse whisper.

Leaning over the edge, Moira watched as he descended into the thick fog.

He reached a hand up toward her. "Place yer foot in my hand," he said. "I will set it upon the right stones."

She did as he said, clinging to the cliff face as he guided her down. Her stomach clenched as their cave was swallowed up by the fog.

Once Aedan reached the ground, he took her by the waist and lifted her down. She clung to him for a long moment, drawing strength from his solid form. He set her away from him and grasped her hand.

Twining their fingers together, he led her off the beach toward the interior of the island. The fog was starting to lift, false dawn lightening the shadows around them.

"Hurry, lass," he urged her. "'Tis almost too late."

Faster and faster they moved, almost running over the rough terrain. Moira stumbled, but this time she had Aedan's strong hand to hold her up.

Too soon, she recognized the trees, standing silent and tall before them.

Aedan stopped, turning her toward him. He tugged her forward for a gentle, heartbreaking kiss. "Ye must go now," he said, his voice rough. "The magic will be gone soon."

Moira looked around. The fog was starting to lift, breaking apart with the coming of morning. A faint glow touched the horizon beyond the grove.

If she was to return to her own time, it had to be now.

Giving his hand a squeeze, she let go. She took one step forward. Then she crossed her arms over her chest, turned around and said, "No."

"No?" Aedan stared at her. "We dinna have time to argue, lass. Once the sun rises, ye will be trapped here."

95

"I won't be trapped." She put her hands on her hips. "I choose to stay."

The blank look on his face turned to disbelief. "Ye would choose to stay here? What of yer family, yer life back in yer time?"

She stepped closer, eyes intent on his. "I haven't heard from my parents in over a year. I doubt they'd notice I was gone. And there is nothing else to hold me there."

"And here?" His voice was low, thrumming with emotion.

"I came to Iona to try to capture some of the joy I had as a child, with my grandmother. She's long gone, but I've found the magic she always wanted me to have."

"There is that in abundance," he agreed.

"I want adventure," she said.

"Also in plentiful supply."

"And you." She reached out and stroked the curve of his jaw. "I find that I can't walk away from you, Aedan ap Crannog."

He said nothing for a long, breathless moment. Then he pulled her into his arms, groaning, "Thank the gods."

Moira opened her mouth to do just that, but Aedan was too quick for her. He swooped down with a passionate kiss that chased away all thoughts of the gods, Samhain and the veil between the worlds.

Long moments later, he lifted his head, breaking the kiss. "'Tis time to go, lass."

"But I thought—"

He silenced her with a brief kiss. "I meant to the skiffs, Moira. Look around. 'Tis the dawning."

The sun had crested the horizon, and early morning light chased away the last of the fog. Moira smiled as she looked around the grove, the tiny island familiar and yet so new.

Gran would definitely have approved.

About the Author

Kate Davies first tried her hand at romance at the young age of twelve. Sadly, that original science fiction love story is lost to the ages. But after many years meandering through such varied writing fields as fantasy, playwriting, poetry, and non-fiction, she's made her way home to romance.

Kate lives in the Pacific Northwest with her husband and kids. When not chasing the rugrats around the house, she loves to write sexy stories about strong, passionate men and women.

Learn more about Kate at www.kate-davies.com, or check out her blog at www.kate-davies.blogspot.com. Join her newsletter group at http://groups.yahoo.com/group/katedaviesupdates/ to keep up to date with new releases, signings, and other news. She can be contacted at kate@kate-davies.com.

Look for these titles

Now Available
Taking the Cake by Kate Davies
Striptease by Kate Davies

Coming Soon:
Challenging Carter by Kate Davies

Babe in the Woods

Lorelei James

Dedication

Thanks to editor extraordinaire, Angela James, for choosing this story for the first Samhain Anthology. I'm thrilled to be in such good company.

Chapter One

Lacy Buchanan fantasized about leaving a size ten boot print on his ass. A very fine ass that'd commanded far too much of her attention already.

The tight male butt stopped. The equally fine masculine body faced her. Brown eyes snapped with barely restrained hostility.

"Would you hurry up?" The guide waited impatiently by a decaying log, wiping away the sweat beaded on his forehead with a dirty red bandana. The compass on a chain around his neck glinted in the harsh sunlight. "We'll never make camp before nightfall at this rate. God, what are you? Part tortoise?"

"Better that than part caveman," she retorted, throwing her Day-Glo orange backpack to the rocky ground. It kicked up clouds of dust. She coughed and flopped down beside it. Something inside it made a horrible crunching sound.

Lacy could care less what survival item she destroyed because her feet were killing her—not that she'd ever mention it to the sullen hiking guide she'd dubbed Ranger Rick. Except after marching the last two hours in near-desert heat, she'd secretly added a silent "P" to his name. Not even her secret attempt at humor lessened her irritation with the man whose facial expressions registered exactly two emotions—anger and frustration.

"Just go on. I'll catch up."

His left eyebrow winged up. "You'd rather I left you out here to wander the woods alone?"

"Yep. I've got water and an excellent moisturizer. Just give me your compass and I'll be set."

A new expression lit his eyes. Disbelief. "Where is *your* compass?"

She was so hoping *not* to have to confess that little mishap to this rugged outdoorsman with the instincts of a wolf and the disposition of a bear. "Umm." She absentmindedly fingered her charm bracelet. Damn thing was supposed to bring her good luck, not bad. "It's kind of funny actually."

His gaze narrowed. He didn't look the least bit amused.

"Okay. It fell out of my pocket and sank to the bottom of the creek when we filled our canteens."

"And you're telling me *now*? What makes you think you'd survive out here?" He expelled a harsh bark of laughter. "Cupcake, you'd last about ten seconds before screaming your head off for me to come back and rescue you."

Cupcake? Lacy ground her teeth. So she wasn't Campfire Girl material, but she wasn't helpless either. For godsake, she worked in the jungle of Manhattan. She'd spent years honing her survival instincts.

"Rescue me? I wouldn't call for you with my last breath."

The first hint of a smile played at the corners of his sinful mouth. "Careful, that can be arranged."

Ooh, his testosterone-laden behavior rankled.

"But, if we don't get going," he continued, "we may be forced to rely on survival techniques that'll offend your delicate sensibilities."

"Like what?"

"Oh, I don't know." He scratched the sexy stubble on his chin. "Eating squirrel or grub worms." His gaze locked on hers. "Conserving our strength tonight by sharing body heat."

Lacy knew he was bluffing, yet something warm and liquid pooled low in her belly. "In your dreams, Grizzly Adams. Not if you were the last man on earth."

"Back at you. But at this pace, the human race might be extinct by the time we reach base camp."

She tossed her head, reaching in the pocket of her cargo shorts for a tube of cherry Chapstick. "Please. Could we hurry back so I can choke down another meal of the prepackaged cardboard you psychos are passing off as food?"

His avid gaze remained glued to her mouth as she spread the waxy substance over her cracked skin.

She puckered and compressed her lips before releasing them with a loud smack. "This is not what I expected."

He inhaled deeply and muttered, "Don't ask. You don't even want to know."

"Want to know what?"

"What exactly *were* you expecting?"

"A nightly campfire with cowboy sing-alongs. Horseback riding through flower-filled meadows. A grumpy old man everyone affectionately called 'Cookie' scrounging up a kettle of baked beans. The only ones eating well on this trip are the mosquitoes."

"Spare me the drama. This is backwoods hiking."

"Well, I didn't know that."

"It was spelled out on the damn brochure. How did a woman like you end up here anyway?" A beat passed. His slow, knowing grin was worse than his disdain. "Aha. I get it now. Was this adventure your boyfriend's idea?"

"*Ex*-boyfriend," she spit out.

His gaze lingered on her white silk tank top permanently discolored gray by sweat stains. "You seem better suited for a bed and breakfast in wine country."

"Instead, I'll spend another night sleeping on pinecones and deer poop with a man whose idea of conversation is grunting."

When his eyes flashed, she backtracked. "When are we going to get back to civilization?"

"If we hurry, we can catch the group before they start the trail ride in the morning. If not. Who knows?" He uncapped his canteen, never breaking eye contact as he took a small sip. "None of this would've happened had you not drifted off from the main group. How did you get so lost in such a short period of time?"

She shrugged.

"What were you doing?"

"I was looking for—" Her mouth snapped shut. No way was she confessing that humiliating tidbit, even if it was a normal bodily function. Even if bears regularly did it in the woods.

"For what? A Starbucks?" His disgusted gaze zeroed in on her red leather ankle boots. "Or perhaps a Saks? No wonder your feet hurt."

Lacy thought she'd been limping pretty discreetly. "For your information, Captain Caveman, I ordered these boots from Eddie Bauer. The premier outfitter of all outdoor enthusiasts." Not that you'd know, she added a mental raspberry. He probably fashioned his attire from the skins of animals he'd trapped. And killed. With his bare hands.

"Figures you'd have blisters, ordering from that useless yuppie store. And for the last time, my name isn't Ranger Prick or any of the other creative monikers you've been muttering behind my back. It's Becker."

"Whatever."

He unhooked the compass and studied it. "It says we're going the right direction…" He squinted at the sun, the woods behind them and the sandstone cliffs rising on both sides of the canyon. He gave her a once over. "So why does it feel like every time I look at you that I've stumbled into a secret passageway to hell?"

"Back at you, *Pecker.*"

His mouth tightened. "Look, Lacy. Break is over. We need to get moving before the sun drops behind those cliffs."

"Your compass tells you that? Let me see it."

"Be careful. Not sure I can find the way out of here without it." Becker reluctantly handed the compass over.

Lacy studied the gadget for several minutes, as if it contained a map. "What does it mean when—"

He sucked in a sharp breath. "Put down your hand. Slowly."

"What now?" He wasn't having a cow about her simply touching his precious compass, was he?

"Don't move."

"Move. Don't move. Make up your mind. I am so sick of being bossed around. First, I got conned about this lousy trip, and now I'm stuck with you, Mr. He-man-woman-hater—"

"Shut-up," Becker hissed. He inched sideways from the log, his movements deliberate and steady as he reached into his backpack to ease out a small shovel. "You can boss me all you want in a minute. Right now, don't talk. Stay still."

"What is it?" She slid her butt lower toward her blistered heels.

"I said. Do. Not. Move."

Lacy froze at his serious tone and the concentration on his face. For once he wasn't pretending to ignore her. That scared her far more than she cared to admit.

"Why?" she whispered.

"Because there is a rattlesnake coiled about a foot from your backpack."

Sure enough, through the sudden silence, she heard an agitated rattling.

Lacy screamed, launching herself off the log like a long-jumper on steroids. She stumbled and face planted in the dirt. For a half-a-second she stayed completely motionless—until something dry slithered over her bare calf, followed by a sharp sting.

She leapt up, frantically beating her clothes, hopping from foot to foot drawing her knees to her chest. Her high-pitched shrieks blocked out the sounds of blood pounding in her ears, but didn't hide the taste of fear lodged in her throat.

A large hand clamped over her mouth. She was pulled against a solid, warm body. "Quiet."

Her heart slammed in her chest, but she stopped struggling.

"Calm down." His breath fanned her ear. "It's dead."

A shudder moved through her. She slumped in Becker's arms.

He released his hand. "Did it bite you?"

"I—I don't know. I felt something touch my leg."

"Okay. I'm going to pick you up and carry you to that log. If it did bite you, and you continue to act like a Rockette on acid, then the poison will move through your bloodstream twice as fast, understand?"

She nodded.

Strong arms hooked under her knees. Her head rested under his chin as they shuffled to the log.

Becker sat, keeping Lacy on his lap. "Which leg?"

She burst into tears. "I don't know."

"Ssh. Calm down. Deep breaths, Lacy. We'll figure it out." He shifted, running his hand down her right leg to her knee. "Lift up. Let me see."

Lacy concentrated on the gentle way his callused fingers slid over her skin and not the idea of poison flowing just below the surface.

He turned her foot, fingers circling her ankle. "Nothing. Good. Next leg."

She remained immobile through the same procedure on the other calf, although his hands caressing her body made her skin tingle. Finally, he eased her from his lap.

"You were lucky. Doesn't appear to be a bite mark. You feel okay?"

Relief soared through her. "If it had sunk its nasty fangs into me?"

He tenderly brushed a strand of hair from her tear-stained cheek. "I carry a snakebite kit in my pack, just in case."

"Bet you were an awesome Boy Scout."

Becker actually flashed a half-smile. "I've never been a Boy Scout."

Whoo-ee. That could be taken the wrong way. Smiling, gentle Becker was far more dangerous than surly Becker.

Maybe the rest of the hike wouldn't be so bad now that they'd come to a truce.

"So you killed the varmint, huh? With your bare hands?"

"Nah. Chopped it in half with a shovel. Want to see?"

"Sure."

Lacy stood frozen in place, horrified by what lay next to her dirty backpack. Her stomach roiled, but not at the sight of a potential snakeskin purse in its rawest form.

No. She was sickened by the chunks of metal and broken glass that used to be a compass—a compass she'd accidentally pulverized during her impromptu snake dance.

Damn.

Her stunned gaze caught his.

She decided a snakebite might've been preferable to the venomous gleam in Becker's eye.

Chapter Two

Sam Becker stared at the broken compass.

I could kill her. Wrap my hands around her lovely sunburned neck and squeeze until her cynical blue eyes popped out of her beautiful head.

No one would find her body. Hell, since they were for all intents and purposes lost in the Bighorn Mountains, there was a good chance they'd never find his body either.

He shoved aside his murderous impulse and jerked the chain holding the powdered compass. Spun on his boot heel and stalked to the other side of the log to consider their options. Although he felt her questioning gaze burning his neck like a laser beam, she managed to keep her smart mouth shut for a change.

The sun beat down. The air was calm and hot without a breath of wind. Even the absence of buzzing insects seemed to mock their predicament.

No way around it. They were seriously screwed.

On a gut level he knew his cousin, Dave Hawk, wouldn't wait for them at base camp beyond a few hours, but he wouldn't immediately send out a search party. Their fledgling business had too much riding on the hike to spook other clients. Besides, Dave had told everyone Becker was a partner in Back to Nature Guided Tours.

Problem was, Dave was the experienced backwoods guide, not Becker. Becker was merely the moneyman. He'd taken the summer off from his financial firm in New York City to reevaluate his life and help Dave build databases. He never dreamed he'd have to fill in as an actual employee.

Without a compass, and mired in one mountain pass that looked like every other, they'd be hard-pressed to find their way back to base camp before tomorrow. He'd be damn lucky to find a way out *at all*.

107

So there he was, lost in the woods with a babe who was pure temptation; silky blond hair, blue eyes clear as the summer sky, long legs attached to a perfectly pear-shaped ass…and a tongue sharper than his bowie knife. He'd known Lacy Buchanan was a wild card before she opened her lush pink lips.

Becker had to buck up. Like it or not, she was now his responsibility— even if it was her fault they were up the proverbial creek.

He might be a novice trail guide, but *she* didn't know that. Somehow he'd get them back, even if they had to march all night. He grinned. She ought to just love that, especially wearing those stupid red boots.

"Can you fix it?" she asked anxiously.

"No."

"So what are we gonna do?"

Becker pointed at the watch on her right wrist. "Don't suppose that has a compass?"

"Nope." She peered at the neon blue face. "But it is waterproof to three hundred feet."

"Like that'll do us any good in the middle of Wyoming."

Pink tinged her cheekbones. "I really am sorry. I didn't mean to stomp on it. I sort of panicked."

"*Sort of?*"

She blew out a frustrated breath. "I'm sure that never happens to *you.*"

Becker cocked his head, studying her coolly. "I take it you don't like snakes?"

She shuddered. "No."

"Well, get over it, cupcake, 'cause it's what we're having for supper."

"You can't be serious!"

"I am. Unless you've got a couple of rib-eye steaks hidden in your backpack?"

Lacy shook her head.

He smirked. "Didn't think so."

"It doesn't matter. I'm not eating rattlesnake. Because I-I—" *Come on, think of something or you'll be picking scales out of your teeth.* "Because I'm a vegetarian!"

"Since when?"

Since about five seconds ago, but *he* wouldn't know that.

When she stayed quiet, he threw back his head and laughed. A deep, rich, warm sound in direct conflict with his brusque demeanor. A sexy timbre that made her stomach swoop.

"Nice try. But I saw you eating jerky on the trail yesterday. I know they don't make the stuff out of tofu."

Why had he been watching her wolf down a package of dried buffalo meat instead of watching the trail markers?

No wonder they'd gotten lost.

"I'll bet if some fancy restaurant offered you snake as the evening special you'd order it without hesitation."

"That's different."

"How so?"

"Because I don't eat something that tries to bite me first!"

Becker shrugged. "Suit yourself. If you don't eat it, I don't want to hear you whining that you're hungry later on."

Of course, her stomach chose that exact second to growl.

He picked up the shovel, muttering, "Chicken" under his breath, but loud enough she heard him.

Lacy demanded, "What did you say?"

"It'll probably taste just like chicken." His cool brown eyes dared her to contradict him.

An enormous black buzzard landed on the log, cawing loudly. Beady eyes zeroed in on the snake carcass.

"Go find your own dinner, scavenger," Becker said, chasing the bird away. He tossed a smug look over his broad shoulder. "You too, cupcake."

Right then Lacy knew she'd *have* to eat the snake. Even if it gagged her. Even if it killed her. Better to embrace the idea now, rather than having to…well, eat *crow* later and admit he'd been right.

Before she lost her nerve, she picked up the tail end of the snake. Eww. It was still warm. "How are you going to cook it?"

Did Becker suddenly look a little green?

"Can't sauté it in a white wine and cream sauce, now, can I?" He chopped off the head, picking up the leftover chunk. "We'll roast it like a hot dog. Let's go. Gotta log a few more miles before dark."

"What am I supposed to do with this?"

"Carry it. The rattle might scare off other snakes."

"*Other* snakes?"

Becker smiled before he shouldered his pack and started down the trail.

Insufferable jerk. She had no choice but to play follow-the-leader. Every once in awhile she rattled the snake tail, just to be safe.

<hr />

Hours later, Lacy's feet were sore, blistered and probably bleeding. Her back ached and she still clutched a dead reptile.

She groaned. "I can't move another step."

Becker stopped and stretched. "Fine. We'll take a break."

"*You* can take a break. I'm done for today."

She lifted her face to the breeze, listening to the birdsong and the faint sound of water trickling nearby. With the mountains rising all around them, this remote area was one of the most magnificent places she'd ever seen. "This is breathtaking."

"I'll say."

Becker wasn't looking at the scenery, but at her.

Oh man. He flustered her with one look. What would happen if he actually touched her? She'd probably erupt like Old Faithful.

She refocused on their surroundings.

They'd left the jagged cliffs behind and hiked into a deep canyon. Pine trees grew on a steep incline towering to reach the periwinkle sky. To the right, a small clearing packed with tall, pale green grass eventually sloped up into another craggy hill. It wasn't the flower-filled meadow she'd expected, but it was stunning.

"We'll make camp here. It's almost dusk anyway. You'd better gather some stuff to burn for the fire tonight before you get too comfy."

"What are *you* going to be doing?"

"Skinning the snake. Of course, if you'd rather do it, I've got no problem trading jobs."

Lacy shuddered. "No thanks." She handed him the limp remains and trudged toward the trees, cursing her swollen feet.

"Don't go far," he called. "I don't want to spend the rest of the night wondering if you've become a mountain lion snack."

"Bite me, Pecker."

His soft laughter echoed around her. Seemed the acoustics in the canyon were better than a microphone. Or Mr. Nature had the hearing of a bat.

Or Becker was more focused on her than she realized.

A shiver ran through her, not one of revulsion.

Half an hour later Lacy proudly eyed the pile of pinecones, twigs and decayed logs she'd gathered. In the flattest spot, Becker had lined rocks in a circle and dug a shallow fire pit.

Home sweet home.

But Becker was nowhere to be seen.

She wiped the sweat and dirt from her forehead with the back of her hand. Ick. Snake germs. She crossed the meadow toward the tinkling sound of water. She stumbled over a tree root and her tongue when she saw a shirtless Becker standing in the stream.

Lacy quickly ducked behind a clump of bushes and gawked.

His wide, muscled shoulders were tanned golden brown. Rivulets of water trailed his nicely defined pecs and followed the lines of his six-pack, disappearing into the waistband of the wet cargo shorts that hung dangerously low on his lean hips.

He was a glorious, gorgeous male animal.

A punch of lust knocked the breath from her lungs. She'd never wanted a man on such an elemental level. No talking. No foreplay. Just an animalistic mating. Hard, fast, sweaty, dirty raw sex. Him pounding into her until she screamed her pleasure, shattering the woodland silence.

Oblivious, Becker bent down and splashed water on his face. Raked his hands through his hair. Droplets of water clung to his dark stubble and glistened on his eyelashes. His nipples were tight.

Lacy ached to feel those rigid points with her tongue. Longed to trace the water's path down his river-cooled body with her hot mouth.

He stiffened. Seemed to look right at her. Then went on cleaning himself. Thoroughly.

Did Becker realize he was tormenting her as his wet bandana wiped every inch of his amazing body?

Probably.

Still, she leered until he returned to camp.

The narrow stream tumbled over a rock-lined bed. In several spots along the grassy edge, water pooled deep. Lacy plunged her hands into the icy coldness, scrubbing with a small stone until her fingers turned pink.

Satisfied all traces of snake oil were gone, she whipped off her tank top and rinsed it. Felt strangely freeing to flaunt her naked breasts and cup the cool, clear liquid, letting it flow down her body like an invisible lover's caress.

Was Becker lurking? Feeling that same inexplicable desire she'd experienced watching him?

She stayed bare-chested until her shirt dried, just in case.

Lacy sat on a bed of moss, hypnotized by the transformation of day into night. Twilight turned the sky a majestic purple. Stars twinkled. A soft breeze wafted by, stirring the hair stuck to her nape. She couldn't remember the last time she'd existed in such peace. No agenda. No people criticizing her. The scent of pine and the underlying earthy aroma of the forest filled her lungs.

When a rank smell replaced the sweetness of the night air, Lacy immediately scrambled to her feet.

Was there a dead animal close by? Or just a stinky, hungry creature hunting for a meal? She started to run, but stopped when she remembered the Discovery Channel warning that predators *liked* prey to run. In the near dark she staggered through the meadow, the stench increasing with every step.

She stopped. A fire lit the darkness surrounding the campsite and smoke drifted toward her.

It appeared that awful smell was dinner.

Chapter Three

It looked worse than it smelled.

Becker eyed the crispy chunk of meat on the end of the stick. Screw this. He didn't have to demonstrate his stubborn streak to her. He'd rather starve than eat barbequed snake.

Lacy limped into view, smile pasted on her freshly-scrubbed face. "What's that delicious odor?"

Odor. Not aroma. Not exactly a ringing endorsement for his culinary skills. He scowled at the red-hot coals. Time to call a halt to this juvenile, I'll-eat-it-if-you-will game.

When she stopped—downwind from the campfire smoke—he glanced up.

The dancing firelight bathed her in an ethereal glow. She looked half-angel, half-temptress. Which one was the real Lacy? How could he find out firsthand?

He was tired of baiting her. Since they were stuck with each other for the rest of the hike, they might as well make the most of it.

Becker mustered his most charming smile. "That stench is dinner. And you're more than welcome to eat my share because I sure as hell am not touching it."

Her eyes narrowed suspiciously. "Really?"

"Scouts honor. I'd rather chomp on pine needles."

She plopped beside him on the log. "Thank God. Honestly, I didn't know if I could—Hey! Wait a minute!" She whapped him on the arm.

"Ouch! What was that for?"

"For making me carry that stupid snake. If we weren't gonna eat it, we could've left it for the buzzards."

Hopefully she'd credit the fire for the red flush on his cheeks, not guilt. "Sorry. Don't know what came over me. I'm usually not such a jerk."

Lacy looked dubious at his declaration. "I know what came over you. Being out in the wilderness does strange things to men."

"Define strange."

"A temporary reversion to caveman ways. You know..." She grunted. "You man, me woman. Me make fire, you make dinner."

"Error in your logic. I've made the fire *and* dinner."

Lacy blushed a delicate rosy-pink, captivating him completely.

"You missed the point."

"Which is?"

"The need for men to prove they're 'real men'."

He lifted his brows, waiting for what promised to be an entertaining explanation. "Like?"

She kicked a pinecone into the flames. "Like Ross didn't have a clue what 'GPS' meant, but put him in Central Park and suddenly he's an expert? Please. He can't find his way out of the men's room."

This guy had soured her on more than the great outdoors. Becker didn't find it as amusing as he'd imagined. "Ross sounds like an asshole."

She blinked. "Whoa. Sorry about the 'men suck' tangent."

"Why didn't you back out of this hike?" He stirred the coals. "Since it was your ex-boyfriend's idea?"

Lacy propped her elbows on her knees and gazed into the fire. "Because I'm sick of being called a marshmallow. A creampuff." She slanted him a sideways glance. "A cupcake. I wanted to prove I'm an adventurous woman."

Oh yeah, he definitely had one way in particular she could prove that. And it sure as hell didn't involve GPS.

Their gazes clashed. By the way Lacy fidgeted, Becker figured his lustful intentions were clearly written in his eyes.

She glanced away quickly. "So, since we're not having snake filets, how about if I cook?" She rummaged in her backpack, unearthing two protein bars, tossing one to him. "Guaranteed edible."

"Thanks." He bent forward to chuck another branch on the fire.

Lacy was frowning at him when he sat up.

"What?"

"You're bleeding."

He craned his neck but couldn't see. "Where?"

"From a scratch on your back. I can't believe you didn't feel it. Then again, I suppose a tough outdoorsman like you is used to getting hurt." She dug in her backpack and waved a big Band-Aid. "Voila."

"You carry Band-Aids?"

"A necessity for wearing stylish shoes. Hold still." Soft fingertips gently danced over his skin.

Goose bumps broke out across his body. He hissed, but not from pain.

"Sorry. Did I hurt you?"

"No." He smiled slyly. "Thanks for tendin' my wound, little lady."

Lacy batted her lashes. "Careful, mountain man. I might think you like me."

"Maybe I do."

The air between them turned sultry, heavy with promise, though neither voiced the obvious. Silence stretched for a time as they listened to sounds of the night.

Becker heard a jingle. He'd noticed she constantly fiddled with the silver bracelet circling her right wrist.

"Where'd you get that?"

"A gift from my friend, Cat."

"Can I see it?"

"Sure." She scooted closer, offering her arm.

"Pretty. What is this?" He pointed to a twisted, dangling blob.

"A *Sita* knot."

"Which is?"

"A Celtic symbol denoting the four phases of the moon, the four stages of life and the four seasons."

"Did Cat give this to you because you've been friends *for-ever?*"

Lacy groaned at his pun. "No. She gave it to me before I left as a symbol of new beginnings." She smiled wistfully. "But crazy Cat kinda runs on her own kooky calendar."

"How so?"

"Well, the traditional Celtic season for new beginnings, Samhain, doesn't happen for a few months."

"I know," he murmured, stroking his thumb over her silky skin beneath the bracelet.

"You do? How?"

He'd never admitted to anyone outside his family that his crazy mother had christened him "Sam" after he'd arrived on Samhain Eve. Since childhood Becker had discounted his mother's warnings about the power of fate and karma, as much as her belief in crystals and superstitions. Nonsense in his opinion. Hard work, not fate, ruled his life. "My mother is into all that New Age crap."

"It's not crap." She attempted to yank her arm away.

Becker held fast. "Wrong word choice."

"Then what did you mean?"

He flicked the charm. "Do you believe this bracelet can somehow change your life?"

"Yes. Not by itself, but I see it as a reminder I *can* choose my own path. I'm not doomed to keep repeating the same mistakes."

"Such as?"

"Bad jobs. Bad relationships. Bad decisions."

"Has your luck changed since you put it on?"

"Into bad luck, maybe. First I got lost, now I'm stuck with you—"

He dropped her arm like a hot coal.

Lacy leaned until their shoulders touched. "Wrong word choice."

"Touché," he said.

"*I* seem to be bad luck. I'd hoped it'd change on this trip."

Becker couldn't help himself. He reached for her, smoothing fine wisps of hair from her velvety-soft cheek. "Maybe it has." His touch lingered when her eyes sparked with desire. With the back of his hand he leisurely traced the outline of her face from temple to chin, sweeping his thumb over her plump bottom lip. "Firelight looks good on you, Lacy."

"Becker—"

"Sam."

"Sam—"

"Ssh. You talk too much."

Her breath caught as he brushed his lips across hers. Once. Twice. As he was about to dive into her succulent mouth for a real kiss, an animal screeched.

Lacy jumped. "W-what was that?"

Bad timing. Shit. Or good timing. What had he been thinking? His responsibilities for her didn't include kissing and exchanging life goals.

He scanned the sky. "Probably an owl." Better to put some distance between them. "I'm whipped. Let's douse the fire and hit the hay. We've got an early start tomorrow."

※⬩⬩⬩⬩⬩⬩⬩⬩⬩⬩⬩⬩⬩⬩⬩※

Surly Becker had returned. Big surprise. No skin off her nose he'd changed his mind. He hadn't asked for her help as he trekked to the stream for water to put out the fire.

Did the cold water have any effect on the heat she'd seen in his eyes? She hadn't imagined his interest or the eroticism in that simple kiss.

As the last embers smoked, Lacy unrolled her sleeping bag.

"Got everything you need out of your backpack?"

"Yeah. Why?"

"Because I need to loop it over a tree branch in case bears come sniffing around."

118

Bears. Her stomach lurched. How could she sleep knowing wild animals roamed nearby? Last night there'd been safety in numbers. But tonight…just the two of them? She watched him tie the flaps together and drape the backpacks over a high tree branch with a long stick.

Becker spread out on the other side of the fire pit.

She tamped down the urge to ask if it'd be safer if they slept closer. Like in the same sleeping bag.

No. Dammit. She'd show him she wasn't scared. Or a cupcake.

"Lacy?"

"Yes?"

"If you need…"

To rip my clothes off and revisit that body-heat-sharing idea… She shook her head to clear it. "What?"

"To…see, ah…man about a horse, wake me up."

"Afraid I'll wander off?"

"Yes."

"Fine. But you'd better not be grouchy as a damn bear when I do. Good night."

Lacy crawled inside her sleeping bag fully clothed. She zipped up, scooting down until no part of her body stuck out.

Eyes squeezed shut, she repeated, *There's no place like home. There's no place like home.* Which really didn't calm her because it brought to mind the other famous phrase from *The Wizard of Oz, Lions-and-tigers-and-bears-oh-my.*

Counting sheep wouldn't help either; it'd remind her of hungry wolves. With red eyes and big gnashing teeth.

She'd actually fallen asleep only to be awakened by a bloodcurdling scream. Hers? Maybe she'd imagined it. She waited breathlessly. And heard the scream again. Louder. Was it closer? After the third one, she scrambled out of her sleeping bag and ran to where Becker slept.

Lacy threw herself on top of him. "Becker!"

"What the…" He squinted at her. "What's wrong?"

"I heard a scream and I-I—"

119

"Shit. You're shaking. Come here." He unzipped his bag and pulled her inside. It was a tight fit.

Lacy didn't care. She plastered herself to him.

Becker stroked her back, murmuring in her hair. When she calmed down, she looked up at him. He was so...

Yummy. Hot. Sweet. Like cinnamon candy. She could suck on him all night.

"Better?"

"Yeah. Thanks."

"Hang on." Cool air wafted in. He climbed out and dragged her sleeping bag over. "Hop out for a sec." He zipped the two bags together.

A shiver worked loose at the thought of lying beside him in close quarters. Without meeting his gaze, she dove inside their cozy nest.

He followed a beat later.

Despite the awkwardness of sleeping with a man she hardly knew, Lacy finally felt safe. She drifted off and was almost asleep when a chorus of howls shot her back to awareness.

"What was that?"

"Coyotes."

"That wasn't what I heard earlier."

"Probably a mountain lion before," he mumbled.

"A mountain lion?" She inched closer.

"Yeah."

"But—"

"God!" Becker wrapped his arms around her, tucking her against his chest. "Happy now? They'll have to chew through me to get to you. Go to sleep."

She shut her eyes. Really tried to think of Becker as protection. Not a man with bulging muscles. Who smelled all woodsy. Who radiated such warmth. She rubbed her cheek over his left pec. Listened to his erratic heartbeat.

"Stop wiggling."

"I can't get comfortable."

"That makes two of us." He loosened his hold on her.

Lacy glanced up.

Their lips were a breath apart.

He growled and covered her mouth with his.

No gentle kiss this time. The second his tongue touched hers desire leveled her like a felled tree.

Becker's masterful kisses alternated teeth-grinding passion with slow, wet, teasing nibbles. His hands cradled her head to position her mouth however he wanted.

If the hardness pressing into her hip was any indication, he wanted her. Big time.

Lacy grabbed handfuls of his T-shirt until he impatiently yanked it off.

Oh. His skin was hot. Smooth. Perfect. Chest muscles rippled beneath her fingertips as she traced his hard contours.

Groaning, he shifted, wedging his muscular leg between her softer thighs and clamped his hands on her ass, grinding her pelvis against his.

She bowed beneath him, greedy to gorge on all the carnal delights his body promised.

Becker trailed openmouthed kisses down her throat, flicking his tongue in tandem with her racing pulse. Then he sank his mouth into the magic spot where her neck met shoulder and bit down.

Lacy let out a moan, lost in his intoxicating masculine scent, and the thrilling feel of his reckless lips branding her skin.

His hands slipped beneath her tank top. Rough fingertips tickled her bare belly as his thumbs lazily grazed the underside of her breasts. He stopped kissing her neck, pressing his damp lips to her ear. "Lift your arms."

Her shirt disappeared. Then his silky mouth closed over her right nipple.

He sucked softly. Forcefully. The teasing nip of his teeth was followed by wet swirls of his tongue. His hot breath beaded the tip into a painful point.

Her brain fogged with pleasure. "More."

The stubble on his chin raked the tender skin on her chest. He soothed the sting with petal-soft kisses and switched to the other breast. "You taste sweet, cupcake."

His hoarse whisper sent a rush of moisture south.

The flannel sleeping bag stroked her flesh as Lacy thrashed. She ached. Every scrape of his beard, every suctioning kiss and deliberate lick made her slick and ready. She turned her head...and saw a pair of beady red eyes staring back at her.

She screamed and tried to roll away—an impossible feat with two hundred pounds of amorous male crushing her to the ground.

Becker went still. "What's wrong?"

"There's a wild animal!"

"Where?"

"By the tree."

He sat up. Paused. "The squirrel? *That's* what scared you?"

Lacy peeked over Becker's shoulder. A fluffy tail swished up the trunk as it scampered away.

She'd freaked about a squirrel. How mortifying. She reached for her shirt, giving Becker her back.

"Lacy—"

"Save it. I'm an idiot. Go ahead and laugh." She pressed herself into the zippered side of the joined bags, leaving a big gap between them.

"I'm not going to laugh at you," he said quietly.

"You'd be the first."

The last thing Lacy heard Becker say was, "I'm not like him. You'd best remember that."

Her heart turned over, but she didn't. She closed her eyes and tried to sleep.

Chapter Four

Becker's snores woke Lacy up. She snuck off, snickering at his quaint phrasing about bodily functions. When she returned, Becker had already rolled up the sleeping bags and their backpacks rested against the log.

He gave her a crusty look. "Thought I told you to tell me when you needed—"

"I don't need you to hold my hand," she retorted sweetly.

"Could've fooled me last night."

Her face flamed. Damn Nordic genes. "Sorry. It won't happen again." She tied her sleeping bag to her pack, grabbed her toothbrush and uncapped her canteen. Empty. Without another word, she headed for the creek.

Scrubbing her face and teeth improved her mood. Until she noticed Becker leaning against a tree, glaring at her.

"What? Hoping to see me fall in and get washed downstream?"

Becker scowled. "You have a real high opinion of me." He sidestepped her and bent to fill his canteen.

"I assume you've got a plan for getting us back to civilization?"

Why did his back stiffen?

"Yeah. I think we should walk east. Because if we keep going west, we'll get deeper into the mountains. There are houses and roads at the foothills."

She considered it. "Makes sense."

"You aren't going to question my plan?"

"No. I trust you."

Relief flitted through his eyes. "What's our food situation?"

"Don't you have anything in your pack?"

"No."

A guide with no supplies? Something about that didn't ring true. "I've got one protein bar left."

"Save it. Keep an eye out for berries or something edible."

"While I'm foraging what will you be doing?"

"Keepin' you safe from wild critters, darlin'."

"I don't—"

"Although, I liked it when you wanted my protection from them last night."

Incredulous, she said, "You did?"

He nodded.

"You aren't upset?"

"Only if I won't get another shot at protecting you tonight."

A sexy smile broke across his handsome face and made Lacy weak-kneed. How was she supposed to hike with him wreaking havoc on her system?

"Come on, cupcake. Let's get moving."

<hr>

"Tell me about your job in New York," Becker said to take their minds off the grueling uphill hike.

"It's not nearly as exciting as what you do. I'm in advertising. I try to sell people things they don't need."

Becker grinned. An apt—and surprisingly honest answer.

Lacy launched into an explanation about the rigors of her day-to-day life that sounded exactly like his. "But I'm ready for a change."

"Like?"

"Like working in a low-pressure job so I can savor life instead of making it a competition."

"Are you competitive in everything?"

"Yep." Lacy smiled saucily before taking off up the steep incline.

He chased her. She won. This time.

They stood atop the rise, wheezing, staring at the never-ending sea of greenish-black pine trees.

She sighed. Sipped from her canteen and handed it to him.

"What?"

"I'd hoped to find a Super 8 on the other side of this hill."

Was she sorry she'd listened to him? Especially when he was winging it about forging a way out of the mountains?

She trusts you. Don't let her down.

Becker wiped the water from his chin, passing back the canteen. "Let's keep walking. Never know what's over the next rise."

Once they'd returned to the shaded woods, she said, "Tell me about your mother. Is she still into that 'New Age' crap?"

"Yes."

"Is that why you are the way you are?"

He knew Lacy meant his persona as a mountain guide, but he answered honestly. "I'm the way I am in *spite* of my upbringing."

"She doesn't approve of your chosen field?"

"No." His mother was half-Irish/half-Lakota Sioux. She'd expected him to help run the family pub after college. Becker preferred to pursue other goals. Now that he'd exceeded his own expectations, he was ready for a new direction in his life. Taking the summer off to help his cousin launch a new venture was shaping up to be the best decision he'd made.

Despite the fact he and Lacy were lost.

"Does your family think you should abandon the ad biz?" He picked up a branch blocking their path.

"No. That's why Cat made me the bracelet. To remind me I'm in charge of my own destiny."

Before Becker could respond, Lacy wandered into a patch of sunshine. He watched her poking around in a cluster of low bushes. "What'd you find?"

"Raspberry canes." She held out her hand. Nestled in her palm were tiny red fruit.

"How does a Manhattanite recognize a raspberry bush?"

Lacy blushed. "My grandmother lived outside of Spearfish. We used to go raspberry picking in the Black Hills the summers I stayed with her."

"So you do have some wilderness skills."

"I thought I did until that time I got lost and my parents forbid me from visiting Grandma again."

Becker froze. "Lost?"

"Ah. Yeah."

"What happened?"

"I wandered off. Grandma thought I'd gone back to the house. She didn't realize I wasn't around until it was dark." She kicked the dirt. "Then it was too late to search so I spent the night in the woods alone scared out of my mind."

"How old were you?"

"Nine."

He grasped her by the upper arms. "Why the hell didn't you tell me this before?"

"Because my parents accused me of getting lost on purpose just for the attention. I didn't want you to think the same."

Another thought notched his guilt. "Did your ex-boyfriend know you'd gotten lost in the woods as a child?"

Lacy nodded.

"And yet he still booked you on this wilderness hiking trip?"

"Yes. He's probably at base camp laughing that I'm missing."

"He's *there*?"

"Yes. Waiting to go in the next group. Instead of canceling, I moved my trip up a week."

Becker's hands fell. He stared at the stubborn tilt to her elfin chin. He spun away to hide his mortification. Jesus. He'd acted the super-macho asshole, just like her ex. She'd been scared shitless last night and he'd used it as an excuse to get his hands and mouth all over her lush body.

Talk about caveman tendencies.

He heard Lacy's footsteps fading He needed a minute to wallow in his self-reproach before he offered her an apology.

When Becker regained control, he tracked her to a sun-washed clearing. She sat on a stump like a beautiful woodland fairy, eating raspberries.

He groaned. The fruit was the exact color of her nipples. His zipper grew snug as he remembered the sweet taste and those rosy tips hardening against his stroking tongue.

She offered her hand. "Berry for your thoughts?"

"Cupcake, you'd run if you knew what I was thinking."

"You don't scare me, mountain man. Besides. I beat you once."

"I *let* you win."

Lacy said, "You wish. But, I'd probably let you catch me anyway."

He gave her a wolfish smile. "Prove it."

***

Lacy trudged after Becker, panting at his breakneck speed. Seemed he was anxious to make good on the lust-filled challenge she'd read in his eyes.

He stopped so suddenly she smacked into his backpack.

"Do you smell that?"

"What?"

"Water. Thank God. I'm out." He shot off, cutting through underbrush, skirting trees and disappearing down a slope.

She found him by a sharp bend in a wide stream.

"See? I told you."

"I never doubted your woodsman abilities, Becker."

He frowned.

Lacy untied her boots, peeled off her socks and waded in.

"What are you doing?"

"Cooling off."

"Be careful."

"I am." The icy water felt sublime. She aimed for a flat rock on the other side when the bottom literally fell from beneath her.

The cold shock of submersion caused an involuntary gasp and her mouth filled with frigid water. She couldn't breathe. She kicked, thrashing to reach the surface for air.

Her head hit a rock. Or was it the bottom? She flailed, dredging up silt and sank deeper into nothingness.

Oh God. She was drowning.

An eternity passed before powerfully built arms lifted her from the black hole.

Becker.

He dragged her to the clearing and wouldn't let her go. Even after she finished coughing up half the river.

Once she could breathe, she slumped against his heaving chest. "Thanks." Several minutes later when Becker hadn't responded, she peered at him warily. "Tired of rescuing me?"

"Stop."

Lacy swallowed hard at the fierceness in his dark eyes. "You were right. I—"

"Shut-up," he snarled, grabbing her shoulders. "Just shut the hell up." His mouth dropped over hers. He consumed her in a kiss so fiery she was amazed the forest didn't ignite from the heat.

Becker kissed her until she was dizzy from the onslaught, drunk on the taste of hot, demanding male.

Then he touched while exploring the depths of her mouth, reassuring them both she was alive and well. Stroking her hair. Face. Throat. Breasts. Between her thighs. Thorough, reverent caresses spiked with passion until her blood heated and steam poured from every pore in her body.

He broke free from her lips to drag wet kisses down the arch of her neck.

She moaned.

He tugged her shirt. "Off."

Lacy's tank top sailed to the ground followed by Becker's T-shirt. Strong hands cupped her breasts. A rough thumb rasped over her nipples.

Her pelvis sought his. She dug her nails into his brawny shoulders, anchoring herself against the storm he'd unleashed between them.

"Lacy," he breathed against her skin, "you scared me."

"I'm sorry."

"I never should've let—"

"Ssh. You talk too much. Touch me."

Impatient fingers unzipped her shorts, slipping them and her underwear off. He cupped her bare ass, picked her up and walked backward until her spine hit a tree.

Once her feet touched the ground, she reached for his zipper.

"No. My way."

One possessive hand covered her breast. Becker fastened his lips to hers. Ran his palm down the center of her body, through the moist curls. He pushed a thick finger deep inside her damp heat, groaning at the creamy wetness he found. He added another finger and pumped in and out, feathering his thumb over her throbbing clit until it flowered beneath his persistent stroking. He ate at her mouth, then those voracious kisses veered south.

He dropped to his knees and licked her quivering belly.

"Sam—"

"Say my name again."

"Sam." Her swollen sex was weeping for his attention.

"Say it while my mouth is on you." He flattened his tongue and made long, calculated sweeps from her opening to her pubic bone, avoiding the hot spot aching for his notice.

"Please—"

"Say it," he growled, retreating to scatter love bites inside her sensitive thigh.

"Sam! Sam, please—" Lacy fisted her hands in his glossy hair, jerking him back to where she burned.

"Goddamn you taste sweet." His thumbs spread her wide. Teasing tongue flicks on her clit turned precise. He settled his wicked mouth on that engorged nub and sucked. The blood in her body gathered in a pulsating rhythm and burst against his darting tongue as she shattered.

The sheer force of her climax elicited a shriek, scattering birds from the treetops. She wilted against the tree, her legs trembling, bark scoring her naked back.

Through her ragged breathing she heard his shorts hit the dirt. Felt his gentle touch on her cheek.

Lacy's mouth went dry even as moisture flooded her core from the raw hunger on Sam's face.

He boosted her against the trunk. "Wrap your legs around my waist and hold on."

She reached for the low-hanging limbs. He leaned back, aligning the tip of his cock to her molten entrance.

Locking his gaze to hers, he slammed home.

Lacy moaned at the luscious feeling of all that male hardness filling her. Her lids fluttered shut in pure bliss.

"Don't close your eyes. Watch."

"Sam—"

"Do it."

In the back of her mind she knew the adrenaline rush from life or death situations created over-inflated primal responses. Becker's domination didn't scare her; it inflamed her.

Their impassioned gazes clashed.

He kneaded her ass and lifted her torso higher. "These are the berries I want." Sam's hot mouth latched onto her nipple. He suckled strongly. "Mmm. Mmm."

The tugs of his teeth along with his greedy sex ramming into her over and over coiled her desire until she nearly burst. "Please. Sam."

Abruptly he changed the angle of his hips, driving deeper until she felt his balls slapping her ass.

"Like that, do you?"

"Yes!"

He growled. "The harder I fuck you the shorter it'll last."

"Then harder." Lacy squeezed her internal muscles as he pulled out.

Sam hissed. "You are so tight and hot it's like shoving my dick into a live electrical socket."

Her body tingled in a line from where his busy mouth seared her skin to where her breasts jiggled from his powerful thrusts. Gradually contractions built deep within her cervix. Then wham! The strength of the spasms around his thick cock caused her to scream.

In the aftermath of another orgasm that blew her mind, her breath heaved. The pulses faded to soft throbs.

He'd stopped moving inside her. His fingers dug into her hips. Sweat dripped down his face and over his clenched jaw.

"Sam? What's wrong?"

"Watch me come, like I watched you." He began to thrust, shallow, then deep, keeping those dark eyes on hers. The deep-seated strokes became piston-fast. He whispered her name, arched his back and exploded inside her with a ferocity that sent another orgasm ripping through her still quaking body.

Exhausted, sated, stunned, they clung to each other.

She whispered, "Tiimmbbberr."

His laugh rumbled against her throat.

Then Sam gifted her with the sweetest kiss of her life. She breathed him in, wreathing her arms around his neck. Being lost in the woods wasn't nearly as scary as the way this man made her feel.

Chapter Five

Becker attempted to stay upright. His cock twitched inside Lacy's snug walls as air billowed from his lungs.

She licked his earlobe. Bit down. Chills racked his system. "You gonna drag me off to your cave now?"

How should he play this? Tough? Tender? Hell, he'd never been the kind to fuck a woman senseless against a pine tree. Never been that out-of-control, in his personal or professional life. "You *want* me to drag you off?"

"Mmm. If you promise to do that to me again."

Becker gazed at her slumberous eyes, cat-like smirk, flushed skin, lips plumped from avaricious kisses. His Neanderthal tactics hadn't bothered her.

He nibbled her jawline. "Next time you don't have to practically drown to get my undivided attention."

She went rigid. "I didn't do it on purpose."

"I know." Becker nuzzled her ear. "I'm surprised you aren't chewing my ass for being so rough."

He held his breath, waiting for her to voice regret.

"Me too. I've never let a man take me like that—" She shuddered, a little moan escaped. "I liked it, Sam. What does that mean?"

"My little cupcake has a submissive streak."

She tipped her head back. "Really?"

"Really. It's sexy as hell." He kissed her. "It also means we're camping here."

"Why?"

"So I can do all the other uncivilized things I've been fantasizing about doing to you before we find civilization."

"Oh." She moistened her lips. "Such as?"

"Bending you over that log by the stream and taking you from behind until you scream like a mountain lion in season."

Lacy's gaze darted toward the fallen tree before her eyes widened with interest.

Becker grinned. "Much as I'm dying to stay buried inside you…" He brushed his lips over her mouth, reconnecting their desire as he disconnected their bodies.

She seemed shy, turning away to get dressed.

Impulsively he snatched her clothes. "Huh-uh. Naked. All day. My rules."

"Caveman rules, you mean."

"Yep."

"Do the rules of the jungle apply to you?"

"Yep."

"Great." Her shyness vanished as she eyed his dick. "I have a few fantasies."

One smoldering look from her and his cock went from semi-aroused to hard-as-nails. "Such as?"

"Tarzan and Jane." Lacy smiled, circling her fingers around his girth. "Can I lay on something soft this time? That bark raked my back."

Guilt beat at him. "Let me see."

"You will. When you bend me over, rutting on me like a stag, you can kiss it and make it all better."

Becker found a flat spot where cool breezes blew off the water and spread out the sleeping bags. He lowered Lacy to the soft flannel, using his mouth and hands to render her mindless. Sucking on her fingers. Her toes. Her nipples. Her juicy sex. He drove her to the brink with gentle kisses. Fleeting touches on every inch of her trembling flesh until she begged him to stop.

Then he'd begin again.

When he entered her, oh-so-slowly, she came on a long sigh that floated away on the pine-scented wind, but boomeranged to implant in his soul.

Not to be outdone, Lacy whispered dirty suggestions in his ear. The leisurely loving became frantic. Harsh kisses and harder thrusts. His sweat-slicked skin slapped hers. His balls pulled up, blanking his mind to anything but pure animal instinct.

He grunted, slamming into her wet channel. Taking them both higher, until Lacy milked him to an orgasm so ferocious he roared like a beast.

Afterward, Lacy's sweet breath tickled the back of his neck as she curled around him.

He'd fallen into that peaceful half-asleep/half-awake state, when she asked softly, "Why did you wait for me, Sam? No one else in the hiking group noticed I was missing."

Because you piqued my interest more than any woman ever has.

Another voice whispered, *Because she's your fate.*

Shut-up, Mom.

Becker kept his tone light. "You were my responsibility."

"That's it?"

Why did she sound disappointed by his answer? "No." He faced her and the truth in himself. "I'd been watching you." Becker caressed her cheek. "Wanting you. Admiring your determination even when the unknown scared the hell out of you."

"You admire that? Why?"

"Because I've been thinking about making changes in my own life."

Lacy gestured to the great outdoors. "But your life is a new exciting adventure every day."

"You'd be surprised at the mundane aspects of my day-to-day existence."

"Does having uninhibited sex in the woods count as mundane?"

"No. This is a first."

She smiled sleepily. "I'm glad." Seeming content, she snuggled closer.

He traced lazy circles on her back. "Tell me something about yourself that no one else knows."

"Besides the submissive side you've uncovered?"

"Smart-ass." He pinched her butt.

Lacy giggled. "Hmm. How about…my dream of making love in a field of wildflowers?"

Becker rolled his eyes. "You and every woman on the planet. Not good enough. Try again."

She ducked her head, delving her fingers into his scant chest hair. "It's hokey."

"Tell me.

"I want to be like my Grandma Ingrid."

"Why?"

"She's always happy. Whether she's living in the woods or in a rest home. She's never afraid and embraces change. Whereas, I'm scared of change, even when I'm hoping for a fresh start."

A fresh start with him?

Surely she wasn't one of those women who altered their life on a whim after meeting a man? But Lacy *had* agreed to undertake the hike at the urging of her ex, even with her frightening past experience. "Like moving to Wyoming to live in a shack in the boonies?"

"With a real, live mountain man like you?" Her smile didn't sugarcoat the bitter tone. "That didn't sound like an invite, Becker."

"Lacy—"

"Don't worry. I'll be on a plane to LaGuardia in another week. It's on my mind because I visited Grandma last week. She told me change is good for the soul."

"Your soul doesn't need to change."

"That's sweet. But *I* need a change. So, I made a decision. I'm going to quit my job and take Cat's offer to manage her store. Then she can concentrate on creating more of these."

Lacy lifted her arm. Her smile died when she realized the charm bracelet was gone.

"Omigod!" She leapt up, blood pounding in her ears as she ran to the river. Why hadn't she noticed it was missing?

Because Sam-the-orgasm-man made it impossible to focus on anything else.

She frantically sifted through her socks and shoes. Nothing. She scoured the rocks and mud on the bank until her feet were submerged in silt.

A large hand circled her upper arm, angrily yanking her back.

"What the fuck are you doing?"

Lacy shook him off. "Looking for my bracelet."

"The hell you are."

Seeing something shiny, she bent down.

And found herself airborne. The sinewy arms circling her waist were striking against her paler bare skin. She gasped. How had she forgotten she was naked?

"Becker! Let me down."

Water splashed.

She kicked, which increased his grip. She swore, which earned her a solid slap on the ass.

He tossed her on the sleeping bag. Imprisoned her flailing arms above her head, using his body on hers as dead weight.

"Let me go!"

"Not until you're acting reasonable."

"But my bracelet—"

"Is lost."

"So I need to find it!"

"Not at the expense of your safety. You don't even know when you lost it, do you?"

"No."

"I'm responsible for you and you aren't chancing another unexpected swim in the river for a trinket. Are we clear on that?"

Sam's eyes were clouded with concern, not anger.

Finally Lacy nodded. She hid her face. Frustrated tears leaked out. She knew Sam was right. But dammit, that bracelet wasn't a trinket. It'd meant something to her. Something he didn't understand.

Sam tenderly kissed the top of her head, folded her in his arms and let her bawl.

When the crying jag ended, he handed her a canteen.

She took a tiny sip.

"Drink more," he demanded.

"No. I'm hungry and confused, not thirsty. I'm—" Lacy started sobbing again.

"Ssh. You're just tired."

She felt like an idiot for many reasons, but mostly for needing Sam to stick around. "You'll—"

"Be right here."

"Okay." Before she drifted off, she whispered, "Since I lost the bracelet, that means I'm doomed to repeat past mistakes, doesn't it?"

Sam stroked her hair. "Don't worry. Just rest."

<hr/>

While Lacy dozed, Becker dressed and dragged deadfall for the fire. Two days had passed. They were out of food. Hiking out tomorrow until they reached something resembling civilization was a must. Dave might've already sent out a search team.

He glanced at Lacy. Possession rolled through him like a hot wind. They'd created a connection deeper than phenomenal sex. Would their lives be simpler if he *could* cart her off into the woods and keep her to himself forever?

Nice fantasy. He couldn't even feed or protect her for the short-term. Speaking of...why hadn't Lacy demanded that he hunt or fish to fill their rumbling bellies?

Did Lacy suspect he wasn't an outdoorsman, but a suit-and-tie wearing workaholic? Since it appeared she'd given him her blind trust, how would she react when she found out he'd deceived her?

She'd be upset. He never wanted to see hurt in her big blue eyes.

He picked up her socks and shoes. Her shorts. He grabbed her shirt and tried to turn it right-side-out. Something was caught on the inside and he gently shook. Charms jingled as the missing bracelet fell from inside the shirt and hit the dirt.

Becker froze. Thank God. Now maybe she'd lose the forlorn look. Maybe she'd get inventive in the naughty ways she'd show her gratitude that he'd found it.

But what if…he didn't hand it over? What if finding her talisman was *his* sign that the changes he'd been searching for started with her? His mother claimed destiny and blind faith were intertwined. Alone the fragile threads could snap. Together they were a steel cable. He fingered the twisted silver chain.

Romantic nonsense? Or the leap of faith he'd been lacking?

Destiny aside, he needed a plan. How could he convince her these past days meant more than a random romp in the woods?

It hit him. Dave had Lacy's address on file. After she returned to Manhattan, Becker could show up at her place, bracelet in hand. Confess his true "city slicker" identity. They could start fresh. Go out for a latte or something.

Right. Like a civilized coffee date would cut it after screwing like wild animals in the forest.

What to do?

Wait, which he was lousy at. He shoved the bracelet in his backpack for the time-being and hoped he hadn't already screwed this up.

Half a protein bar didn't slake Lacy's hunger. Sam hadn't complained about the lack of food. He hadn't said much either.

There were plenty more interesting things to do besides talk.

Did she have the guts to make the first move?

The fire crackled. Sam caught her leering as he swiped a damp bandana over his face. "What?"

Lacy swallowed the fear that surly Becker had returned and would rebuff her. "I watched you cleaning up in the stream yesterday."

"You did? Why?"

"Duh. Because you were half-naked."

He grinned.

"I wanted so bad to—"

"To what?"

"Touch you."

"Why didn't you?"

"You didn't like me much."

He lifted a brow. "What's stopping you now?"

She seized the dare and gave him a once-over. "Your clothes."

Sam stood. Shed his shorts and shirt in a flash.

The red glow from the fire threw shadows over his sculpted form, making him appear cast from bronze. Her mouth watered. Slinging the canteen over her shoulder, she eliminated the distance between them.

Lacy placed her hands on his chest. Smoothed her palms over his chiseled pecs. "Yum." She took his flat nipple in her mouth, sucking until it puckered on her tongue. Then she gradually slid her hands down his center. His flat belly quivered from her touch, giving her an incredible sense of power.

As she kissed a path to his neglected nipple, she urged his body against hers by grabbing his muscular ass. Sam's erection fit perfectly in the cradle of her hips. She ground into him.

His head fell back, but his heated gaze remained on hers.

She circled his impressive shaft and pumped from root to tip.

Sam hissed when she flicked her tongue over the hard nipple in time with her thumb sweeping across the weeping tip of his cock.

Lacy nibbled the column of his throat, swirling damp kisses up to his ear where she blew softly.

Sam moaned.

"You want my mouth on you?"

"God yes."

"Do you trust me?"

"Yes."

"Stand still and close your eyes."

Her heart raced as he obeyed. She retreated, uncapped the canteen and dumped cold water on his straining cock.

He jumped. "Jesus—"

She dropped to her knees, sucking his water-cooled dick deep into her warm mouth.

"Christ!"

Lacy's teeth scraped the length as she slowly released the silky hardness. Mmm. He tasted clean. Musky. Her sex grew wet, her thighs sticky as she tightened her lips around the thick, purple head, licking the glans with her curled tongue.

Sam clutched her hair.

She made soft, passionate noises as he thrust in and out of her eager mouth.

"Say my name," she demanded before taking him deep again.

"Lacy."

She increased the rhythm, hollowing her cheeks, gripping him in her hand as she sucked his rod to the back of her throat.

"Say it again when you're as far in as you can go."

"Goddammit—"

"Say it!" Her hand pumped rapidly, the wetness from her mouth made the faster pace easy as she sucked.

"Lacy! Enough!" he bellowed.

Sam hauled her up and carried her to the sleeping bag.

"What? Didn't you like it?"

"Jesus? Are you kidding? I loved it."

"But I wanted to—"

"Another time, okay?" He crawled on her, a male animal on the prowl. "I want you. I'm finding I want things with you I've never wanted."

Lacy's heart slipped.

Her clothes vanished. Sam stretched out and lifted her over his bronzed body so she straddled him. "Ride me."

Her silken hair tantalized his chest as she leaned forward and angled her hips. His shaft slipped in and they groaned simultaneously. Her hands clutched his shoulders; she moved in long, sensuous strokes.

Sam let her control the pace. His hungry mouth suckled her nipples as his fingers stroked her clit. She came immediately. Then he whispered sweet words across her passion-dampened flesh until she was lost to anything but the feel, the sound and the taste of him. Of Sam.

When neither could hold back, Lacy rocked her pelvis at the same time Sam fixed his lips to hers in a bone-melting kiss. Together they went spiraling into the abyss of pleasure.

Later, after the embers died, Lacy said, "What about the log?"

"There's still a few hours until sunrise." Sam tugged her closer and murmured, "We have to find our way out tomorrow."

"I know. I'd rather stay like this."

"Me too, cupcake. Sleep now. We'll talk later."

Chapter Six

Lacy yawned and poked Sam. "It's dawn."

He groaned. "I'm tired."

"Your fault, you fiend." Her insides liquefied as she remembered Sam waking her with ravenous kisses. Coaxing her to the log like some mythological god to ravish her in the moonlight. It'd been hedonistic, magical and perfect.

"Mmm. Was worth it. C'mere. I like waking up with you."

"You do?"

"Mmm-hmm."

She scooted away from him and the temptation to put faith in words he'd uttered when he was half-asleep. "Move it, Becker."

"Slave driver."

Once they'd packed up, Lacy stared at the swath of clear water disappearing around a steep curve.

"What?" Sam asked.

"I think we should follow the river today. There's bound to be fishermen or others close by."

"Okay."

Why didn't Sam argue and remind her he was in charge? Or discount her suggestion?

Because he's different from any man you've known and he trusts you.

"Anxious to get back?"

Sam crouched to fill his canteen. "Yes."

He appeared to be dealing with their upcoming separation much better than she.

They talked about everything and nothing on their journey through swampy spots and around boulders. As the hours passed her steps dragged and his pace increased.

"Sam, wait. I need to catch my breath." Lacy rested her backside on a rock.

"What's the first thing you'll do when we get back?"

"Throw these boots away. You?"

"Eat a steak the size of Wyoming." He stalked toward her with an unmistakable gleam in his eyes. "Will you have dinner with me?"

She studied his face. "Just as long as snake isn't on the menu. But we—"

"We'll talk later. Give me this mouth. God. I crave the taste of you."

These beautiful, sensual kisses chock-full of promise didn't happen every day. Her heart beat crazily. His familiar scent, the certainty of his mouth moving on hers, the heat of his body, inundated her and felt…right.

Just as her blood reached the boiling point, Sam ripped his mouth away. "Did you hear that?"

"Probably a deer."

"No. Listen."

Then she heard it. A sputtering motor.

"You were right to have us follow the river. Come on." Becker raced toward the sound.

Her energy level was rock-bottom. By the time she reached the source, a humble aluminum fishing boat nestled in the rushes along the shore. Sam and a wrinkle-faced fisherman were deep in conversation.

"Hey! There's your missus."

Sam didn't correct the old man. "Lacy, this is Jeb. He says we're only seven miles upstream from the lodge."

"The lodge we started out from five days ago?"

"Hard to believe, isn't it? Anyway, Jeb's got cell service and I've left a message for my partner Dave to meet us there. We'll be docking within an hour. Isn't it great?"

"Yeah. Super."

His eyes narrowed. "What's wrong?"

"Just hungry. And tired." *And heartsick at the thought of saying goodbye to you.*

Sam stepped closer, shielding her from Jeb. "Everything will work out."

"How can you be so sure?"

"Fate."

"B-b-ut. You don't believe in that crap."

"Yes I do."

"Since when?"

"Since the moment I set eyes on you. I didn't want to believe it or admit what it means because it scares me. And proves my mother was right."

Lacy was stunned into silence.

The boat engine whined. Jeb shouted, "Let's get you folks back where you belong."

Sam helped her aboard the narrow boat. He sat in the rear seat, Lacy in the middle. Jeb steered the craft into the center of the river and offered Lacy a package of jerky. She ate it, but she might've been chewing bark her mouth was so dry.

Luckily the spectacular scenery kept her distracted from her tangled emotions. Sam didn't speak as they putted down the twisty river. He clasped her hand, absentmindedly stroking his thumb over her knuckles.

Black-tailed hawks dove into the silvery water, spearing fish with sharp beaks, then soaring off into the cloudless blue sky to enjoy their meal.

Seemed they'd been trolling for hours when Sam's breath tickled the back of her neck. "Lacy?"

"Hmm?"

"Before we get back, I have to admit I haven't been completely honest."

A fission of fear crawled up her spine. Followed by visions of a rustic cabin in the woods, a pregnant wife and little tykes running out to greet "Daddy".

Wrong image. She didn't know everything about Sam Becker, but her heart knew he wasn't the type of man who'd cheat. Or share. He'd be loyal and demand the same from his mate. Hadn't he shown her his protective and possessive streak ran as wide as this river? "What?"

"I'm not who you think I am. I—"

The engine revved loudly, cutting off his declaration. Jeb swerved around a floating log, nearly tossing them overboard. He yelled, "I'll be. Your party's already waitin' for ya!"

Lacy and Sam looked at each other then at the wooden dock in a sheltered cove.

Five horses and five men waited. Dave, the main guide, Clarence, the cook...and her ex-boyfriend Ross, plus Ross's two smarmy friends.

Great. Ross had tagged along. No. He'd probably insisted on going along hoping to witness her humiliation.

Sam clutched her hand. "What?"

She didn't want Sam's pity. Besides she was no longer Lacy Buchanan, city mouse—she was Lacy Buchanan, outdoor adventuress.

Dave shouted, "You all right?"

"We're fine," Sam said.

Jeb helped her off the boat. Sam stuck to her side like pinesap.

Ross, that self-important asshole, stepped in front of Dave before Dave spoke again.

"Should've figured you were the one who'd screwed this up, Lacy. I'm surprised you went through with the hike after I dumped you."

"Hah! I dumped you. I'm surprised *you're* here. Isn't this the time of month when you get your back hair waxed?"

His face turned cherry-red. "Still got a smart mouth. This poor schmuck got stuck with you?" He gave Sam a pitying look. "I would've left her there as wolf bait."

Lacy started to retort, but Sam draped his arm over her shoulder. "We were stuck together a couple of times, but it was completely consensual, right, cupcake?"

She froze.

"Or should I say *sensual*," he amended, nuzzling her crown with his cheek.

It was quiet enough to hear a pine needle drop.

"You…and s-she…" Ross sputtered and pointed to Dave. "H-he said you were lost without supplies."

"Technically, we were lost after an accident with the compass. We managed to entertain ourselves…food wasn't a big priority." The sexual heat in Sam's eyes made her thighs tingle. "But our delay getting back to base camp was my fault."

"Your fault?"

"Mm-hmm." Sam brushed kisses across her temple. "I wanted Lacy all to myself."

Her back snapped straight. He didn't have to lie for her. Pretend he felt more than he really did. "But Sam—"

"Who are you anyway?" Ross demanded.

"Sam Becker," Dave supplied. "He's my cousin and business partner."

Ross' jaw went slack. "Partner? I thought you said your partner was some big time stockbroker from New York City?"

"Yep. He is. They're one in the same."

Lacy's eyes went wide.

"Trust me. I'll explain everything later," Sam whispered to her, praying she didn't bolt before giving him a chance.

"So you're telling me this hiking outfit left two city dwellers alone in the woods? For three days?" Ross sneered. "When word of this gets out, you might as well close-up shop. Nobody will trust you. I sure don't."

"Wait a minute—"

Ignoring Dave, Ross directed his comments to Sam. "How did you find a way out without a GPS?"

"I didn't, Lacy did. She has great instincts. We'd still be wandering around in the trees if not for her."

Ross flashed his teeth. "Must be hard on your ego to realize a powder-puff like her is a better outdoorsman than you."

"No, but it'll be hard on your ego if I let Lacy kick your pansy ass in front of your buddies, like she wants to." Sam mock-whispered, "I saw what she did to a rattlesnake. It was ugly. I wouldn't stick around for a personal demonstration if I were you."

Ross looked torn—act macho or save face. He cleared his throat. "Well, I don't care. I want my money back."

"Fair enough." Becker motioned to the cook. "Clarence, take these guys back to the office. Dave will be along to write him a refund check. Good luck finding another outfitter, Ross."

Ross opened his mouth to protest, but thought better of it. He and the two stooges scrambled on their horses and trailed behind Clarence into the forest.

"I'm glad they're gone," Dave said. "Okay. 'Fess up, cuz. What really happened out there?"

"Later. Right now Lacy and I need to clear up a few things."

Dave nodded and moved to tend the horses.

Lacy held up a hand, stopping his explanation. "Thank you for making me seem tough and capable in front of Ross."

"You are tough and capable."

"That means a lot coming from a fellow New Yorker. Bet you're having a big laugh about pulling one over on me."

"Stop thinking I'm secretly laughing at you."

"Then why didn't you tell me the truth?"

"Because you gave me your trust. You made me feel I could protect you. I wanted prove to you and to myself that your faith wasn't misplaced."

"So that's why you assured me 'everything would work out' and spouted that speech about fate?"

"Not entirely." Becker reached into the pocket of his backpack, pulling out her missing charm bracelet. "I believe in fate because of this."

Lacy gasped.

"When I found it, I realized not only had fate led me to it, fate had led me to *you*."

"But—"

"Let me finish. Yes, I'd planned on dropping by your apartment with the bracelet and then confessing the truth. I thought we could have a fresh start.

But I don't want to start over with you, Lacy. I want to go forward on what we've already built together." He let his heart show in his eyes. "The last three days have been the most amazing and enlightening of my life. I don't want this to end."

"Really?"

"Really." He fastened the bracelet, tenderly kissing the inside of her wrist up to her elbow.

"Oh, Sam. I'd hoped you felt it. I was afraid you'd blame this strong connection because we had no choice but to rely on each other."

"True. The sex is pretty rocking too. But somewhere between the name-calling, the snake scare and sharing secrets by firelight, I fell hard for you."

Lacy blushed.

It charmed the hell out of him. If he had his way, she'd spend the next fifty years charming and exasperating him. "What do you say we get out of here?"

She nodded.

Dave waited in the clearing, probably making sure they didn't get lost again.

"You afraid of horses?" Becker asked after he mounted.

"I'm not afraid of anything when I'm with you."

God. He adored this woman.

Lacy grabbed his hand. He hauled her in front of him on the saddle, nuzzled the side of her neck, losing himself in her sweet scent and the sense of rightness of having her in his arms.

Becker yelled to Dave, "Call Clarence and have him send our things to the honeymoon suite in the Lodge."

"Honeymoon suite?" Dave repeated. "Something you wanna tell me, cuz?"

"Not yet, but I'm working on it."

Lacy relaxed against his chest. "Riding off into the sunset with you is much more romantic than making love in a field of wildflowers."

"Yeah?"

"Absolutely."

"Probably snakes in the flowers anyway."

"True."

After awhile Sam asked, "Maybe on our next outdoor adventure we can find a bed of wildflowers?"

"Definitely next time."

"Although, I can't wait to make love to you in a real bed."

She sighed dreamily.

The horse meandered down the trail, content as his riders.

Finally Lacy spoke. "You really didn't mind being lost in the woods with me?"

"I was lost, Lacy, long before we entered the woods. It was you who found me."

"You sure talk romantic for a stockbroker."

"I liked it better when you thought I was a wild man."

She looked up at him and smiled. "Can't you make this horse go any faster, my wild mountain man?"

He grinned. "Hang on, cupcake."

About the Author

To learn more about Lorelei James, please visit www.loreleijames.com.
Send an email to lorelei@loreleijames.com or join her Yahoo! group to join in
the   fun   with   other   readers   at:
http://groups.yahoo.com/group/LoreleiJamesgang

Look for these titles

Now Available
Dirty Deeds by Lorelei James

Coming Soon
Running with the Devil by Lorelei James

A Touch of Magic

Cassandra Kane

Universal Alliance Settlement Exploration Unit: Report 17836ZE-C

Target:

"Samhain" Type M planet on outer edge of Ekabadian System. Nine year cycle.

Atmosphere: Habitable. Terraforming unnecessary. Possible instability due to proximity of Ekabadian Black Hole.

History:

Year 2395 Illegal colonization by New Wiccan cult, *Lalith's People* (Cross Reference), in privately chartered starship *Goliath*. Contact with Universal Alliance severed immediately. *Goliath* reported missing. Assumed crashed on Samhain, no survivors. No resources to verify. Status: Code F (Extreme Low Priority).

Year 2552.9 Status Change: Code C (Medium Priority). Black hole proximity considered stable. Universal Alliance green light colonization into Ekabadian System.

Year 2553.2 Settlement Scouting Unit SU-SEU5821 dispatched. Preliminary report on Samhain: Highly ionized atmosphere. Frequent electrical storms causing equipment malfunction. Small colony of *Goliath* survivors detected. Scouting Unit classified "Missing" following preliminary report. 13 days in field.

Year 2559.4 Settlement Scouting Unit SU-SEU6073 dispatched. Confirms preliminary by first scouting unit. Civilization: Primitive, barbaric. Observation of restrictive New Wiccan rituals amongst *Goliath* settlers. Scouting Unit classified "Missing" following secondary report. 19 days in field.

Current Status:

Year 2561.7

Final reconnaissance mission. Type: Scouting / Military

Primary directive: Ascertain whereabouts of missing scouting units

Secondary directive: Ascertain Samhain readiness for colonization

In case of mission failure, SEU to hand over Samhain exploration to UA Special Forces for full military intervention.

Chapter One

"So that's Samhain," Colonel Stodd Orson sneered, staring at the small green planet on the ship's viewscreen.

Scout Leader Captain Tirana Albaster nodded. She despised the man but it was best if she treated him with civility. These Universal Alliance Special Forces military types were known for their short fuses—and their trigger-happy fingers.

"There's something in Sector 12A," the ship's science officer reported, reading the data from his console.

"Signs of life, Lieutenant?" Tirana asked.

"Affirmative. Looks like a small settlement."

"Send the location co-ordinates to Shuttle 4. I'm going down."

"*We're* going down," Colonel Orson corrected as he followed her from the navigation pit.

"That goes without saying, Colonel." Tirana's voice was polite even as she lengthened her stride to shake him off. "I'm fully aware that you were assigned as protection on this mission."

Colonel Orson stopped her with a thick hand on her shoulder and gave it a deliberate squeeze.

Tirana spun around, shrugging out of his hold. "I'd appreciate it if you stopped pawing at me, Colonel."

The colonel grinned, showing crooked teeth beneath thin, stretched lips. She tried not to look at the scarred eye-socket, wondering again why the man refused to wear an eye-patch. She suspected he liked the fear—if not downright horror—it inspired.

"I've already apologized for my...accidental...visit to your quarters last night, Captain," he said, not looking sorry at all. "But an attractive woman like you must surely be used to such...accidents?"

Tirana stared at him with unflinching distaste. "I don't care for what you're implying, Colonel. But let me tell you this—if there is another incidence of inappropriate behavior, I will be forced to report it to your commander. I'm sure Special Forces wouldn't want another scandal on their hands after the Dilorac incident."

Orson's good eye narrowed. "Are you threatening me, Captain?"

"Take it as you will," she said coolly. "And please remind your men that this is a peaceful recon mission. I don't want their excessive use of *chi'kle* to jeopardize it by putting any of my team in danger. Native life forms are to be treated with respect, Colonel. We'll meet in Shuttle 4 at oh eight hundred."

She turned on her heel and strode down the corridor to assemble her scouting team.

Behind her, Orson spat out the *chi'kle* he'd been chewing. The masticated gob stuck to the corridor wall.

"Uptight bitch," he snarled.

After the Dilorac debacle, where a Special Forces unit had wiped out an entire native settlement following a bar brawl, the performance-enhancement drug had been made illegal. Fifty thousand addicted Special Forces men were forced to quit or take the drug in secret. Colonel Orson didn't believe in hiding because of someone else's stupid mistake. No one had dared pull him up on it until now.

He fingered his gun and thought about the places in Tirana Albaster's curvaceous body he'd like to shove it. And the part of his anatomy he'd definitely be shoving there eventually, whether she liked it or not.

***

Electrical storms raged overhead as Tirana and her three-man scouting team cut their way through the thick forest undergrowth with machetes. Following on their heels, weapons cocked, came the ten-man Special Forces unit headed by Colonel Orson.

Orson had been professionally distant since the encounter in the ship's corridor. She hoped she'd made her point but somehow she doubted it. She was aware of his gaze lingering on her backside in the tight rubberized comms suit.

Tirana swallowed the urge to turn around and claw out his remaining eye. Then took a steadying breath and shook her dark hair to remove all thought of Orson. *Keep your mind on the job.*

Successful completion of this mission would fast track her career in the Settlement Exploration Unit. That's why she'd volunteered for it. As far as she was concerned, failure was not an option.

She looked down at her locator link. The tiny screen showed they were close to the original coordinates for the settlement. Trees crowded close around them, thick-branched and tinged with purple, towering into the angry sky. She couldn't see more than a couple of yards in front, but the locator indicated a rapid rise in the ground ahead. A hill. Any settlement would more than likely be situated at the summit where it would be easier to protect itself from possible attack.

"What the fuck…!"

Tirana heard the soldier's shout and whirled as he pumped a volley of laser fire into the undergrowth. The bushes at the foot of a large tree fizzled and burned, leaving a charred mass.

"Stop it!" She ran at him, aiming a kick at his hand. The impact catapulted the rifle into the air and the soldier jerked back his hand with a yowl of pain.

Outraged, he turned and raised his fist at her in fury.

"Stand down, soldier!" Orson barked.

As the soldier lowered his fist, Tirana noticed Orson and his soldiers had their rifles aimed squarely at her chest.

She froze.

Orson took out a square of *chi'kle* from his pocket and popped it in his mouth. Chewing, he gave his sneering grin and lowered his rifle. "You attack my men one more time and I can't guarantee I'll be able to hold them back."

"Should I remind you *again* that native life forms are to be respected?" Tirana almost spat at him. "We know nothing about Samhain. We don't know what type of native life forms we're dealing with, and we have sketchy data on the culture that has developed from the descendants of the Goliath. This mission is still under the jurisdiction of the SEU, Colonel, and we'll play by *my* rules."

Orson's eye glinted. He turned to the offending soldier. "Son, what did you see out there?"

"An animal." The soldier glared at Tirana. "Looked like some sort of— some sort of gargoyle. Ugly as sin. Sir, it was *grinning* at me."

"I don't care if it was mooning you, from now on keep your finger off the trigger." Orson turned to his men. "That goes for all of you. No firing unless by my express orders." He raised an eyebrow at Tirana, his lip curling in contempt. "Happy?"

Tirana gave a curt nod before picking up the locator link she'd dropped when she'd kicked out at the soldier. Her scouting team observed her and Thurley, her second-in-command, curled his right finger to his chest, signaling for instructions.

Continue, she signaled with a raised thumb. Then shot out her little finger. *But be on your guard.*

It was bad enough being on a planet that had already swallowed a starship and two previous scouting units, she thought in suppressed fury as she wiped the mud off her locator link. Now they had to watch their backs for the men who were supposed to be protecting them.

A roll of thunder growled overhead and a sudden flash of lightning sizzled from the empty sky and struck the treetops. High above them, a branch broke off and came crashing through the thick foliage to land with a heavy thud at her feet. Tirana's heart pounded as she realized it had only narrowly missed her head.

In her hand, the locator link beeped once and then died.

The stink of burning reached them first.

They'd been climbing uphill for the past hour, crunching over a thick mulch of dead leaves, their thigh muscles straining against the deepening gradient of the slope. Cutting through a final tangle of undergrowth, they emerged from the crowding trees. Orson gave a series of hand signals and everyone spread out along the edge of the forest, hiding behind tree trunks and in the scant undergrowth.

Crouching behind a dense bush sparkling with purple berries, Tirana peeked out to survey the landscape.

The top of the hill rose like the bald pate of an old man, rounded and smooth amongst the lushness of the crowding forest. A few yards away, a two-foot high stone wall swept to either side, rounding the curve of the hill. She surmised it was more a boundary marker than an attempt to keep anyone out.

The hill rose in a steep incline from the boundary wall to a ring of tall standing stones circling the summit. Inside the stone circle an enormous bonfire of dried faggots blazed, shooting sparks and billowing acrid smoke into the purple twilight. A whorling mass of clouds churned in the sky, criss-crossed with flickers of lightning.

Beneath this disturbing backdrop, a group of people in long robes gathered around the bonfire, chanting. She figured them to be at least a dozen, though it was too dark and they were too far away for her to accurately make out how many.

Tirana looked across at Orson, who knelt on one knee behind a neighboring bush with the butt of his weapon resting on his thick thigh. She signaled that she and Thurley were to go closer while everyone else remained behind. Orson frowned, looked as if he would argue. Instead, with an abrupt movement, he signaled agreement.

Tirana nodded at Thurley. They picked their way over the rough stone wall and crept up the side of the hill. Nearing the top, they slipped behind neighboring standing stones, or menhirs, and hid in the black shadows. Tirana crouched down and peeked around.

The chanting had grown more intense as they neared, and now the robed men raised their hands to the sky in gestures of supplication. But they weren't alone. Beyond the bonfire on the downslope of the hill, a crowd had gathered. Their stark, white faces watched the chanting group with a mixture of worship and fascinated horror.

The chanting stopped. A black-robed figure detached itself from the group around the bonfire and approached the crowd.

"Bring forward the son of Amun and his familiar." His voice boomed in the sudden quiet.

A man and what looked like a dwarf, both with hands tied behind their backs, were shoved out from the crowd.

Tirana snuck across to another menhir where the view was unhindered by the bonfire. As she peeked again, a blaze of lightning slashed across the sky, illuminating the scene before her.

For that flashing instant, she saw the man in clear relief. He was tall, slim-hipped and wide across the shoulders. A coarse tunic opened at his broad chest, revealing a long necklace of blue gems hanging around his neck. Dark thick hair hung to his shoulders, framing a strong, square-jawed face. Tirana was struck by his male beauty, but what captured her attention were his brilliant eyes as he stared at the robed figure in blazing fury.

By his side, hopping from foot to foot as he gibbered, was what looked like a tiny gargoyle.

"Silence your familiar!"

The gargoyle stopped, his bulging eyes glaring at the priest.

The glacial voice boomed out again. "What is your plea to the charges?"

Tirana leaned forward, angling to get a closer look at the man with the necklace. The gargoyle screeched and stared straight at Tirana. The man's head snapped around. His blazing eyes met hers. She was held, transfixed and breathless, as their gaze locked for what seemed an eternity.

Then a volley of laser fire shot across the top of the crowd, scorching the sky with red.

Colonel Orson and his Special Forces team stormed the stone circle.

Chapter Two

Orson's soldiers thundered past, manic grins fixed to their faces as they fired indiscriminately at the crowd. Tirana felt someone's hand on her neck, shoving her to the ground, a body throwing itself over hers. She nose-dived, felt the scrape of grass against her cheek, the smell of damp soil pressed against her nostrils. Screaming and shouts reverberated around her, punctuated by sharp volleys of gunfire.

"Get off me!" She fought against the dead weight forcing her down, managed to jab her elbow into his ribs. The body slid off her. She pushed herself away, struggled to her knees and pulled the stunner from her holster, turning to protect herself.

Thurley lay sprawled facedown on the ground beside her. Laser fire had blasted a gaping hole in his back, his flesh blackened beneath the edges of his singed jacket. He was dead, taking the shot obviously meant for her.

The hot sting of fury wiped out the shock of horror. She rose and pushed through the frightened crowd running to escape the battle being fought on the far side of the hill. The bonfire had toppled beneath the weight of two robed men lying across its scattered centre. Loose embers fluttered into the sky from the trail of fire spreading over the hill.

"Orson!" Tirana strode towards the knot of soldiers herding the crowd. It was difficult to see more than the circling shadows of their uniforms, the points of their rifles. A scatter of bodies littered the area.

Someone slammed into her, screamed. Tirana stumbled, gripped her stunner firmly. She heard the sobbing of women, the cry of children. *Children!*

Damn Special Forces. Damn Orson. She would make him pay for this outrage.

Orson was standing in the exact same spot where only minutes before the man in the necklace had stood. In the flash of lightning, she saw a smug smile settle over his countenance as he watched his soldiers rounding up the crowd. Half a dozen of the robed men knelt before him, the soldiers' weapons digging into their backs. Their hoods had been yanked back to reveal spider-like tattoos engraved on their bald heads.

"Orson!" Tirana raised her stunner.

Orson turned and saw her. A nasty smirk spread over his face.

A blazing heap of embers obscured her view, making a sure shot difficult. She stepped closer and flicked her stunner to its highest setting.

"I wouldn't try that," Orson called, raising his voice to be heard over the space separating them and the sobs from the crowd. "You're outnumbered, Captain. I suggest you stand down."

"You'll be court-martialed for this." Tirana aimed at him through the shimmer of heat. "I'll make sure of it."

Orson laughed in derision. "Who do you think authorized this?"

No. Oh, no. She stared at him in horror.

"You think they'd give something like this to you without a reason?" His voice rose in scorn. "You were in way over your pretty head from the start, Tirana."

Her shoulders jerked when he said her name. There was menace and rage in his voice, a desire to hurt. And in his eyes the lust to control, to make her submit, to destroy her.

"Come here, bitch." Orson's mouth thinned into a vicious twist. He lifted his laser rifle, aimed it, and took a step towards her.

Standing in the open was suicide, her stunner no match for a rifle. She wheeled and ran, stumbling over the bodies strewn in her path as Orson shouted her name. Laser fire sizzled past her ear. Up ahead, she saw Thurley's body beside the menhir. Beyond the standing stone lay the bare hill, where Orson would get a clear shot if she ran. She'd have to make her stand there.

She ran and jumped over Thurley's body. Someone caught her arm as she landed and dragged her behind the menhir. She smacked up against the solid chest of the man standing there. He gripped the top of her arms and held her still against his hard body.

Tirana gazed up into blazing green eyes. A shock of recognition shivered through her body. The man with the necklace stared at her, his beautiful face austere in the shadows of the tall stone, his mouth set in grim determination.

"Come with me."

She heard the low authoritative growl of his voice and shook her head, twisted out of his grip. Something screeched. At her feet, the gargoyle jumped from foot to foot, his tiny leathery hands pulling at the edge of her trousers.

Shock had her stepping back involuntarily, out into the line of fire. Something sizzled, slapped into her arm. There was a moment of excruciating pain before everything went black.

Loren caught her unconscious form as it fell, dragged her to safety behind the menhir. He sat the woman's body up against the stone. A jagged wound had torn the skin at the top of her arm, pouring blood over his hands. The wound wasn't fatal, but the shock had knocked her cold. He ran his hands over the severe clothing that cupped every curve of her lush body, searching for other wounds, trying to ignore the surge of blood to his groin. Even unconscious she stirred his blood.

The devil is upon us! deLoren's voice screeched in his head, demanding his attention.

Loren turned and held his hand down for his familiar, waited as the tiny *hekarten* scampered up his arm to his shoulder. He winced as deLoren gripped a fistful of his hair and held on tight.

"Calm yourself," Loren murmured. "I know how to deal with him."

Loren stood and summoned his power. He felt deLoren whisper on the outskirts of his mind, felt a great push, and deLoren's energy joined his, pumping through Loren's body until it surged to his fingertips.

The one-eyed devil soldier ran around the menhir, his face contorted in triumph. He would have expected to see the woman unconscious on the ground and stopped short, startled, as he faced Loren instead.

His reflexes were good, Loren admitted, as the soldier raised his rifle with barely a pause and squeezed the trigger. But Loren's were better. Loren snapped up his hand and evoked a force field that shielded them from the burst of laser fire and sent the shots skidding to one side in a trail of blue sparks.

The soldier's mouth gaped open, then fury washed over him at having been thwarted. Instead of shooting again, he was smart enough to pull out a club clipped to his belt and came at Loren shouting, the club swinging over his head.

A moment later, his thickset body shot back in the air, propelled by the force of the *powrbal* Loren threw at him. The ball of blue energy smashed the soldier hard to the ground, crackling over his body in a thin sheet before it dissipated. The devil soldier groaned, attempted to move and fell back.

Loren wasted no time. He crouched over the woman's body, lifting her limp form over his free shoulder while deLoren balanced on the other. With both burdens weighing him down, he ran down the hill and slipped into the forest.

Tirana came around with a start, crying out at the pain shooting along her left arm. Her hand flew to touch her shoulder and instead touched the warm skin of the hand resting there. Snatching hers away at the unexpected contact, she opened her eyes and met a brilliant green gaze.

"Have no fear." His voice soothed her. "You are safe."

She was lying against a tree trunk in a small clearing in the forest. The gorgeous man knelt beside her, studying her in a way that made her breath catch in her throat. He was even more beautiful up close, with fine, molded lips and a straight patrician nose that drew her admiration, though that almost feminine perfection was tempered by the sprinkle of dark stubble over his jaw and the thick brows drawn close over startling emerald eyes. But it was the pressure of his hand over the wound that sent shivers along her body from the heat radiating at his palm.

"You were wounded, I am stopping the flow of blood," he said before she could formulate the question.

The arm of her uniform and her left side were covered in slick blood, as was the right side of the man's tunic. Her stomach lurched, sickened by the sight of blood spattering their clothes. She realized she would be dead now if this man hadn't taken her away from the fighting at the stone circle. She would have confronted Orson, but with his superior strength and Special Forces training he would destroy her in one-to-one combat.

Something chattered across the clearing. She swung her head around, saw the little gargoyle sitting on a fallen tree trunk pulling the skin off the soft fruit held between his small hands, the same fruit which hung ripe and purple from a nearby bush. He revealed a flash of tiny sharp teeth before he bit into the fruit and sucked at the juicy insides.

"deLoren says we should leave." The man's breath caressed her ear.

"You understand him?" Tirana turned her gaze back to him in surprise.

"deLoren and I mindspeak." He watched her reaction to this news.

Telepathic communication. She absorbed the fact with some excitement. There were telepaths on other worlds but interspecies telepathy was almost unheard of. She turned back to study the little creature in fascinated curiosity as it pulled out the seeds from the center of the oval-shaped fruit and threw them over his shoulder. The leathery texture of his dappled brown skin set deep wrinkles at the joints of spindle-thin arms and legs, and his chunky body boasted tiny brown nipples and no genitalia that she could see. A large head balanced on a stick-like neck, distinguished by pointed ears, a wide mouth, bulging eyes and two round holes above his mouth serving as nostrils.

"deloren. Is that his name?"

"deLoren, *hekarten* to Loren." The man's tone flowed with the smoothness of formality.

"Loren?"

"I am Loren."

She swiveled her head back to look at him. This close to her, his lips were only inches away. He'd been observing her while she watched deLoren, studying her with the same intensity. She gazed at his generous mouth and wondered what it would feel like to be kissed by him. Loren's lips twitched into a smile, and a slow blush crept over her cheeks as she realized he knew exactly what she'd been thinking.

"Your name?"

"W-what?" She wondered why this man's—Loren's—proximity set her nerves to jangling. A prickly heat spread over her body, and her nostrils flared at the scent of his earthy masculinity that had her nipples tightening. "Tirana."

"Tirana." Her name rolled around his mouth as though savoring a rare delicacy. "I am pleased to meet you, Tirana." His lips lowered and brushed hers.

Tirana's eyes widened in shock. She'd read about this custom in ancient societies on Terra, where people greeted each other with a kiss—a custom she'd always found disturbing in its over-familiarity. But her shock sprang more from the sudden electricity that sizzled between them. The touch of his lips branded her with their soft touch.

She stared at him as he pulled back from the kiss. Loren's hand cupped her face, his gaze traveling over her features as though imprinting it to memory. Her stomach lurched with the sudden urge to feel his mouth on hers, and she licked her dry lips, her heart battering against her ribs.

The color of his eyes darkened with unabashed lust as he watched the flick of her tongue. Then he lowered his mouth to hers in a passion-filled assault that had nothing to do with the first gentle greeting.

Sparks of pure desire shot over her body as his tongue parted her lips to explore the warm cavity. Swept up in the sensation of his mouth plundering hers, she met his assault fiercely. She arched against him when the hand at her face lowered to curve around her breast, his thumb flicking at the taut nipple straining at the comms suit.

A fear-filled screech from deLoren had Loren breaking away, wincing.

"What's wrong?" Her bruised lips ached for Loren to continue his devastating exploration.

"The devil soldier is near." Eyes glazed with unabated lust, his gaze swept over her. "We must go."

She felt a surge of disappointment. As if on cue, they heard a thrashing in the undergrowth somewhere behind them. deLoren screeched and scrambled off the tree trunk. Bounding across the clearing, the small creature launched himself from the ground to Loren's shoulder where jerked in desperation at Loren's long hair.

Loren pulled Tirana up with him as he rose to his feet. She winced, expecting to experience pain at her arm. Instead, there was only a vague discomfort. She eased her arm up and around and shot Loren a look of surprise.

But Loren had turned away and watched the surrounding undergrowth with a frown. Suddenly the fruit-laden bush deLoren had been eating from burst into flame. deLoren screamed and clasped his thin arms in panic about Loren's head.

Loren pried deLoren off and tucked him under his arm. Grabbing Tirana's hand, he turned and ran.

Tirana steeled herself for a long sprint through the forest, yet they had barely crossed the clearing when Loren skirted an outcrop of rocks behind the nearest line of trees. She stumbled as the thick mulch of the forest gave way to pebbled dirt. Loren pulled her around a boulder leaning like a sentinel guarding the rocky mound.

Loren bent to squeeze in the narrow space between the rocks leading to a dark hole gaping beyond.

Tirana stopped. "Where are you going?"

"This passage leads to *Laliata*." Loren tugged at her hand.

"No." She didn't know what that meant, but there were other priorities. As much as she longed to follow him, craved the taste of his mouth, she'd come here on a mission and needed to fulfill it. "I have to get back to my shuttle so I can radio for help—"

"Tirana!" Orson's rage-filled voice shattered the quiet of the forest.

Tirana froze.

"I know you can hear me, you and that fucking alien freak."

Tirana stared at Loren. His face had hardened into an austere mask. He set deLoren on the ground and the *hekarten* scrambled between his legs and disappeared into the dark void between the rocks.

"Come out, you bitch." The sound of snapping branches nearby indicated he was close. "Or I'll fry you both."

Loren's gaze raked over her with hot possession before his expression transformed into one of cold determination. He pushed Tirana behind him, shielding her, then picked up a couple of large round pebbles at his feet and weighed them in his hands.

He meant to protect her, Tirana thought in wonder. He barely knew her and he was going to pit himself against Orson's laser fire with a couple of stones. He would put his life on the line for her—while safety lay only a few feet away down the hole deLoren had disappeared into. It was madness.

She pulled at his arm. "Let's go."

Loren frowned. "Hide behind me. I will get him as he—"

"No." She drew him around, tugged urgently at his arm. "Take me to La-latita?"

"Laliata." His mouth quirked at her mispronunciation.

A volley of laser fire scorched the edge of the boulder, sending a shower of crumbling rock over them. Loren moved to cover her, his arms wrapping around her. Pressed against his chest, she breathed in the heady scent of his maleness. Their eyes met and his filled with a hungry possessiveness that had a blast of heat pooling between her legs.

Fragments of rock rained on them from the top of the boulder. Orson was getting closer.

With a last hungry look, Loren caught her hand and dragged her after him through the dark hole between the rocks.

Chapter Three

Loren found it hard to run with his stiff member rising hard between his legs. He wanted nothing more than to throw Tirana down and ravish her. That and beat the devil soldier to a pulp for his threats. He'd been too lenient with him back at the Sacred Circle and he would not make that mistake again. If not for his own sake, then for Tirana's. He knew the soldier wanted her, but the thought of that monster's hands on her lush body sent a cold fury sweeping over him.

Tirana was his.

He'd known that the moment his lips had met hers. A fire had coursed through his veins then, a deep need that had stiffened his staff with urgent force. He knew she would be his mate. Had known, if the truth was told, when deLoren had pointed her out at the Circle, watching them like a beautiful, otherworldly apparition.

He'd given quick praise to Lalith that the soldiers had saved him from the judgment of the Priests—a judgment that would have had him sacrificed in the pyre together with deLoren. It had given him a chance to work himself free of the rope binding his wrists and make his escape with the surging crowd.

His first thought had been to find her. deLoren had shouted in his ear, frantic to get away, but Loren had gone to look behind the Sacred Stones, cursing when he realized she'd disappeared. Then she'd found him. A sure sign she was meant to be his.

His hand tightened over hers.

The entrance to the underground passage had been left far behind before he slowed. They were deep in the bowels of Samhain, winding their way along slick, slime-covered walls wet with the rain filtering through the earth and rocks above. He was sure the devil soldier would never venture this far after them. If he tried, he would be driven out by the *ba-hekarten*. It had happened to more than one of the Priests and their followers when, in the frenzy of their hatred, they had organized hunting parties to root them out.

For this was the domain of the True People.

"What's that noise?" Loren heard the fear in Tirana's voice.

This deep down, the passages were lit by the cold glow of the phosphorescent lichen clinging to the walls. Apart from the steady drip-drip-drip of filtering water, he could hear the faint shuffles of the *ba-hekarten* following them. They could sense Tirana and were drawn by the ripeness of her life-force.

"The *ba-hekarten* live here. Don't be afraid. They won't harm you."

"*Ba-hekarten?*" She grasped his hand tightly, her voice sounding nervous. "Isn't that what deLoren is?"

"deLoren is *hekarten*."

"I don't understand."

He remembered she was an offworlder, that what seemed natural and familiar to him was strange and alien to her. "*Hekarten* have chosen from the True People. *Ba-hekarten* are still searching."

"What are they searching for?"

"Their host."

She does not understand. deLoren's impatient voice came into his mind. Loren could sense him in the passage somewhere ahead, sure-footed in his home ground. The forest scared him, and he would throw up a stink whenever Loren went overground. His fear had proved justified when they had been captured by the Priests.

Why don't you show her the hekarten-jal? *That might make her understand.* deLoren's tone was openly sly.

There's no need for us to follow that route to Laliata. Loren frowned.

You need to mate, and so do I. Our time is due. Loren could almost feel the *hekarten's* hunger, mirroring his own.

No, I won't force it on her. But his tumescent cock had stiffened involuntarily at the thought.

So let her decide. And deLoren capered off into the darkness.

Tirana was afraid of the dark. It was a weakness she was loathe to admit, even to herself. When the rocky passageway had begun to lighten, she'd breathed a sigh of relief. But the fear had returned when she realized they were being followed. Not by Orson, whom she hoped they'd left behind in the forest, but by the shuffle of tiny feet.

Hekarten and *ba-hekarten*. Loren's explanation had only left her more confused. She had too many questions that needed answering, all of them jumbled about in her head. One of them lay uppermost.

Why had Orson called him an alien freak?

Loren was human, a descendent of Lalith's People, of that she was sure. Yet deLoren was undoubtedly a creature native to Samhain. His fierce attachment to Loren seemed unnatural. The robed men at the stone circle had called deLoren his "familiar". In Terran mythology, only black witches had familiars.

Adherents to the New Wiccan religion were sprinkled in small pockets in planets all over the galaxy, but Lalith's People had been a breakaway cult, more rigid in their religious beliefs, holding the mystical Lalith as True Goddess over the numerous deities of other wiccans. A small colony on an alien planet separated from the rest of the UA for over a hundred and fifty years was bound to develop in unique ways. Already she could see two strata—the robed priests reigning over the frightened crowd of followers, and the True People with the *hekarten*. All of this she could extrapolate from what she had witnessed, using logic to slot the pieces together.

It was Loren who remained the greatest mystery. She trusted him, trusted that the *ba-hekarten* meant no harm although she sensed them everywhere, scurrying on the edges of her vision like frightened rats. It was getting to know more about Loren—*everything* about Loren—that made her swallow her fear and keep to his side.

Her hand was still clasped in his although she had to walk behind him in the narrow passageway that glittered from the lichen clinging to the glistening rock. His dark head almost brushed the ceiling, his broad shoulders the edges of the wall. She sensed a deep power in him, a power that called to her wildly, heated her whenever she met those amazing emerald eyes.

Her gaze lingered on his tight butt and she wondered how it would feel cupped in her hands. At the forest clearing she'd felt the hard length of his member against her body through the material of his trousers, had shivered with desire at the thought of easing it free and holding it warm in her palm. Feelings she had rarely, if ever, experienced on first meeting a man. She just wasn't built that way.

Or maybe she was, and it needed the right man to unleash it.

Loren stopped and she bumped against him, caught in her erotic musings. The passageway had opened wider and they were at a junction that split into separate tunnels. deLoren crouched by the rock wall separating the entrance to the tunnels, staring intently at Loren.

"I would like to show you something." The strange, flat tone of Loren's voice instantly aroused her curiosity. "If we go this way—" he pointed to a passage to their right "—we go straight to Laliata."

At his pause, she glanced at the dark opening of the passage to their left. "And that way?"

"To the *hekarten-jal*."

The very blandness of his voice indicated this was where he wanted her to go. "What is it?"

"A place sacred to the True People."

Their gazes locked. He wanted her. And she wanted him.

"Are you sure you want to show me this sacred place?" She needed to know if she could trust him.

"If you choose to, yes."

Tirana had the giddy feeling she was on the brink of a life-changing decision. A decision Loren was leaving entirely in her hands.

She took a deep breath and followed her instincts. "Then yes."

deLoren broke the silence with a gleeful chattering and shot off into the tunnel to the left.

Loren smiled, tightened his hold on her hand, and followed him.

They walked for what seemed an hour before the passageway began to widen. The lichen covering the walls took on a warmer, pinkish glow, heating the air until the sweat began to trickle down Tirana's neck and into the back of her comms suit.

Finally, a blast of warm air, damp and earthy, hit her in the face. The passage opened into a huge cavern, the floor lost in the darkness far beneath. Stalactites aimed down like pointed spears from the ceiling, stalagmites rose like twisted columns to greet them, both covered in glittering pink lichen. She gazed in awe at the shapes of strange forms twisted in fanciful displays. From somewhere up ahead came the steady drip-drip of water.

They picked their way along a narrow rocky path sweeping along the side of the cavern, leading down towards the bottom of the cave. Tirana heard the scrabble of feet and once or twice caught tiny blinking eyes watching them from behind twisted rock formations before the creatures disappeared with a flourish of warm air.

The atmosphere became warmer and more humid as they went deeper into the cave. The comms suit became sticky with her sweat-slickened skin. Finally, the rock beneath her feet turned to sand and leveled out. A splashing rumble of water came from up ahead, swathed in darkness. She looked up, saw stalactites twisting around the sides of the cave, curving like the giant flutes of a cathedral organ.

Loren took her along a well-worn path to the center of the cavern. A tall waterfall fell from an aperture halfway up the wall of the cave. The gushing water poured onto a ledge and bounced off the edge in a stream that danced and played over rocks in bright sparks before plunging into a small rock pool below.

Tirana marveled at the beauty of the sparkling curtain of water and the clear pool at her feet. "Where does all the water go?"

"There is an underground stream that becomes a river near Laliata."

"What is this place? It's so beautiful. All of it." She swept her hands about the cave.

"A place of meditation and ablution for the True People." He gazed at her with a fixed intensity. "When we are of age, we use this place for our prayers, and the pool for purification before entering the *hekarten-jal*."

A feeling of unease gnawed at her gut. "If this is your sacred place, perhaps I shouldn't be here. Loren, I'm an offworlder. I don't have a religion, I don't believe in a god or a goddess. You believe in something that I can never believe in. You should know that."

Loren nodded, his gaze never leaving her own. His eyes glowed here, Tirana thought in alarm, with a phosphorescent brilliance not quite human.

"I expect nothing from you." A strong emotion crossed over his features, and he qualified it by saying, "Nothing you would not choose freely."

Drawn into the brilliance of his gaze, Tirana felt her body heat at the meaning behind his words. He wanted her, but it would be her choice.

She pulled down the zipper at the neck of the comms suit to ease the warmth flushing her face. Loren's burning gaze followed the slide of the zipper before he lowered his hands over hers and teased her fingers free of the tag. She held her breath as he pulled down the zipper, exposing the rounded swell between her generous breasts.

"You are very hot." His fingers traced over the damp skin at the curving top of her breasts, watching her mouth. "And we are both very dirty after the ordeal at the Sacred Circle."

Shivering at his touch, Tirana glanced with longing at the waterfall and the pool at their feet. She slanted her head and smiled up at him. "Are you trying to seduce me with a swim?"

His eyes laughed down at her. "Perhaps."

She stepped back and crossed her arms over her chest. "You first."

Loren raised an eyebrow at her challenging stance and grinned. He drew the necklace of blue stones over his head and dropped it on the sand between them, quickly followed by his tunic. Tirana caught her breath at the play of muscles over his shoulders and arms. His solid chest was covered by fine dark hair arrowing over well-defined abdominal muscles to the edge of trousers. Kicking off his soft boots, Loren planted well-formed feet in the sand as he untied the leather belt knotted at his waist. He watched her reaction as he slowly removed the belt and let the trousers slide over his hips and pool at his feet.

For a beat she stared into his eyes, noted the playful challenge in them, before she made herself look at him. His legs were long and lean, rising to muscular thighs. Between them, from the flare of dark hair at his groin, his staff rose hard and long, tipped with a large, smooth head.

A magnificent specimen, Tirana thought as her breath caught. And totally human.

A small smile teased the corners of his lips. She realized she was staring a little too hard. Not that he seemed to mind as he was evidently proud of his physique—with good cause.

"And you?"

When she had issued the challenge, she hadn't thought ahead to the fact that it would be her turn to undress before him. A flush of embarrassment crept over her cheeks. Tirana reminded herself brusquely that she had nothing to be ashamed of, that she could be just as proud of her body as Loren was of his.

Smiling at him coolly, she lowered the zipper of her comms suit to her midriff, shrugged off the shoulders and wiggled the tight rubber over her hips. Her naked breasts swung as she bent to remove her boots—which she should definitely have taken off first—before peeling off each leg. Her face was red as she straightened, wearing just a tiny pair of panties snug against her hips.

Loren's expression heated as his gaze ran over her breasts, yet he still waited expectantly. Sighing inwardly, she slipped off the panties, threw them over the pile of clothes and faced him. He considered the trim thatch of hair between her thighs before his gaze moved back to her breasts in a way that had her nipples hardening. A long leisurely look that took its cue from her own careful study of his assets.

Smiling, Loren stepped forward and took her hand. She trembled at the warmth of his palm sliding over hers, yet he only pulled her after him, skirted the edge of the pool and went to the waterfall. A mound of rocks rose to the ledge where the stream poured before bouncing off into the pool below. A narrow set of stairs had been cut into the rocks. Tirana followed Loren as he climbed them—trying hard not to gaze at the tight muscles of his butt at face level, but nevertheless taking time to admire them—before they came out onto the ledge.

Tirana saw deLoren sitting on a boulder beyond the curtain of water. Beside him sat a tiny furry creature with large, soulful eyes and pointed ears. It looked like a cross between a small monkey and a rabbit. Was this one of the *ba-hekarten*? Not as fearsome as she had imagined, even though both creatures observed her with an unnerving intensity.

Loren pulled her under the waterfall. Tirana gasped as the blast of freezing water poured over her head and shoulders. Raising her face to the pounding water, she sighed as the grit and sweat washed away.

Loren touched her arm and she opened her eyes. He rubbed the dried blood off her arm, and she noticed with shock that the wound from Orson's laser fire had disappeared. As she turned to ask how he had healed the wound, Loren caught her face in his hands and crushed his mouth to hers.

She moaned beneath the onslaught of his tongue as it pried into her mouth and explored the moist interior. Her legs weakened and she clung to his broad shoulders, caressing the firm muscles, reveling in the slick feel of his skin. Loren lowered his hands over her breasts, cupping them, before sweeping to the small of her back. He pressed her to him, hip to hip. Caught between them, the head of his cock nestled comfortably at her belly button, hot and hard with need.

Desperate to feel his butt in her hands, she wriggled her arms between his until her hands closed over the firm rise of muscle. His mouth left hers to trail over her jaw and down to nibble at the tender spot where neck met shoulder, until he lowered his hot mouth over one taut nipple.

Tirana arched back at the explosion of need that gushed between her legs, sending a wanton heat shooting over her body. She pressed her groin to Loren's as he tongued her nipple while a thumb circled the other. As his teeth pulled at the tight nub in his mouth, his finger rubbed the other nipple between his fingers until her legs weakened with the restless heat of desire that threatened to engulf her.

Loren groaned in frustration as she extricated herself from his embrace and stepped back. His eyes glowed through his wet hair, his chest rising rapidly with his excited breath. The waterfall pounded over his lean body. He was beautiful, raw and untamed.

The intensity of her feelings for him frightened her. The hunger coursing through her veins pulled at her as much as the fear deep in her gut. Fear of the urge burning inside her to join with him forever.

"Tirana." He reached for her.

She turned to face the pool and dove head-first off the platform into the depths below.

Chapter Four

Tirana was dragged down into a vortex of cold water, spun and twisted, dragged downwards to the bottom of the pool. Her chest burned as she expelled her last breath and a freezing cold wrapped itself around her. She flailed her arms, mouth open in a silent scream, trying to hold on to anything that would keep her from the relentless pull of the current.

Something hard gripped her wrist, hauled her up through the water. She broke the surface with a desperate gasp, drawing the air deep into her burning lungs. An arm caught her around the chest as she gulped in air, drew her to the edge of the pool, pulled her out. On all fours, she vomited a lungful of water into the sand as Loren smoothed back her hair.

She spluttered, wiping water from her face, looked up at him. "Thank you."

"If I had known you found me so distasteful you would rather risk death than my arms, we could have bathed safely in the pool."

Tirana flinched at the coldness of his tone, the edge of anger on every careful word. She had meant to get away from the intensity of her own feelings, had almost killed herself by that childish and foolish reflex. And she had hurt him, when he had done nothing. Nothing but desire her.

"I'm sorry." She touched his arm. He drew away, the look in his eyes distant and dismissing, and rose to his feet.

"We'll go to Laliata now." He reached for her comms suit from the pile of clothing, threw it so it landed beside her in the sand.

"No." Panic made her voice harsh as she stumbled to her feet and faced him. He ignored her, crouching as he gathered up his boots and sifted through the pile for his trousers. "You haven't shown me the *hekarten-jal* yet."

"There will be no *hekarten-jal.*" Loren lifted his trousers and shook off the sand.

A piercing scream filled the cave. She saw deLoren hopping from foot to foot in a dance of anger on the rocks above the waterfall. Loren winced. Then his face set hard as he flicked a hand at deLoren. The creature toppled backwards onto the rock.

"Loren!" Tirana stared at him in shock. Somehow Loren had made deLoren fall, she was sure of it. A lash of anger that should have been directed at her.

In a temper, she tore the trousers from his grasp. "I said I'm sorry. What more do you want?"

"My clothes." His face was impassive, eyes hooded.

Furious, she cupped the back of his neck and dragged his head down to her. Her lips burrowed into his cold mouth, prodded at an unresponsive tongue. She growled in frustration, catching his fleshy lower lip in her teeth, pulling and nipping. She glared at him, saw the flash of anger in his eyes, lowered both hands and gripped his cock. It jumped to stiff attention in her grasp.

Loren shoved her back. Then his hand clamped over her wrist. He turned on his heel, storming off into the darkness at the far side of the pool.

"Loren!" Her feet skidded in the sand as she tried to tug her arm free from his iron grip. Darkness enveloped them, and a moment later they were in another warm passage. Here the rock glowed red around them. There was a low round entrance at the end, so small Loren had to bend his head to enter. She barely had time to duck under the rock as he dragged her after him

"Here!" Loren pushed her into the cave before him.

She stumbled and fell. Her hands landed on a soft, cushiony substance the texture of cotton candy. A soft cloud of fibers stretched over the floor of a small cave, warm and snug like a cocoon. Or the pulsing red insides of a womb, for the walls were covered in glittering red lichen.

Loren fell to his knees behind her, hooked her legs apart, and slipped his stiff member between her thighs, resting the hard shaft on the slit of her sex. He hauled her up and slid his hands around to cup her breasts, squeezing them. She gasped at the pleasure/pain as Loren lowered his mouth to her ear.

"This is the *hekarten-jal,*" he growled, his hot breath fanning her face. "The mating place."

Heat spurted at her core as he said the words. *Mating.* This was what he'd wanted all along. What *she'd* wanted since she'd set eyes on him back at the stone circle but had been too cowardly to even admit to herself. Until now.

One of his hands swept over her midriff, burrowed between her thighs, found the hot, pulsing nub. She arched back against him at the first flick of his finger, and he caught her head and dragged it around so he could crush her mouth beneath his. His tongue devastated her, plundered and ravished, even as his fingers rubbed over the slick flesh of her throbbing clit. His cock jerked between her thighs as the blood pumped to his extremities, and he moved his hips to slide it back and forth between the moist folds of her sex.

His mouth left hers, his breathing harsh, and he bent her forward and worked his hand between them to position his cock at the entrance to her vagina. She vibrated with the need to have him fill her, held her breath in excited anticipation as she felt the nudge of his thick head pushing at her tight entrance.

Loren suddenly stilled and pulled away. Her juices slid out, dripped over the inside of her thighs. She felt the desolate thud of abandonment clenching at her stomach as his warm body left hers. Slowly, she turned to face him, saw him crouching back on his heels.

A war of emotions—regret, desire—swept over his features. "I'm sorry." He covered his eyes. "I cannot take you this way."

"Why can't you?" She was no longer afraid to reveal the raw need in her voice. She dragged his hands away from his face so he could see the truth in her eyes. "I want you, Loren. What I did back there—when I jumped—that was fear. Not fear of you, but fear for what I felt for you."

His eyes blazed with fierce hope before the fire in them banked. He shook his head. "Tirana, I have not been honest with you."

"About the *hekarten-jal?*" She smiled. "Because you brought me here to mate?"

"It will not be a simple mating." His beautiful eyes were full of guilt. "You said you didn't believe in gods or goddesses. That you believed in nothing. But if we mate here, you will become *si-heketarten.*"

She shrugged helplessly. "I don't understand that word."

"Touched by magic." He paused for a beat. "As are all the True People."

"Magic?"

He nodded, held out his hand. She saw a blue flame lick over the palm, gather itself into a ball of light, pulsing and spinning. When it had grown to the size of a small orange, Loren threw it in the air. It shattered against the low ceiling and spilled over them in a shower of rainbow sparks. Tirana felt the prickles where sparks touched her wet skin.

Magic. He could communicate telepathically with deLoren, he could perform magic—or manipulate energy so that it seemed like magic. And it seemed that mating with him would allow her to do the same. There were mysteries here that would take a long time to unravel. For starters, she doubted that magic could be sexually transmitted.

"Tell me about what was happening in the stone circle when I first saw you," she asked softly, looking at his empty palm. His fingers clenched in a fist.

"The Priests captured deLoren and I. The True People are heretics to them, to be sacrificed to their cruel goddess, the one they call Lalith and is not Lalith."

"What were you doing there, risking capture?"

"The *ba-hekarten* told us you had come. I was searching for you, to bring you back to join the others in Laliata."

"Others?"

"Those who came from the skies before."

He could only mean the previous SEU scouting missions. Tirana experienced the heady sense accomplishment as the mystery unraveled. "They're in Laliata? They're all alive?"

"Only those who chose to be *si-heketarten*."

Joy gripped her. "I'll take them back with me on the shuttle. The SEU needs to know they're alive."

Loren frowned. "They cannot leave."

"Of course they can. We'll find a way to get past Orson and his men—"

"They are True People now." His tone was patient.

"If they've converted, which isn't surprising after all this time, they can safely practice their religion anywhere in the galaxy."

"You don't understand. The True People can never leave Samhain. Your friends can never go back. They chose to be touched by magic, to be one of the True People. They said others would come and that we must find you before the Priests did. This is true, Tirana."

"Yes but—"

The impatient flash of anger in his eyes stopped her further arguments. "Look where you are, Tirana."

She stared at him without comprehending. "I'm in a cave."

"No. You're in the *hekarten-jal.*"

She gazed around her. The walls weren't rock, she realized, but something soft and living, pulsating with heat. And the fibers beneath her, they were part of it, the soft hair of a living creature.

"What is this place?" she whispered.

"The soul of Samhain. Lalith's womb."

Tirana felt the *hekarten-jal* enveloping her in its pulsing warmth, infusing her with a sense of safety and acceptance. Her heart beat fast, her breath felt shallow and labored.

"The *hekarten-jal* wants you, Tirana. As I want you."

Her body quivered at the heat in his voice. "I don't—"

"You can go back to the Priests, or you can join the True People. There is no other choice."

She shook her head. "You asked me to choose at the junction, to go to Laliata or come here. I could have chosen Laliata."

Loren nodded. "And there you would be asked to make the choice again. The Priests or the True People." His voice deepened as his eyes grew in brilliance. "I brought you here for mating but have no doubt that, with me or alone, here you would eventually come."

Tirana's thoughts twisted and spun, verged on the edge of control, tumbled over. And yet...and yet a slow excitement was building within her, insinuating itself in her mind, pressing against her body. She knew she was on the brink, on the precipice of something that would change her life in unimaginable ways. Loren was telling her she had no choice, yet he was asking her to make that choice, now, with him.

The key to it was Loren, whom her body ached for, whose eyes blazed for her, whose mouth she would never forget. Would never want to forget.

He sat quietly, observing her. And held out his hand, silently asking her to take it. To take him.

She made her choice—and slipped her hand into his, palm against palm.

Loren closed his fingers over her hand and came to kneel before her on the soft fibrous mattress of the *hekarten-jal*. His hands cupped her face, lifted it, and he rested his lips on hers. The kiss was sweet and gentle, a soft exploration, a token of love. It sent a shiver through her, and she trembled with the force of it. She loved him.

He murmured against her lips, lifted his mouth to kiss her nose, her eyelids, her forehead, before swooping down on her mouth again. She felt his passion, his demanding need for possession, like a bolt through her center that had her clutching at his shoulders.

He lowered her back, pressing himself along the length of her body until she was cushioned deep into the soft, thick fibers. Loren's hands swept over her tender breasts, and his mouth followed, teeth nibbling at the taut nipples that still ached from his earlier assault. Tirana felt the hardness of his staff lying hard against her sex, rubbing across the slickness of her exposed clit. Loren eased his fingers between them, circled fingertips over the engorged nub, dipped into the wetness between her legs, and circled some more until her legs fell open in the ache to accept him.

He shifted, his lips lifting from her breast, his gaze meeting hers. She drowned in the brilliant green of his eyes as his cock nudged at her entrance again. This time, he shafted her strong and sudden, burying himself inside her. She cried out at the burst of pain and pleasure, heard him murmuring endearments as his lips slid over the moistness of hers. When she settled, he began to move with a slow rhythm, pulling back and then penetrating her again and again, until she was meeting him thrust for thrust, arching her hips to meet the pistoning of his. Tirana could feel the unfurling at her core, the rise of her orgasm. Loren's eyes were blazing into hers, his buttocks clenched beneath her squeezing hands as she locked her legs around his waist.

He stopped, his breathing ragged, and lifted her as he sat back on his heels, drawing her with him, her legs clenched around his waist. He was buried deep inside her, her breasts pressed against his chest. She grabbed a handful of his hair and kissed him. He moaned beneath her devouring mouth, and she rode him hard and fast, driving him deeper and deeper, until he stiffened. She felt the spasm of his hard shaft throbbing inside her, and her own orgasm tore through her body. She cried out, arched back, as the waves of pleasure shot over her.

Something soft dropped to her neck, clung, and stung her hard between the shoulder blades. She screamed, twisted to take it off—and a sensation of pure ecstasy shot through her. Colors burst beneath her eyelids, shattered like crystals, sent her flying and floating until she was caught up on a breeze of color. A warm gust pushed into her mind, trickled through her consciousness, sent a pulse of energy to every extremity until every cell of her body vibrated. It seemed to go on forever, ebbing and flowing, until it subsided like the pulling back of the tide.

Tirana opened her eyes and found herself clinging to Loren, her arms wrapped around his neck. She felt something slide over her back and drop into the fibers behind her. Loren's gaze met hers, and he swept a wet strand of hair from her sweat-slicked face and kissed her.

She eased herself off him and, heart beating fast, turned to look behind her.

The small, soft creature that had been with deLoren at the pool lay huddled on the fibers, curled into a ball. Tirana recognized it. Knew it. No, *her*. It was the sighing breeze in her mind.

Her voice soft, she called to it. "deTirana."

Her *hekarten* unfurled itself and blinked at her, eyes groggy, tiny ears twitching.

Hello. The voice swept weak and gentle over her mind.

"Hello." Tirana smiled.

Chapter Five

Tirana didn't know how long they spent in the *hekarten-jal*, but it felt like days. Her tentative attempt to communicate with her *hekarten*, deTirana, was abandoned as the creature drifted off to sleep. Soon she and Loren followed, wrapped in each other's arms, and when they woke Tirana found only a soft pelt beside them. deTirana's fur.

"She is becoming *hekarten*." Loren soothed her fears. "She will become like deLoren. Don't worry, deLoren is with her. They will return."

They made love again, taking each other with a fierce desire, a heat that smoldered at her molten core. She couldn't get enough of him, of his touch worshipping her body, of glorying in the splendor of his. She came time and time again, crying out his name, as he drove himself into her. When they were both sated, embraced by the *hekarten-jal*, they slept again.

Wake.

Tirana opened her eyes at the soft sigh in her mind. deTirana's presence was close, timid and afraid. Loren curled in sleep at her side, his warm hand clasping her breast.

She stretched, feeling extraordinarily relaxed and fulfilled. There was a warmth at her center that had never been there before, not just contentment but…power. As though a restless ball of energy had wound itself around the base of her spine, spinning, ready to be released.

Sliding from under Loren's grasp, Tirana padded out of the *hekarten-jal* into the great cavern.

Here. She looked about the cavern for deTirana and saw her sitting on the steps leading to the waterfall.

The small creature had transformed into the spitting image of deLoren, who sat at her side, grinning. His eyes twinkled in glee as he bit into the round fruit in his hands from the pile at their feet. Tirana felt her stomach rumble with hunger.

She took one of the oblong pieces of dark fruit and bit into the pulp. It was sweet and delicious. deTirana observed her with sombre curiosity and Tirana studied her in turn. The *hekarten* was smaller than deLoren, with tufts of hair on the tips of her tiny ears, softer eyes and a smaller mouth. A feminine version of Loren's *hekarten*.

Sitting beside them, she ate her fill of fruit. At her last mouthful, deLoren and deTirana scampered away into the darkness. Her stomach full, juice covering her chin and chest, Tirana climbed the steps to the ledge and stepped into the pounding curtain of water.

She could never go back, she knew that. In the *hekarten-jal*, she and deTirana had become one. Leaving Samhain would mean the death of the *hekarten*, and her own death. She belonged here now, on this strange world. Belonged to Loren—as he belonged to her.

She closed her eyes, moved out of the waterfall, brushing back her wet hair as she remembered Loren's hard body taking hers. She'd wake him, let him know how much she wanted him, and—

"Very nice."

Tirana's eyes snapped open in shock. Orson leered at her, his yellow teeth exposed in a snarling grin. Dried blood had pooled in his scarred eye socket from the scrapes across his face—or what she could see of them under the smears of dirt. A large backpack was slung over his shoulders. He must have gone back for that before he'd come looking for her. Had taken the time to prepare. And she understood that his obsession with having her, destroying her, knew no end.

He jabbed the muzzle of his weapon between her breasts, let it trail down over her midriff to her belly. Lowered. She jerked away. He snatched her arm and yanked her, dragged her down the stairs after him. She slipped, cried out in pain as her ankle scraped against stone. He threw her like a rag-doll on the sand.

She turned to crawl but he was on her in a second, his knee planted between her thighs, forcing them apart. He struck her across the face with the back of his hand, a blow that sent her eyes rolling back into her head in agony.

"Thought you'd get away, did you? Bitch." She heard him as she struggled up from the blackness, opened her bruised eyes to see him throw the rifle and the backpack to one side. He wrapped a hand around her neck, pressing down hard till she gasped for breath.

"I'm going to enjoy tearing you apart." His rank breath rolled over her face. She felt him fumbling at his trousers, jerked against him in panic, choked as he pushed his thumb into her windpipe.

His cock pressed against her thigh and he groped between her legs. Her eyes widened in horror as he pushed himself at the entrance to her vagina, ramming against the tight constriction of her muscles denying him passage.

"Lemme in you fucking wh—"

Suddenly he was off her. Gasping, she gulped in a lungful of air. She heard blows, the sick thud of flesh against flesh, a moan of pain. Turning in the sand, she saw Loren leaning over Orson's prone body, the lapel of his army jacket twisted in one fist. Loren's expression was contorted with fury as he pounded and pounded at Orson's face.

Tirana struggled to her feet, hobbled over to Loren, dragged at his shoulder. "Stop it! You'll kill him."

Smashing his fist into Orson's face one last time, Loren threw the soldier to the ground in disgust. The soldier's face was a sickening, bleeding pulp of raw flesh. But he breathed, moaned softly with pain.

"Loren," she whispered.

Loren turned and caught her as she fell. She savored the strength of his arms, the sanctuary of them. There was a stricken look in his eyes, the glitter of tears, as he touched her face.

She tried to assure him. "He didn't—he didn't—"

"Sshhh. It doesn't matter. You're still here. Still here." He clasped her close to his chest, lowered his head to brush his lips gently against hers.

They heard Orson moan and twist on the sand. Tirana pulled away as she glimpsed Orson reaching for the rifle. She aimed a kick that sent it skittering over the edge of the pool to fall into the water with a plop. Loren turned to crouch, ready to spring at him.

Orson crawled back over the sand, his one eye a slit between slices of raw flesh. "Get away from me!" he screamed at Loren. "Don't touch me."

He caught the strap of the backpack and dragged it with him, scrabbling at the fastening until its contents spilled on the sand. Clothing, food and a square black box with cables attached. A long-range transmitter.

Tirana burned with sudden hope as she saw the transmitter. Orson threw the delicate instrument carelessly to one side, and she felt a hot wave of anger sweep over her. A ball of energy formed at her core, rose through chest and shoulders, shot over arms and out through her hands—which she had pointed at Orson. It hit him square in the chest, sent him flying back into the sand. Away from the transmitter.

She slumped back into Loren's arms, drained by the outpouring of energy.

A piercing cry filled the air, reverberated around the walls of the cave. It was followed by the chattering of a thousand angry creatures who scraped and scrabbled over sand and rocks through the darkness in a frothing sea of fur. Orson screamed as the *ba-hekarten* surrounded him, over him, under him, until they lifted him beneath the carpet of furry bodies, thousands of tiny feet running towards the blackness at the far end of the cave, carrying him away into its depths. He screamed once. And then a deafening silence.

Shaking, Tirana turned to Loren. He stared at deLoren and deTirana sitting on the rocks beside the waterfall, grinning. Loren grinned back.

He caught her bewildered expression and said, "The *ba-hekarten* don't like the devil soldier. They'll throw him out of the caves, just like they do the Priests."

She sighed in relief. She didn't want Orson's death on her conscience, as tempting as that was.

She saw the transmitter half-buried in the sand and crawled to it. Loren followed, watched curiously as she lifted it onto her lap.

"There'll be more like him," Tirana told him quietly, wiping the sand from the metal box. "Special Forces will take Samhain. They'll destroy everything." She stared at him. "Everyone."

Loren took her hand, squeezing gently. "What will be will be. There is nothing we can do but prepare."

"I have another idea."

She packed the transmitter into the backpack, snapped on the seals, went to put on her comms suit.

"Where are you going?" Loren sounded alarmed.

"Topside. I need to send my final report."

Loren was at her side, dragging her into his arms. "No. More of your soldiers may be sitting in wait. And if not them, then the Priests. I cannot lose you."

He held her close, whispered, "Tirana, if I lost you I would lose everything."

She wrapped her arms around his waist, saw the despair blazing in his eyes and felt love for him bubble through her.

"You'll never lose me, Loren. That I can promise you."

His mouth covered hers hungrily and she arched up to meet his passion and her destiny.

Epilogue

Universal Alliance Settlement Exploration Unit: Report 17836ZE-C

Update:

Year 2561.7

Settlement Scouting Unit SU-SEU9107 first transmission: Reported plague on Samhain's surface. Origin suspected parasitic, estimated 99.9% fatal. Suggest immediate quarantine of onworld Special Forces and SEU teams. Transmission incomplete. Scouting Unit declared "Missing". 4 days in field.

Recommendation:

Immediate withdrawal of UA Special Forces' troop carriers enroute to Samhain. Special Forces' mandate over Samhain returned to the SEU for further investigation. Exploration of Samhain coded black for extreme low priority.

About the Author

Cassandra Kane grew up in Australia and now resides in the UK. A graduate of the University of Sydney, Cassandra divides her time between the day job and her writing. She enjoys good food, interesting conversation and exotic travel, not necessarily in that order.

To learn more about Cassandra, please visit www.cassandrakane.com. Send an email to Cassandra at cassandra@cassandrakane.com or join her Yahoo! Newsletter group at http://groups.yahoo.com/group/cassandrakane-news to find out about the latest news and releases.

Look for these titles

A Warrior's Witch

Mackenzie McKade

Dedication

To my wonderful editor, Angela James. Thank you for your guidance and the opportunity to express myself through my writing.

Acknowledgements

A special thanks to Cait Miller, Christine H., Patti Duplantis, and Cheyenne McCray. You are the special people in my life.

Chapter One

Scotland welcomed Conall Lachlan back to her moonlit shores by pitching him on his arse. One minute he was astride his horse cantering along the cliff side—the next airborne when a rabbit darted across their path. While his skittish mount ran one way, the hare sped in the opposite direction.

Conall struck the ground hard and rolled with the momentum of the fall.

As pain splintered across his backside, he caught sight of the Barney drifting back out to sea. With the ship's departure went his freedom.

Unexpected sorrow pierced his heart. At fourteen, travel, adventure and exotic tales of the Orient lured him away. Now, ten years later, his father's death called him home.

Eyes pinched closed, he remembered their argument, words exchanged in anger.

"Lad, ye'll be back," Hamish Lachlan, the Lachlan clan's chieftain had growled. "With yer tail 'a'tween those scrawny legs."

"Dinna hold yer breath," Conall shouted, without glancing back.

He never returned, until now.

The message he had received from his cousin Eacharn that his father had died had been a shock. Although Eacharn had promised all was well, Conall knew it was time to come home and fulfill his duties as clan leader.

Unmoving, he lay where the horse pitched him upon the sandy ground sparsely covered with patches of rough grass. Sounds of the ocean's unrest rose and crashed against the jagged rocks below mimicking the turmoil churning inside him. He let a calming breath fill his lungs, gathering scents of pine and oak with the salty air. When his eyes opened, he rose and dusted off his leather tunic and leggings. Scotland had changed little, except the ground seemed less forgiving.

With a tug, he straightened his red and gold plaid, adjusting it over his shoulder and waist. As soon as they disembarked the ship, Conall had sent his men ahead to a neighbor's castle to announce their need for accommodations. He and his men were still a day's ride from home and would need a place to stay the night.

His destination was the grey, majestic castle looming ahead. Years ago, the Earl of Loch Tower, Edmond Macleod, had been an ally. Conall hoped that was still the case. The earl was not a man he cared to have as an enemy, especially since they shared an ancient bloodline.

They were a breed apart from humanity.

Beserka.

Men neither fully human nor fully animal gifted with shape-shifting and preternatural abilities rumored to exist as far back as the Nordic gods. Known as Odin's warriors, each blessed with an animal totem.

The wolf was Lachlan's totem. The feline was the Macleod's.

He bent at the waist, gathered a stone off the sandy path, chucked it and watched it bounce and roll away.

Odd what one remembered. As a child he'd heard claims the earl's daughter possessed her mother's witch heritage and, strangely, her father's lineage. She possessed not only the Beserka totem, but the ability to shape-shift into whatever form she chose.

Impossible. The child was only eight when he had left. Beserka abilities surfaced around puberty for boys, never a girl.

Female Beserkas did not exist.

A sudden breeze stirred his shoulder-length blond hair, whipping the thin braids along each side of his cheeks. Thunder boomed. Threads of lightning raced across the sky, one after another. The scent of rain filled the air.

He glanced askance at the angry clouds above. "Och. Ye threaten tae spit on me?" He stepped over a fallen log, stumbled, nearly falling as the earth trembled beneath his feet. Again, lightning flashed illuminating the heavens.

A sudden blast of heat surged through the soles of his boots grinding him to an abrupt halt. Feet temporarily paralyzed, his skin prickled as the hairs on his arms rose.

Lightning strike?

He glanced at his feet. No blackened spot lay beneath him. No tree or bush nearby was afire.

And he still stood.

"Good sign indeed," he chuckled. Yet the beast inside him wasn't reassured. It moved silently below his skin, forcing his chin upward to scent the air. The distinct smell of honey and cloves and something—no someone—female caused his groin to tighten. Not with a mild stirring, but an ache that bent him so that he had to brace his hands on his thighs, forcing a groan from his throat.

"It canna be," he murmured, slowly rising to his six-two height.

The Beserka were a dying breed, only able to procreate with a true lifemate. Finding that mate was a lifelong challenge.

If his body's reaction was an indicator, Conall's search was over. He had found his mate.

Samhain was strengthening.

As it neared the witching hour, Sabine Macleod could feel its magic calling. Soon the great Shield of Scathach would lower its barriers between worlds to allow the spirits of the dead and those yet to be born to walk amongst the living.

It was a magical night.

Still, a whisper of unease raced through her body. The wind tugged at the hem of her long white robe, tossing her waist-length black hair around her shoulders.

Throughout the village bonfires flickered brightly. Before the night ended, they would extinguish all but one—a common flame—to light their hearths and bond the families of the village together.

It was tradition.

Sabine gazed around the sacred clearing surrounded by tall oaks and alder. Tonight she would ask for clarity of thought and thank the Goddess for guidance, because something was amiss.

The sackcloth Sabine held slipped to the ground. With a shrug, her robe followed to reveal her nudity.

Was her anxiety due to Samhain? Or perhaps it was her father's invitation for every eligible Beserka in Scotland to court her. He worried the Beserka curse would leave her unwed.

That aspect worried Sabine naught. Loss of independence and the unknown were her concerns. At Loch Tower the clan understood and accepted who and what she was. Strangers were either frightened of her differences or wished to use her unique gifts for their own benefits.

From the bag, she retrieved a flask of saltwater and sprinkled half of the contents about, purifying the area. Even as she poured the remaining water over her body, she knew Loch Tower's dining hall was filling up with visitors who had two goals in mind—to celebrate the final harvest and witness the possible pairing of mates.

Sabine had stayed away as long as she dared. Her father would send his men in search of her. She had to hurry.

"It will be my choice," she stated firmly. Yet her frustration came from knowing that if the Beserka legend was true and if her mate existed among her father's visitors, when the sun rose on the morrow her life would change forever.

Conceived on Samhain, witch blood ran deep in her veins, clouded with that of the beast. The mischief of an evening just like tonight had caused the phenomenon.

"Beserka lust is an impellin' force that must be answered—a matin'—the joinin' of two lifemates," Sabine's mother, Isobel, had said on numerous occasions.

Another wave of anxiety swept across Sabine's skin but she pushed it aside.

To connect with the earth she focused on the core of light inside her body. She faced the east calling upon the air.

The element responded, stroking her body with an intimate breeze. A gentle caress circled her breasts and weaved between her legs. Her nipples grew taut, stinging. Moisture dampened her thighs. She wiggled her hips, trying to shun the strange tightening in her loins that appeared out of nowhere.

"From the forest, South, I call tae thee." The sudden rush of heat stole her breath. Visions of two naked bodies, hot and moist, intertwined, came to her.

"Saints preserve," she gasped.

Aye. The Goddess was sensual, but never had Sabine felt these sensations.

Sabine spun to the west. "From the sea, West, I call tae thee." Like a dolphin leaping the waves, her belly did several flip-flops. Her pulse sped. The increasing throb between her legs turned her breaths into small pants.

What is happenin' tae me?

She swayed. Eyes clenched shut, her knees wobbled as she fought to continue.

"...ground, North, I call tae thee." The temperature in her body soared.

Her voice shook as she lifted it to the sky. "Join in the circle, Center, I call tae thee."

The elements came together in a rush, slamming into Sabine. Raw power surged throughout her. She felt alive, standing on the pinnacle of something new and exciting.

With a thrust, she raised both hands into the air, invoking the Goddess. A moment of meditation followed. She prayed for peace, healing and guidance, closing her invocation to thank the Goddess for her presence.

The earth's melody rose. Sabine's slender form began to move in slow undulations to raise the Cone of Power needed to strengthen the vision of her destiny.

Invisible hands washed over her body. She spun in circle after circle, loving the way her skin felt, tight and tingling. Eyes remained closed, her palms moved boldly across her heated flesh, until she cupped her breasts. The peaks of her nipples were sensitive, hot nubs of sensation, as she rolled them between her fingers.

Uninhibited, no maidenly shame rose, only the excitement to follow where the Goddess led.

As the music in Sabine's mind grew wilder, her back arched and flexed, a fluid wave that rippled through her like water rushing over stones. Her hips swayed as she tried to ease the ache between her thighs.

The wind's caress was no longer a whisper across her skin. Instead, warm, firm hands guided her wrists above her head. It felt right to lean against the wall of muscle that appeared, spooning her from behind, because she was safe—no evil could enter the sanctity of the circle.

Salt and spices permeated the air. Heavy breathing warmed her neck. A seductive touch slid down her arms and around her waist, holding her close.

Sabine thanked the Goddess for sending this ethereal being to fill the emptiness inside that she had never voiced. Something was missing in her life, she just didn't know what.

Strong hands guided Sabine around. Heavy-lidded, she gazed into the intensity of eyes a crystal blue. Golden hair swept his shoulders. Thin braids hung at each cheek.

As their mouths touched, his tongue slipped between her lips.

Sweet Jesus. She'd been kissed before, but never like this. It was a spell, an attack on all her senses. She felt helpless, melting in his embrace. As he tasted her, their naked forms continued to strengthen the Cone of Power in movement.

When their kiss broke, his lips traced a path down her throat. His hands caressed her from shoulders to hips. Slowly, he eased her down upon the rough grass and heather. His large, muscular frame draped hers, pinning her to the ground.

"Yer an innocent?" His deep, sexy voice smoothed across her flesh like a warm breeze.

She couldn't respond or think, not past the echo of discomfort thrumming throughout her body. She clung desperately to him, needing him to silence the storm raging inside her.

His hand slipped between them. Skillful fingers touched her where no man had ever. She whimpered as he parted her folds, and then pushed a finger deep within.

Fire raced across her womb. "What's happenin' tae me?" The ache low in her belly pulsed, growing to an unbearable peak. A sliver of anxiety slid up her spine.

"Fate." His tone sounded hoarse, strained. "I will be gentle as I can, lassie, but the beast begs not tae be denied any longer." He wedged his knee between her legs, spreading her thighs wide and moving between them.

Before Sabine knew what was happening, he replaced his fingers with something bigger and harder, slowly pushing inside her. A sharp tearing sensation made her tense as he broke through the thin layer of her virginity. Pain too real to be her imagination made her cry out. Her fingers dug into solid flesh—too firm—to be an apparition.

"A moment of discomfort—a lifetime of pleasure." His promise was followed by a sense of fullness Sabine had never experienced. Buried deep inside her, he remained motionless for only a moment, long enough for her to catch the breath that had deserted her.

"Mine." His husky declaration made her gasp. A rainbow of colors rippled across his eyes. Canines pushed from his gums, pressing into his bottom lip. He held back the change, but Sabine knew the truth.

Beserka!

It was too late to stop the inevitable. He sank his teeth into her shoulder, marking her.

The sudden pain only heightened the moment as her inner muscles clamped down on him. A swell of pleasure made her arch, causing her to buck beneath him. Hot spasms shot from her core. She groaned low and long as her body milked his cock.

Another growl rumbled from his throat as he smoothly disengaged their union, rolling her on her stomach. She didn't have time to savor the smell of grass and heather mingling with scents of their mating. His hand slid quickly beneath her belly, raising her hips as he entered her from behind, but this time the penetration was deeper. His thrusts were faster—harder.

The sounds of flesh slapping flesh threw her into another orgasm. As it ripped through her, she threw back her head and her beast called to his. Her canines dropped. She struggled to keep the cat within from rising.

One more pump of his hips and his beast answered, filling her with his warm seed.

Saints preserve!

The man atop Sabine was real. A pulse still beat where their bodies joined.

Although she wanted nothing more than to bask in his warmth, her mind screamed that he was a stranger, someone who could change her life forever.

The truth was she was afraid. Afraid of losing her freedom and afraid of the hot, uncontrollable desire this man stirred inside her.

Chapter Two

Conall's naked body hummed with satisfaction. The heat of arousal cooled as he rolled from atop his mate, reaching to pull her near. Instead, she yanked from his grip and scrambled to her feet, retrieving the white robe crumpled upon the ground. With short, jerky movements, she dressed, tying the sash.

"Dinna hide from me, lassie." He chuckled, sliding his hands beneath his head. Her beauty lay carved into his memory. Firm breasts, taut rosy nipples, and a heart-shaped bottom had fit perfectly in his palms. His favorite were her long, slender legs, legs that wrapped around his waist while he drove his hard cock into her hot, wet quim.

He strained to hear the words she began to murmur. With a swipe of her hand through the air, she closed her witch's circle.

A witch. And a strange one at that. He could have sworn he touched a beast within her. In the grip of Beserka lust, he even believed he had seen sharp, white fangs retract between those lovely full lips.

Damn. His imagination was running wild. If finding one's mate did this to a man, he had better beware.

The heavy tread of horses' hooves approaching from the north ripped his gaze from the woman gathering her things. He had known when his arrival at Loch Tower was delayed that his men would backtrack to find him.

Slowly, Conall pushed to his feet. As he reached for his clothes, Ewen, Cameron and Fitzer, his friends and traveling cohorts, burst through a copse of trees, heading straight for him.

Pulling his horse to a stop, Ewen haughtily cocked a brow. "Methinks there be a story here." Conall's childhood friend was always seeing stories where stories did not lie. But in this particular case there was.

Conall would be returning home to take his place as chieftain with a bride in tow.

"Ghosties?" Fitzer whispered. His wild mass of red hair bounced as his rusty-colored eyes looked suspiciously about. "Or would it be evil fairies renderin' ye bare-arsed and stealin' yer horse?" From Ireland, he was full of superstition and beliefs.

Cameron was the quiet one. His shoulder-length black hair fell forward as he leaned his wrists on the saddle and waited patiently for an explanation.

When Conall turned to introduce his friends to his bride-to-be—

She was gone.

At the top of the stairs overlooking the great hall, Sabine paused. What had she done? Before she realized the truth, she had given herself to the man in the glen. Damn her Beserka heritage.

The soft kirtle of blue she wore felt binding, too tight. Her breasts were still sensitive and the emptiness between her thighs refused to go away.

In front of one of eight long tables, her father stood. Edmond's deep baritone voice rose with glee as several new guests entered the large communal room where the clan congregated for meals.

Sabine's beast rose to scent the air. Among the scent of freshly baked bread, fish, chicken and boar, one of the visitors smelled of warm, salty air with a hint of spice.

Nay. She worried senselessly. Her true mate was somewhere wondering the glens, not seated at her father's table.

If her father ever discovered the truth—

Sabine startled as her mother's gentle hand settled upon her shoulder.

"Mother, I feel queasy. Must I attend the evenin's celebration?"

Isobel's expression softened. "He only seeks yer happiness."

Gray whispered through her mother's elbow-length ebony hair. The resemblance between them was remarkable, except Isobel's eyes were brown, Sabine's blue.

"I am happy." Stubbornly, Sabine's chin raised. "Marriage would be a chain around my neck."

A frown tugged at Isobel's mouth. "Dinna yer dreams embody the love of a man? Children?"

"Nay." Behind a wall of indifference, she forced the emotion threatening to surface away. She couldn't allow herself to think of how the stranger made her body burn. He would take her away from everyone she loved to a world of unknown.

Isobel brushed a lock of hair from Sabine's face. "Yer father will be sadden if ye dinna make an appearance."

Sabine raised a single brow. "Then I may return tae my chamber?"

A knowing twinkle sparkled in her mother's eyes. "An appearance."

Panic raised its ugly head. Surely her mother had no knowledge of what occurred earlier. The woman always knew things others did not.

Nay. It wasn't possible.

Sabine inhaled a deep breath of courage, squared her shoulders, and began to descend the stairs. Light-footed, she crossed the room.

As her heart leaped into her throat, she jerked to an abrupt halt. For a moment, she couldn't breathe.

"It canna be," she whispered. Her beast stirred with both excitement and fear.

The man from the glen sat next to her father.

Before she could flee, their eyes met. The intensity of his dark stare made her pulse race. Like fire to dry tinder her body went up in flames, her nipples drew tight. Butterflies fluttered in her stomach.

Quietly, he placed his eating knife down. Palms on the table, he pushed to his feet. His approach sent a wave of heat radiating through her body.

When a growl rumbled from his chest, she noticed the room had gone silent and her father had risen. Servants paused where they stood. Friends, family and strangers gathered around the eight tables drew their attention toward her and the man who could change her life forever.

The iridescent glow of Beserka rippled in his eyes, shimmering colors of heat that caressed her skin. Then his nostrils flared—he scented her.

"Nay!" Sabine gasped, cupping her hand over her mouth. A tremor assailed her as she fought the invisible pull beckoning her into his arms. Instead, she stumbled backward.

"Sabine?" Concern furrowed her father's forehead as he moved to her side. "Have ye met young Lachlan?"

"Nay," she lied, at the same time as the man said, "Aye."

Sabine tried to center herself—gain the control she felt slipping like water through her fingers.

"Lord Lachlan, may I introduce my daughter, Sabine." Edmond's sharp gaze remained on Sabine, watching, waiting for the telltale signs that a match existed.

"Daughter?" Lachlan snapped his attention to her father. "Then we must speak."

Edmond shot Lachlan a questioning glance.

Invisible chains tightened around her. She felt the noose around her neck slip and squeeze as Lachlan said, "She is my mate."

Perched on the knife's edge of desperation, Sabine forced a laugh. "Da. He jests. Come let us eat."

Every muscle in her body clenched beneath Lachlan's scrutiny. Her nipples were hard pebbles against her bodice. She refused to think about the rush of moisture between her thighs. She felt achy and tense.

Lachlan contracted his brows, his displeasure evident. "I jest not. We are mated."

Embarrassment heated Sabine's face. Perhaps not everyone heard him, but she knew those who shared her lineage did, no matter how far away they sat. Her skin shrank two sizes too small. For the first time in her life, she stood speechless.

Edmond's face turned red. "Enough! Both of ye—in the library." He didn't wait to see if they followed as he stormed out of the great hall.

Sabine leveled Lachlan with a frown.

Isobel came up beside her. "Please, Sabine. Dinna anger yer father. We can resolve this peacefully." Together they followed Lachlan out of the room.

As Lachlan entered the library, Sabine held back. "Mother, please dinna let this happen." There was a shrill rise in her voice.

Isobel cupped Sabine's face. "Destiny will reveal yer course. Come, let us face this together."

Her mother's words didn't comfort Sabine. As they entered the library, shutting the door behind them, Edmond poured *uisge beatha*, a distilled brew called the water of life, into two glasses.

Lachlan's intense stare met hers, sending flames licking across her body.

Breathe.

She gathered her resolve. "Father—"

Edmond held up his hand. His stern expression pinned Lachlan as he handed him the glass of scotch. "It is true?"

"Aye. Have ye a priest? We leave on the morrow," Lachlan stated.

Sabine's heart stuttered. "Mother!"

Isobel stepped forward. "Edmond, must we act so promptly?"

Edmond hesitated. "Lachlan, since we have no proof of a match I must side with Sabine."

"Proof?" Lachlan's voice rose sharply, which didn't bode well for Sabine. "Yer daughter bears my mark. Her right shoulder."

Sabine whipped her hand over the evidence that would seal her fate.

Shock flickered across Isobel's face. "Sabine?"

Without a word, Edmond brushed Sabine's hand away, pulling the sleeve of her kirtle so it slipped from her shoulder. He released a heavy sigh. "Wake the priest."

"Da. Listen tae me. A mistake it was. Please." Sabine's pleas went unheeded.

"Prepare yerself, Sabine. Ye wed within the hour," Edmond announced.

Sabine was not one to cry, but tears seeped from the corners of her eyes. With a sharp pivot, she ran toward the door, jerked it open and fled.

Isobel watched as an array of emotions filtered across Lachlan's face. Sabine had wounded his pride, not a good way to begin a relationship. He bowed to both her and Edmond and quickly left the room, no doubt in pursuit of his mate. When Edmond had marked Isobel, he hadn't let her out of his sight for nearly two days. She smiled at the tender memory.

"Isobel. He has nary an idea what Sabine is. D'ye think he stands a chance?"

"Sabine is powerful," Isobel said. "Perhaps I could bind her magic toward Lachlan. Her destiny would be revealed and…"

Edmond's brows pulled together. "Yer hesitance warms my heart, naught."

"…and maybe she wouldnae kill him before they are wed," Isobel replied sheepishly.

"Then let me suggest ye cast yer spell right away. Lachlan appears tae be a man who gets what he wants. And, my love, he wants our Sabine."

Chapter Three

Sabine's magic had gone amok.

Twice she attempted to transform Lachlan into a frog as he chased her out of the keep's front entrance. Each time her spells fizzled and rebounded to change her voice into hoarse croaks. She had to get away from him, had to feel the forest beneath her feet.

Only by a stroke of luck did she escape the beast trailing her when he stopped to speak with a man who looked at her appraisingly.

"This canna be happenin'." She trudged through the dimly lit forest using Beserka sight to lead her way. The night wind whispered through the trees, tugging at her kirtle. She glanced at the cloudy sky looking for the answer.

Sabine felt like a forsaken child, instead of the woman she was. And where was her aplomb? The man confused her on so many levels. Her body screamed to be near him. Yet she feared leaving the safety of her family.

Frantically, she tore her chemise and kirtle over her head and tossed them aside. The beast within her rose to the surface, sending a tingling sensation across her skin as her body began to shimmer. Heat waves rose as every muscle clenched and shifted, rolling across her body until a leopard, black as the night, stood in her once human footsteps.

She raised her head to the heavens, releasing a sorrowful mewl. Then she began to run, fast and furious, away from the castle—away from her destiny.

Light raindrops fell as she bounded over fallen logs and large boulders in her way. She ran fast and far, until her lungs burned, felt as if they would explode. Then she slowed. Panting, she gulped breaths of air to quell the ache in her chest. When the beat of her heart was almost normal, she stretched, and laid her lithe form upon the ground. Soft, non-aggressive puffing sounds came from her nostrils as she called her friends to her side.

From a copse of trees emerged a reddish-brown fox. He sniffed the air. Reynard had been one of the first animals she befriended as a child. Beneath a bramble a rabbit appeared. Kasha's long ears twitched as she hopped closer.

From high in the treetops, a gray squirrel jumped from one branch to another, until he perched on the limb above where Sabine lay. She mewed, urging the skittish animal from its sanctuary. Rubus's encounters with humans and animals alike had left him untrusting, but not so with Sabine. As he crawled closer, Sabine began to purr. Among her friends, she was content.

For a moment in time, all was well. At the rustling of a bush, her friends each startled and began fleeing in opposite directions. Sabine jumped to her feet, crouching low to discover the largest wolf she had ever seen staring at her. He held her chemise, kirtle and a pair of breeches in his jaws.

Devil take the man.

Slowly the change rippled across his body. What was once golden fur was now tanned flesh stretched taut over firm muscle. He was magnificent from his clear-blue eyes, broad shoulders, taut abdomen, to—

Saints perserve! The man was endowed.

"'Tis time, Sabine." He held his hand to her.

She crouched lower. Her tail jerked with agitation, then it beat the ground as her top lip rose in a snarl.

He answered her defiance with a low, ominous sound that rumbled up from his chest. As he began to slip his leggings on, he said, "Change now or I will haul that bonnie arse of yers over my shoulder."

How dare he speak to her in such a way? She barely held her temper as she released her beast's hold, allowing the change to whisper across her body.

She refused to allow Lachlan to dominate her. With a proud stance, she raised her chin. That was until his cock jerked alive, lengthening. She gasped, hastily making tracks to gather her chemise and kirtle and quickly dressed.

"I dinna wish tae wed," her voice trembled.

A shadow raced across his face as he fastened his breeches. Had her words hurt him? She thought differently when his features hardened. "'Tis done. Come." He pushed by her, and then headed for the castle.

Anger surfaced hot and fast. Impulsively, she shoved her hands in front of her. "Rat!"

Nothing happened as she watched his muscled back draw further away from her. Once again, her magic failed. Instead, her nose began to twitch. When whiskers began to appear on her face, she released a high-pitched cry.

Tears fell from Sabine's eyes as her father held her. "Dinna cry, sweetlin'. Ye'll be but a day's ride. We will visit often."

Her sorrow tightened Conall's chest.

Was joining with him that repulsive?

"Da, please." She sniffled and her long whiskers twitched. Conall would have laughed if the situation hadn't been so serious.

The rumors were true. Sabine was a Beserka, as well as witch. Not a very talented witch, if he judged her magic by the bristly vibrissae growing on each side of her upper lip.

A touch of apprehension moved beneath his skin. Would his clan be as accepting as those individuals seated around him?

Edmond firmly set Sabine from him, placing her hand within Conall's. "Let it begin."

Not exactly how Conall pictured his wedding day. The bride's parents, and Sabine's twin brothers who glowered at him, looked bereaved. His friends, Ewen, Cameron and Fitzer stood beside him, but even their expressions lacked the support he sought.

And his bride?

Her tears had dried, but she stood like a statue. The priest began to recite from the bible, never pausing as he lunged right into the wedding ceremony.

"Sabine, do ye take this man tae be yer wedded husband?"

Silence.

The priest cleared his throat and repeated the line.

Mackenzie McKade

A deep warning growl from Edmond made Sabine startle beneath Conall's hand.

"Aye," she whispered so softly it was nearly inaudible. Her whiskers grew faint, dissolving.

Within several minutes the deed was done.

Conall was married.

216

Chapter Four

Conall glanced at his new bride. Backbone rigid, Sabine sat astride a horse for the journey, choosing to refuse the carriage her father offered. Blindly, she stared ahead. Still, she appeared regal wrapped in her red velvet cape and hood.

Beautiful and defiant.

Since departing Loch Tower earlier that morning, not a word passed between them. Dark circles shadowed her eyes. She slept not a wink. He knew because she insisted on sleeping in a chair next to the hearth, instead of beside him in the bed.

He hadn't touched her last night, though he had wanted to. Even now, his cock hardened with the need to feel her warmth surround him. Images of their coupling were never far from his mind.

The afternoon was cool and crisp. The trees exploded with color—brown, gold, yellow and russet red. He had missed the changing of seasons in Scotland. High above a golden eagle soared. From the tree line just beyond the road they traveled, a majestic red stag watched them. Oddly, so did the fox, rabbit and squirrel he had seen cuddled next to Sabine in leopard form last evening.

He pulled back on his horse's reins. "We'll rest here." He dismounted, and then moved to assist Sabine. She felt small as he lifted her from her mount. He should have avoided touching her. His body throbbed with need. A need only she could fulfill. "Come, walk with me."

She followed, but remained silent.

A distance away from his men, he halted. "I displease ye?" Graced with no response, he continued. "Fate can be cruel, Sabine. What is done canna be changed." He placed a finger beneath her chin and drew her troubled gaze to his.

So beautiful.

Desire hit hard, blood rushing to his groin. No way would he be able to sleep beside her this evening and not mate her. "Dinna think tae deny me my rights." In a show of his authority, he pulled her into his arms and firmly pressed his lips to hers.

Her mouth remained pinched until he bit her bottom lip. She yelped. He took advantage to deepen the kiss, thrusting his tongue inside to taste her.

Sweet. Innocent. Fiery.

"All mine," he growled, before devouring her lips again. When he cupped her breast, she whimpered softly. It was hell holding her, tasting her, and not being able to part her thighs and bury himself deep within. "This eve, wife." He left her with the promise, before releasing her and walking back to his men.

Sabine couldn't breathe. Her aplomb melted the minute he kissed her. Her body thrummed, begging for his caress—his hot, wet mouth working its magic.

She couldn't deny Lachlan, even if she wanted to. The heat between them was wild—animal instinct. Even now, her nipples were taut, her inner thighs wet with desire. Last night had been a test of her will. She had won, but paid the price. Her body ached and he was seldom far from her mind.

As Lachlan stood beside her horse, she hastened her steps. His strong hands around her waist as he hauled her up onto her mount made her think of Samhain and their night together.

It was a woman's lot in life to leave the shelter of her family, wed and bear children. The Goddess, as well as Sabine's father, had spoken. Whether Sabine agreed or not was moot. It was time she accepted her fate.

Astride her horse, she gazed down at Lachlan. "I am not displeased, Lachlan."

Surprise filtered across his handsome face. "Conall," he said.

She kicked her horse and the beast lurched forward.

Hours passed and soon Lachlan Tower came into view. Surrounded by a moat, the tall grey castle stood ominously before Sabine.

Lachlan's expression was noncommittal as they drew nearer. The grinding of wood against wood sounded as a drawbridge lowered. Horse hooves clicked across the planks covering the moat. They passed beneath the wall of the bailey and gatehouse to enter a weathered courtyard in need of attention.

A hearty cheer rose. Hands waved, people crowded to get a glimpse of the new chieftain. Lachlan sat erect in his saddle, an aristocratic image, handsome and regal. If he were apprehensive, one would not know.

Then all eyes turned to her.

The breath she inhaled froze in her throat. Smiles turned to frowns. Whispers followed. Tension felt alive and thick in the air. She pulled another breath that didn't fill her lungs.

"Abomination," she heard murmured.

Conall drew his horse to an abrupt halt and pinned the man who spoke with a menacing glare. "Insult my wife, ye insult me." His palm lay upon his sword.

The man bowed, color draining from his face. "My apologies."

Sadly, her notoriety had reached the castle before she had. Her Beserka blood offended them, unlike her own clan who loved her.

A large redheaded man stood in the middle of the courtyard, a half-smile upon his hairy face. When Conall dismounted, the man stepped forward and he embraced him. "Cousin."

"Eacharn. Yer lookin' well." Conall released him and moved quickly to Sabine's horse. "Give 'em time, Lachlan's be a suspicious lot," he whispered to her, before turning back to Eacharn. "My wife, Sabine, of the Macleod clan."

Eacharn's smile vanished. "We must speak." He willfully ignored Sabine.

She stiffened midway in her curtsy. Her gaze darted from Eacharn to Conall. Heat crawled up her neck, sweeping across her cheeks. Slowly, she rose.

Eacharn leaned into Conall, but spoke loud enough so Sabine heard. "The clan's troubled with yer weddin' a woman cursed by the beast."

Beads of perspiration dotted Sabine's forehead. Her pulse sped in anticipation of her husband's response.

"Careful, Cousin. We share that so called curse with many of our clansmen." Conall's ominous warning hung in the air. With a brush of his hand, he pushed back her hood. Long ebony hair fell down her back. He slipped his arm around her shoulders and gave her a little squeeze. "If anythin', she is a gift tae our clan." His smile was heartwarming. "Now let us not hear any more on this matter. We are tired. Hungry."

Eacharn nodded. "The evenin' meal is bein' prepared. I am sure yer new bride is eager tae assume her duties." There was a snarl in his voice as he led the way into the castle.

A short, stodgy woman greeted them at the door. Conall took her into his arms and swung her around in a big bear hug. "Cait."

With a pinched expression, she snapped, "'Tis about time ye showed yer ugly mug." Then she grinned, standing on tiptoes to ruffle his hair.

Affection sparkled in his eyes for the woman. "Come. I want ye tae meet my wife."

Hands on hips, Cait wagged her head. "Wife? And who'd be crazy enough tae marry ye?"

Sabine liked her.

The woman's sharp gaze assessed Sabine quickly, before she curtsied. "Milady."

Sabine returned the curtsy. "Sabine, please."

"Cait." Eacharn's rough voice boomed. "Show the woman her duties."

Conall's face flushed with anger. "Eacharn—" His deep voice halted, as Sabine placed her hand on his arm.

"Aye. I would like tae see the keep," Sabine said to stop a confrontation between the men. She could feel Lachlan's beast rising, held lightly beneath a guise of calm.

"Best hurry. The light of day will be gone in a whisper," Cait warned.

As Conall disappeared into a room with Eacharn, Cait led Sabine downstairs to the cellar. Torches hung from the walls lighting their way.

"Milady, the castle stands five levels high. The cellar houses the dungeon tae the right. Tae the left be storage." She pushed the door open, then placed the key ring into Sabine's hands. "Keys tae the spice chest and every lock in the keep." Bare shelves spoke loudly of the impoverished condition of the castle.

From behind a tall crate, Sabine saw a set of tiny toes. They wiggled. When Cait's back was turned a wee lass peeked around the corner. A lighthearted giggle followed.

"Iris?" Cait planted her hands on her hips. "Lassie, ye hidin' down here again?"

A child around the age of seven eased into view. "Aye." Blonde curls bobbed as she nodded. Her gown was dirty and hung off one shoulder.

A grin teased Cait's mouth. "Who be huntin' ye now?"

A frown deepened the lines on the child's forehead. "Dugan."

"What did ye do?"

Blue eyes as large as platters gazed innocently at the older woman. "Nothin'."

"I...ris?"

A big smile brightened Iris's face. "Hid his sword."

Cait shook her head despairingly.

"I only wanted tae play with it."

"Get up those stairs." Cait swatted the child on the arse. "And leave that lad be." Her light laughter followed Iris up the stairs.

"She's adorable," Sabine said.

"Aye. But the child is everywhere and nowhere at the same time. Nothin' goes unnoticed."

As they climbed the stairs, Cait wheezed, a scratchy sound. "The ground level contains the kitchen and entrance hall. Third floor the Great Hall. The fourth contains the private apartments." She stopped and took a deep breath. "Servants' siege quarters are on the next level. Above 'em is the gallery and a large spiral-stair tower. Ye be wantin' tae visit the gallery?"

Cait was in no condition to be traipsing up and down stairs. "Nay," Sabine answered.

Lachlan was a large castle in much need of attention.

Sabine had her work cut out for her.

Chapter Five

Conall sat at the seat of honor, his father's chair, as his clan filled the great hall. To his left sat Eacharn. The right saved for his bride, whom he hadn't seen since they arrived. He held tightly to the beast stirring beneath his skin, needing to find its mate.

He scented Sabine before he saw her. Honey and cloves. She entered, a vision of loveliness in lilac. All around him smiling faces turned cold. A chill iced the room.

In a show of bravado, she raised her chin. As elegant as a queen, skirts brushing the floor, she moved to his side. The only sign of nervousness was the rapid rise and fall of her breasts accentuated by a deep purple bodice hugging her mid-section. Breasts he needed to feel and taste the second the meal was completed.

The thought hardened his cock against the ties of his black breeches. He stood to greet her, extending his hand. She trembled as he folded his fingers around hers, guiding her to the chair to the right of him. Her hand still in his, he brought it to his lips. "Bonnie lass."

In an attempt to draw his clan's attention away from Sabine and onto filling their bellies, he said, "Shall we eat?"

For a moment, everything returned to normalcy, and then several people begin to sputter. More joined, even Eacharn.

He coughed, before jumping to his feet. "Salt. Someone has added salt tae the wine."

"The witch," a woman cried from the crowd.

Surprise, then anger brightened Sabine's eyes. Her fingers curled into fists. She shifted in her chair. He scented her beast rising. Any show of magic or worse—shape-shifting—might incite the clan.

"Sabine," Conall warned softly. He placed a hand on her shoulder, rising to his feet. She tensed beneath his palm as he shouted to those gathered around the table, "Silence."

As the crowd calmed, he stared from one and then the other. "Who possesses keys tae the spice trunk?"

"I do." The head cook buried her meaty palms against her hips, as if to dare him to accuse her. "As well as Cait."

Cait's gaze darted to Sabine and back to Conall.

"Cait?" he asked cautiously.

She cleared her throat. "Milady, has mine. I gave 'em tae her upon arrival."

The crowd grew loud again.

A flush of heat raced up his neck as he turned to his wife. "Sabine?"

"Me?" As she jumped to her feet, her chair skidded across the stone floor making a screeching sound. Disbelief widened her eyes. "Ye think I did this?" The last came out a growl as her fangs dropped.

The crowd gasped as one.

"Hold, Sabine," he said firmly. He took a moment to silence the chaos roaring inside him and forced a smile. "Nothin' but a child's prank. Cait, see tae it everyone's glass is refilled." He pulled Sabine's chair close. "Sit."

Damnation. This was indeed a quandary.

She trembled, blues eyes nearly black with anger. "Nay."

"Sit," he ordered beneath his breath.

Slowly she complied, but the grim look on her face showed her displeasure. "I wish tae retire."

He placed his refreshed glass to his lips to hide his words. "Afterward ye may do as ye please. For now, eat. We shall talk of this later."

For over an hour, Sabine bore the suspicious and condemning glances of those present. Every morsel placed into her mouth was tasteless and odorless, colored by the anger and hurt burning inside her. The clans' treatment of her was beyond disrespectful. Even the few glances her husband gave her felt condemnatory.

When Lachlan finally rose from the table, she breathed her first sigh of relief. As he spoke to a tall, brown-haired man, she took the opportunity to escape, fleeing out the front entrance.

Torches burned brightly around the inner walls. As a guard approached, she slipped behind a pillar, hiding. Without a second thought, she removed her slippers, gown and chemise, allowing the change to roll over her, shimmering through her with life. A domestic cat was her guise for the night. In a flash, she raced through the courtyard and straight out the front gates.

The night air was crisp. She ran as fast and as far as her small legs could carry her. Her muscles stretched against the tightly wound tension. When the forest closed around her, she stopped. Nails extended, she took her frustration out on an old oak tree, scratching the bark until long deep grooves appeared.

The devil take them all.

"M'lady." Sabine's back hunched as she hopped sideways. Big-eyed, Iris stood motionless. Her small hands clasped in front of her. "Dinna be afraid." She ventured a step and then another, until she was positioned before Sabine. Squatting, she ran her fingers down Sabine's back. "Soft."

Her girlish giggle made Sabine relax for the first time since arriving at Lachlan. The child's touch of kindness was like a raft saving Sabine from drowning in self-pity. As Iris rose, Sabine wove in and out of the girl's legs, rubbing against them gently.

Iris scratched Sabine behind the ears. "Yer innocent. This I know." Then she froze.

Lachlan stepped from the shadows. Sabine's lilac gown and chemise were in his hand.

"What have ye, Iris?" The rumble of his deep voice sent shivers up Sabine's spine.

Devil's breath. How did the man find her?

Iris dipped into a curtsy. "It be a cat, m'lord." She scooped Sabine into her arms. "My cat."

Strangely, Sabine felt safe in the child's arms, safer than in the arms of the man who strolled forward. When he reached out to pet her, Sabine hissed and swatted his hand.

Before her claws met skin, he jerked back. "More like a wildcat." He frowned.

Iris hugged Sabine closely. "Nay, m'lord. Tame as a kit'en if ye treat her well."

From the mouth of babes. The child was wise beyond her age, thought Sabine.

He bent to the child's level and smiled. Something in Sabine's heart melted. He had a beautiful smile. "What say ye we take ourselves and yer feisty feline back tae the keep?"

Iris hugged Sabine closer. "If ye wish, sire."

"That I do. Now up with ye." With gown and chemise in hand, he hoisted the girl into his arms. "Hold tight tae that beastie. We dinna want her tae get away."

His furry wife looked content in Iris's arms as they traipsed through the woodland. Had she been attempting an escape or had she simply needed to release the animal within? Either way, he couldn't allow her to spook the clan.

"M'lord." Iris had been quiet since they passed the gates and entered the courtyard. "M'lady is nary tae blame fer the salted wine."

He carefully let Iris's feet touch the ground. "And how would ye be knowin' this?"

She rubbed her cheek against Sabine's fur. "Please dinna tell Cait."

"I make no promises, lassie." He opened the heavy wooden doors of the keep to let Iris enter. "Tell me what ye know."

"After m'lady and Cait left the cellar I hid there. Nary a soul returned."

Sabine meowed and pinned him with a pointed stare, before she jumped from Iris's arms. With a haughty stride, she strolled toward the stairs, stopping to glance back and twitch her tail at him, before bounding up the steps.

A chuckle rose in his throat. *Saucy wench.* "Good-night, Iris." He headed for the stairs, looking forward to what the night promised.

Iris curtsied. "M'lord, ye will not hurt her?"

Shock drew him to a halt. He faced Iris. "Nay, lassie. Why would ye ask?" His gaze met innocent eyes.

"She's scared and lonely, sire. A friend she'd be needin'."

Leave it to a child to see what others refused.

Blinded by his own insecurities returning home, he hadn't realized how this change would affect Sabine. "Aye." He nodded, then continued up the stairs. As he pushed open the chamber door, he saw the change roll over Sabine. Where only moments ago a black cat stood, his beautiful bride appeared.

Naked.

His pulse sped. His cock hardened.

He expected her to lunge for the blanket on the bed. Instead, she rose boldly. Her shoulders back. Her chin held at an obstinate angle.

It was a pretense. As he grew closer her breathing elevated, chest rising and falling rapidly.

He leaned past her to pinch off the flame next to the bed, throwing them into darkness, except for the sliver of moonlight peeking through the window and the faint glow from the fireplace.

Sabine didn't need the light to see his face or the lust raging in his eyes. The scent of ocean and spices surrounded her as his arms did the same. "Yer people hate me."

Soft lips brushed hers. "Give 'em time." He kissed a path to her ear and lightly blew.

"They branded me a witch and accused me of workin' spells tae harm their kin."

His voice hummed, "Let me speak the obvious, lassie. Yer a witch." He nipped her earlobe. "'Tis the Beserka blood that frightens 'em."

She angled her head wanting him to bite her again. "Why? The clan accepts ye and the others."

"Ye be a woman."

"Surely—"

Irritation surfaced in the puff of air he released. "Lassie, must we talk of this now? My thoughts are more tae the likin' of havin' my way with ye."

Sharp prickles raced across her flesh. Memories of their night in the glen filled her head. As much as she wanted to deny it, she wanted the same. Destined to be tied to Lachlan, why not make the best of it?

Already her breasts felt heavy, nipples tingling with the thought of his hands playing at their tips. Desire moistened her inner thighs.

When his fingers parted her folds, she was wet and slick.

"Lassie, ye be a mon's dream come true." He whisked her into his arms, crossing the room to lay her upon the pillowy bed.

Without hesitating, he began to undress. The sounds of leather sliding against leather only heightened Sabine's arousal. She loved the scent of rawhide. Shadows rose and fell across his face.

Anticipation was killing her.

The bed creaked beneath his weight. Lissome and sinewy, he crawled toward her, sensual movements of a predator that called to her beast.

She mewled.

He answered with a deep growl. "I need tae taste ye."

Sabine parted her mouth upon a sigh, ready for his kiss.

When he spread her legs and dipped his head, a squeal squeezed from her lips.

"Relax, lassie." His warm breath brushed across her moist flesh. "This ye be enjoyin', I promise."

"Nay—"

As his wet tongue slid across her slit, her hips flew off the bed in surprise. The strange sensation was wicked—sinful—and she wanted more.

"Nay?" Eyes filled with laughter gazed up the length of her body. He licked another path that sent shivers down her spine. "Is it nay or aye, lassie?"

"Aye," she released on a breath.

His chuckle filled with male pride.

With a flick of his tongue, he teased the swollen bud, making her stomach flip-flop and tense. Golden hair tickled the inside of her thighs. He pressed deeper, licking and sucking, devouring her. The animalistic sounds he made hummed through her body. Heat simmered across her flesh, her beast waking—needing to mate with his. She felt like at any moment the animal inside her would be unleashed.

"Conall. Please..." Tied into knots, her insides threatened to come undone.

"Lassie, ye taste so good." His tongue continued to work in and out of her channel.

When he latched on to her swollen bud, her climax burst. Her womb clenched and released, repeatedly. With a cry, her beast roared to life, the sensation of human and animal coming together was beyond anything she could imagine. It was magical, sending shards of bright lights through her body.

In the heights of her orgasm, he moved atop Sabine. His thick, hard cock stretched and penetrated her quim. Fast and hard, he slid in and out.

Breathing labored, he thrust once more before his head lolled backward, lips parting as he released a deep, low groan. His face was tight with what appeared more pain than pleasure. Then he collapsed atop her. Two-hundred pounds of sinewy muscle pressed her deep into the bedding, constricting her breathing, but she wasn't complaining.

Seconds passed. When he moved, he crawled from the bed and padded barefooted across the room to open a chest against the wall. Then he returned.

"Give me yer hand." He accepted her outstretched hand and slipped a large ruby ring onto her finger. "My mother's ring. I'd be honored if ye would wear it."

Sabine couldn't help being moved by the gesture. The ring fit perfectly, as if meant to be.

A semblance of pride softened his face as he stared at the precious stone glistening on her finger. He leaned over and gently kissed Sabine. The moment was tender and sweet as he moved to sit beside her. Then he took her into his arms.

"Lachlan," she moaned.

"Conall."

"Conall, we must talk—"

He stole her words away with another kiss. When their lips parted, he said, "Give 'em time. It will get better."

"What about—"

"No more talkin', woman. I need ye again."

Chapter Six

A fortnight passed and things at Lachlan Tower became worse—not better.

The afternoon sun was warm against Conall's back as he held the wooden post Ewen hammered into the ground. Each strike sent vibrations through Conall's palms. An animal had attacked several of their cattle. The pen they built would house those still alive but injured until well enough to join the others.

Post securely buried, he picked up another and moved down a ways.

Sabine's presence had borne the blame of the cattle incident, as well as several clanfolk who had fallen ill of late. Many of his people were calling for her return to Loch Tower.

Conall couldn't allow that. With each day, he grew closer and closer to her. She calmed his beast, gave him the strength to face the work required at Lachlan. But was he asking too much of her?

Her sadness was becoming more difficult to hide.

Conall's beast awoke, scenting Sabine near. Alone, she entered the woods carrying a basket. Earlier she had informed him that she and Iris were hunting truffles—mushrooms—for the evening's meal. He was wondering where Iris was when his thoughts were interrupted.

"Bonnie lass." Ewen struck the pole hard with a mallet.

"That she is." Pride filled Conall's chest.

Though the days hadn't been easy for Sabine, she always came to his bed eager and willing. Yet, he knew that in the wee hours of the morning she rose to sit by the window, blindly staring into the dark. Several nights, he heard her crying and rose to comfort her.

She had a good heart. Iris and Cait had discovered it. Now only if the clan could see what he saw in her. She wanted to please them—she wanted to please him.

Ewen took another whack at the pole, driving it deeper. "It dinna bode well the clan's treatment."

Ewen was right.

"I canna force their acceptance. Already I've threatened half the clan." Conall braced himself for another strike against the pole he held.

Like a boil festering, either the clan or Sabine would come to a head. Someone would break.

God help them if it was Sabine.

At times, he felt strong energy surrounding her beast. She had restrained the animal, as well as her magic, at his request. Like all Beserkas, emotions triggered her totem. He prayed the clan would accept her before she released the fury of her true form—or worse, he released his own.

"'Tis rumblings about." Ewen glanced at Conall.

Tension tightened the muscles in his shoulders. "What now—"

Sabine's scream halted his words.

Sabine's heart stuttered. Torn and bloody, Iris's battered body lay upon the ground. Like with the cattle, the scent of an animal was present. Yet something masked its identity.

Anger and fear collided, tearing the beast from Sabine. Where the change had always been a welcoming peace, this time it was compelling and violent, shifting and twisting her muscles and limbs until an angry black panther stood in her place. Her ruined gown lay at her feet.

The roar that tore from Sabine's throat was raw with emotion. Standing over Iris, she heard the weak flutter of the child's heart.

Desperation pulled at Sabine's soul. Her magic rose like an eminent wave to blanket Iris with every healing property she possessed. As the invisible force surrounded the child, Sabine inched closer to lie vigilantly beside Iris.

Eacharn must have heard her cry as he broke through the copse of trees to her right.

From a distance away he stopped. "Ye killed the child," he accused.

Sabine didn't have time to protest as he began to shape-shift into his family totem of a wolf. The red and gold plaid he wore draped across his shoulders fell to the ground. Fingertips turned into sharp claws as he yanked at his shirt, only managing to rip and tear it from his body. His breeches were shredded by the time he stepped out of his boots.

Rich red fur sprang from his pores and began to cover his body as the change was completed. Growling, he hunched low and began to approach, every muscle and tendon tight as he prepared to attack.

Sabine released a mournful cry of protest. It didn't stop Eacharn as he continued to stalk her.

Sabine lunged to all four feet. Ears lying flat against her head, with a watchful eye she waited.

Iris couldn't be disturbed. Nor Sabine's magic as it continued to heal the wounded and bleeding areas within the child.

Eacharn perched low.

Sabine sensed his impending attack, when she heard the pounding of feet and raised voices. Teeth bared, she snarled to warn Eacharn back. Then she glanced quickly at the oncoming crowd.

Conall, Ewen and several of the clansfolk arrived.

Gasps of disbelief followed by accusations. "The witch killed Iris."

They thought she did this dastardly deed.

"Sabine!" Conall's voice snapped out at her like a whip. "Back away from the child." Wariness in his eyes disappeared. Instead, the beast shimmered in their depths. "Now," he demanded firmly.

Her magic was stronger in cat form. Iris needed her.

Sabine released another mournful mewl. Somehow, she had to get him to realize her innocence and that Iris should remain untouched.

As he approached, she whimpered, before releasing soft non-aggressive puffing sounds from her nostrils. She drew protectively to Iris's limp body.

Sabine's gaze was cautious, alert, as she leaned forward and began to lick Iris's wounds. Among the metallic taste of the child's blood a bitter flavor rose, sending a tremor through Sabine—animal saliva—but not.

Beserka

A woman cried out in horror at the ministrations Sabine performed.

An impatient growl rumbled from Eacharn. In wolf form he crouched low, ready and poised to spring.

Conall's outstretched palm halted his cousin's attack.

Sabine breathed a sigh of relief. She didn't want to kill Eacharn to save Iris's life, but she would.

"She's protectin' Iris. Not harmin' the child," Conall said, as he ventured forward.

Ewen stepped to his side. "Truth or what ye wish it tae be, my friend?"

"Truth. 'Tis the puffing sounds. She uses it tae call her friends tae her side." Conall knelt down beside Sabine. She purred softly as she continued to lick Iris.

"The child needs attention," Ewen insisted.

"Nay. Look. Her wounds are healin'." Conall's eyes widened with wonder.

Blood stopped flowing from the angry tears in Iris's skin and began to pull together and close. Sabine could feel the child's internal wounds mending. Part of the healing process was sedative in nature, rendering Iris unconscious while the worst of the injuries remained.

"'Tis wrong," someone yelled.

Conall picked up the remnants of her gown. "Sabine." She'd done all she could do for the child so she let the transformation slip over her. Quickly he wrapped the gown around her.

Her appearance set the gathering clan into hurling insults and names at her.

"Witch."

"Abomination."

With a growl of contention, Conall silenced them. "Hear me. The next person tae curse my wife will die at my hands. There is no proof Sabine hurt Iris, only evidence that she sought tae help the child."

Eacharn snarled as the change from wolf to human rippled over him. Bare-assed, he reached for his red and gold plaid and wrapped it around his waist. He glowered at Sabine, his glare filled with contempt.

Conall didn't care for the wild look in the peoples' eyes as the crowd began to close around them. They wanted blood. Sabine's blood.

"Cousin, ye know what must be done," Eacharn whispered in his ear. "If ye canna prove her innocence, she must die for her sins."

Conall couldn't believe what he was hearing. They wanted Sabine's, his wife and soulmate's, death?

His beast partially slipped. Fangs pushed through gum and bone, a soft down of golden fur sprung from his pours as he retained his human form.

Surprise filtered over the crowd and they stumbled backward.

"Dinna anger me," he roared, giving no purchase.

Hugging her tattered dress closely, Sabine said, "This is not of my doin'. I would never hurt Iris." Sorrow rimmed her reddened eyes.

"Can Iris be moved?" he asked.

"Yes, but gently. There's much damage." Sabine placed her hand on Conall's arm. "An animal dinna do this."

He frowned, as he gathered Iris into his arms. She felt so fragile, the stench of blood strong. "What are ye sayin'?"

"Beserka," she murmured for only him to hear.

The lines in his forehead deepened. "Nay. I would know."

He felt the tremor in her hand as she added, "He hides his scent."

"Impossible." Conall would be able to scent his own kind. If not, who would have the ability to mask their scent?

Cautiously, but in haste, he made his way back to the castle. Sabine and the entire clan followed.

As he bedded the child down in a spare bedchamber, Sabine moved quickly to stand vigil. "I'll stay with her."

Eacharn motioned Conall across the room. "Ye canna allow this, mon. Yer woman will kill the child before she is allowed tae speak the truth."

"Be careful, Cousin. My patience is growing thin," Conall warned as turmoil churned inside.

"Aye, as it be for all." Eacharn didn't back down. "Ye must see the truth for the child's sake."

If Eacharn was right then Sabine couldn't allow the child to wake.

"Ye must treat yer wife as ye would any others accused of this crime." Eacharn paused. "The dungeon, until her innocence is revealed or yer ready to mete her punishment."

A thousand stones weighed Conall's chest.

The dungeon?

Ice slid through his veins. He couldn't do such a thing to Sabine.

"Conall." Her voice was tight as she approached him. "Do what ye must, but dinna leave Iris attended by one of our kind." Her sullen gaze shot to Eacharn.

Insulted, Eacharn raised his hand.

Sabine flinched.

Conall caught his cousin's wrist midair. "Dinna force me tae kill ye." He let the menacing tone in his voice remove all doubt—he meant it.

Then he faced Sabine. "I canna lock ye in the dungeon."

She gently cupped his face. "Ye have no choice."

Chapter Seven

Cold and damp. The dungeon held no comfort for Sabine. Nor did the dour expression on Conall's face. It was as bleak as the gray walls surrounding her.

With a satisfied smirk, Eacharn stood in the distance, overseeing her imprisonment.

"Sabine," Conall whispered next to her ear. "If I canna prove yer innocence tae the clan, I will return at nightfall and take ye tae Loch Tower."

"Conall—"

"I canna let ye die. Nor will I give ye up."

A shudder raced up her back as she pulled her torn gown closer around her body. She didn't know if it was from the caring she heard in Conall's voice or the calls for her death that rang from the courtyard.

This canna be happenin'.

He held her tight, as if he would never let her go, but he did. "I will return." He kissed her soundly on the lips, and then turned and walked through the open door that clanged behind him. The screech of the lock moving into place made her eyes mist. Conall faced her again, then without a word left, taking Eacharn with him.

Standing in the middle of the cell, she looked about. The dirty pallet in the corner spoke of longevity and she didn't plan on being around to use it. Nor would she allow Conall to choose between her or his clan. He was chieftain. Sooner or later, the truth would be revealed. She just needed to buy some time.

A mouse skittered across her foot and she squealed, followed by an ironic chuckle.

As like is tae like.

A mouse I shall be.

Tingles of sensation spread across her skin. Her gown dropped to the floor. The shrinking transformation completed in a heartbeat. She twitched her whiskers and, as a mouse, she slipped through the steel bars easily. The door lay ajar. As she squeezed through the opening, she came to a sudden halt.

Ewen stood guard.

Cautiously, she moved past him.

"M'lady."

Sabine froze, turning her tiny head to gaze at Ewen.

An uneasy smile touched his mouth. "Lachlan will not be pleased of yer choice, but if ye must go, move with haste."

Saints preserve! The man recognized her.

Her eyes moistened. Conall had placed someone he trusted to watch over her.

If she returned home, she might never see Conall again. Then again, if she didn't leave now she might not see the light of tomorrow.

Without a second thought, she ran for the stairs. Freedom led in the direction of the front entrance, but Sabine couldn't leave, not without checking on Iris once more.

Little mouse legs left a lot to be desired. She shifted quickly into her domestic cat form and leaped up the stairs. As she approached Iris's chamber door, Eacharn spoke quietly to the guard.

With a lightning flash movement, Eacharn grabbed the man's head and twisted. Muscle and bone popped, startling Sabine as the guard tumbled lifelessly to the ground. Eacharn heaved the man over his shoulder and stepped into Iris's room.

Sabine barely slipped inside before the door closed. In a hurry, she lost her footing, scrambling to hide behind a large chest.

A dull thud sounded, as the guard's body fell from Eacharn's shoulder. Then he moved to Iris's bedside.

"Troublesome lass. Ye be a hard one tae kill." Eacharn's words lit a fire beneath Sabine. Before she realized it, her body stretched and transformed into a panther. She growled low and long.

Eacharn spun around. "Witch." An ominous smile tugged at the corner of his mouth. "'Tis my lucky day. After I dispatch ye, the lassie be next, then me dear ol' cousin."

Conall?

As Eacharn rounded the bed where the sleeping child lay, Sabine crouched low, ears plastered against her head. Her tail twitched. She'd kill this man before he touched Iris or Conall.

Slowly, his gaze slid across her panther form. "Ye be a beauty. Tae bad fates matched ye tae Conall instead of me." He took a step toward Sabine. "Yer magic would be handy. Impressed I was at what ye did for the lassie. Nosy chit threatened tae reveal me."

Sabine's stomach churned. Her tail moved faster in agitation.

A frown pinched his face. "If only Conall had remained gone. The clan is mine."

This wasn't about her lineage. It was about Eacharn's desire to be chieftain.

The change swept over Eacharn fast. One minute a man—the next a red wolf, clothes discarded at his feet.

Sabine was ready. Her body was a mass of tense muscle. Her upper lip curled in a snarl, baring her teeth.

They both lunged simultaneously.

She caught a glimpse of something tawny before it crashed hard against her side. She skidded across the floor, feet scrabbling to gain purchase. When she did, Conall in wolf form stood between her and Eacharn.

Eacharn attacked, but Conall was quick jumping out of the way.

Then Iris cried out in her sleep.

Conall's head snapped toward the sound and Eacharn lunged for his throat. Conall went down beneath the massive jaws of the red wolf.

The transformation surged through Sabine, rendering her to human form. She was unconcerned with her nakedness. Her fingers closed into a fist as she reached mentally for Eacharn's heart. He cried out in pain, releasing Conall to grasp his chest and stumble backward.

The man was strong fighting her magic. On unsteady feet, Eacharn moved toward Conall's unmoving form. The coppery scent of blood filled the air.

Sabine flung her hand through the air, lifting Eacharn with her magic and tossing him hard against the wall.

Thud! He yelped, falling to the floor.

In disbelief, he rose crawling toward Conall, determined to finish what he started.

Conall's death.

Sabine had never killed another. She didn't want Eacharn to be her first. Yet he left her no choice as he neared Conall. She wouldn't watch her husband die.

With another pass of her hand, her invisible force ripped Eacharn off his feet and slammed him against the wall once more. This time when he slithered down the side he didn't rise.

Sabine ran to Conall's side. Blood caked his throat. Quickly, she shifted into animal form, sending all her magic into Conall so he would live.

Silent tears fell from her eyes as she waited to see if her magic would again answer her prayers.

Chapter Eight

The bedchamber was dark. Conall woke to a scratchy throat, dry, in need of water. His hand skimmed the bed linens. He needed to know his wife lay beside him, but he was alone. Glimpses of memory flashed in his head. Iris wounded and bleeding. Hurt in Sabine's eyes as she looked at him through steel bars. Sabine and Eacharn poised to battle.

"*Sabine!*" He jerked to a sitting position, his head spinning. He swayed and fell back upon the pillow.

"Ye must not move in haste." Sabine's sweet voice caressed his ears. She sat in the shadows next to the softly glowing hearth. Firelight danced across her face as she rose, dressed in only her chemise.

He rolled to his side. "Why are ye not abed?"

She brushed her palm across his forehead. "I dinna want tae disturb ye."

He caught her by the wrist. Their eyes met. "It disturbs me that yer not beside me."

"How do ye feel?"

With a yank, he pulled her next to him upon the bed. "With my hands." He saw the smile that teased the corner of her mouth. He kissed the hollow of her shoulder. Then he tugged at her chemise. "Remove this."

"Nay. Ye must recover fully."

"Ye doubt my ability, woman?" he growled playfully.

Laughter like bells upon a breeze caressed his ears. "Nay. M'lord. 'Tis it wise?"

"'T'would be foolish to have me strip ye naked."

"I see yer point." She slipped from his arms and stood before him. Slowly, she raised her chemise, baring her glorious body, inch by inch.

He loved her long legs. Firm calves, knees, slender thighs and hips rounded perfectly to fit into his hands. She moved leisurely, revealing the dark, curly patch of hair, a tucked waist and breasts that made his mouth water, as she slipped the chemise off and threw it aside.

He breathed in the fragrance of honey and cloves and woman. "Beautiful." Arms wide, he welcomed her into his embrace. He rolled her upon her back, pressing his length to hers. "Lord, ye frightened me."

In the dark, their eyes met. "Me?" He saw the worry in her gaze clearly.

"Aye." He pulled a strand of her hair. "When I saw ye in Iris's bedchamber confronting Eacharn, my heart stopped." He paused. "Does he live?"

All color drained from her face. "Nay. I'm sorry—"

He placed a finger against her lips. "'Tis I who am sorry. I knew not of his treachery."

"Ye know?"

"Aye. I heard him." He leaned forward, his mouth a breath away from hers. "How's Iris?"

"Well." Her lips brushed his. Their eyes still locked.

Then he drew back sharply. Damnation take him. He'd been unconscious for some time. He had left Sabine alone to face his angry clan. "How did ye fair with the clan?"

Color dotted her cheeks. "Ewen is quite persuasive."

A whisper of jealousy touched Conall.

"He told of how it was." She continued, "And he said he'd kill the person who lay hands on me."

Conall burst into laughter. "I owe him much. I owe ye more."

Her brows burrowed with confusion.

"Ye accepted what fate decreed and remained faithful tae me through hardship."

She cupped his face. "Fate may have brought us together, but 'tis my heart that keeps me here." Her eyes grew misty.

Did she speak of love?

Something in Conall's chest tightened. "I care deeply for ye, lassie."

Before she could speak, he captured her mouth with his.

The kiss was tender, a soft endowment of oneself to another. She swallowed the knot of emotion in her throat, returning his sentiment as she angled her head to deepen the caress.

Callused fingers smoothed across her back, until he held her tightly. His knee wedged between her thighs, parting her legs as he moved between them.

His cock was hard against her moist folds. In gentle strokes, he rocked against her cradle.

Anticipation drew her nipples to hard peaks, sending stinging rays of sensation throughout her breasts to tighten low in her belly. She needed him buried deep within. Still it was almost serene the way he held her, not asking for anything but a moment of closeness.

The night existed for the two of them alone.

His sigh was one of contentment, as he released her to kneel between her thighs. Then he looped his arms beneath her knees, spreading her wide, before his firm erection pressed against her slit. Slowly, he thrust his hips, stretching and filling her, drawing out the sensation until she felt like she would scream.

"Conall." She breathed his name. Desire coiled into a tight ache begging for release.

His eyes were pools of blue intensely watching as their bodies came together. His nostrils flared, and she knew he scented her arousal, because he growled. Golden braids framed his sexy face. Muscles in his arms tightened and clenched beneath skin kissed by the sun, as his fingers dug into her hips.

He was beautiful.

When he reached to fondle the swollen bud between her legs, she nearly lost control. Her back arched as she held her breath, to prolong and heighten their coupling. Her body drew taut around him.

"Ah, lassie." He rubbed the sensitive organ harder, faster. "Release for me. Let me hear ye scream."

Sabine couldn't hold back the cry of ecstasy if she had wanted to. Her body felt like a glass suddenly dropped to shatter into millions of pieces. Sharp,

241

penetrating sensations pushed, pulled and scattered to all parts of her body, awakening her beast with a roar.

She felt her fangs burst from her gums. The animal in her moved beneath her skin seeking Conall's. When they met, Conall groaned low and long, filling her with his warm seed and triggering another passage of ripples to wash over her.

Their beasts intertwined, mated, came together—to become one.

"I love ye, witch." Conall's voice was scratchy with emotion that glistened in his eyes, before he collapsed atop her.

"As I do ye, my beastie warrior." And she meant every word.

About the Author

A taste of the erotic, a measure of daring and a hint of laughter describe Mackenzie McKade's novels. She sizzles the pages with scorching sex, fantasy and deep emotion that will touch you and keep you immersed until the end. Whether her stories are contemporaries, futuristics or fantasies, this Arizona native thrives on giving you the ultimate erotic adventure.

When not traveling through her vivid imagination, she's spending time with three beautiful daughters, two devilishly handsome grandsons, and the man of her dreams. She loves to write, enjoys reading, and can't wait 'til summer. Boating and jet skiing are top on her list of activities. Add to that laughter and if mischief is in order—Mackenzie's your gal!

To learn more about Mackenzie McKade, please visit www.mackenziemckade.com. Send an email to Mackenzie at Mackenzie@mackenziemckade.com or enroll in her Yahoo! group to join in the fun with other readers as well as Mackenzie!

http://groups.yahoo.com/group/macsdreamscape/

Look for these titles

Now Available
Six Feet Under by Mackenzie McKade
Fallon's Revenge by Mackenzie McKade

Coming Soon
Lost But Not Forgotten by Mackenzie McKade

Night Music

Charlene Teglia

Dedication

Special thanks go to Crissy and Angie for bringing The Sirens out of my file cabinet and into the world! Thanks are also due to my real-life hero who makes so much of what I do possible.

Prologue

"Is there something you want to tell me?"

Meghan Davies didn't have to turn around to know who was talking to her. Or to verify that the question was aimed at her.

"Don't think the rest of the band won't notice," the voice behind her went on. "You've always had a little bit of an edge, but lately we could use you to cut glass."

Meghan closed her eyes and let out the breath she realized she'd been holding since Lorelei started to speak. *She knows. Of course she knows.* Stupid to think she wouldn't know.

Lorelei wasn't just the lead singer of The Sirens, the band that was their business, their livelihood and their life. She was the leader and she was psychic. *Don't try to keep secrets from a psychic, dummy.*

"You know already," Meghan answered without turning around. She didn't want to look into Lorelei's eyes. Didn't want to see the sympathy that would be there. Dammit, nobody was going to feel sorry for her. She was young, rich, famous, a musician in a top rock band. She was living a dream come true and if a nightmare had come for her, well, that was life. Sometimes life was a bitch.

And then you die, the thought finished unbidden.

She drew a deep breath and let it out slowly, forcing herself to speak clearly and carefully. "I don't want the band to know. I want to keep working for as long as I can and I don't want anybody treating me any differently."

Lorelei was silent behind her for a minute, thinking it over. "I won't tell them. But you'd better improve your acting or they'll guess. Or start asking questions."

247

Meghan knew Lorelei was right. They were all too close. They'd known each other too long, worked together, traveled together on tour, lived together when they were home in Seattle and now that Lorelei had gotten married, they spent about half their time on the island retreat Lorelei shared with her husband, recording in the studio built for them there.

If she didn't act like her usual self, Paige and Lisa would know something was up. Lisa hadn't been with them as long as Paige, she'd come in to replace their original drummer when Sara quit the band. But still, she was bright and tenacious and while Paige might be too ladylike to pin her to the wall with questions, Lisa wouldn't hesitate. And she would be relentless.

Meghan didn't want to deal with Lisa's questions.

"I'll do better," she promised.

"Okay. We haven't booked any tour dates for the rest of the year and nobody would expect us to until I've had the baby," Lorelei was saying now. "There's just the studio sessions and you can come in whenever you want to do your tracks."

Meghan nodded. That was good. She'd need some flexibility.

"So that just leaves the Seattle concert dates, two more nights. Are you up for those?"

"Yes." She was. She could do the local performances, no problem. She'd make sure to rest first and she'd take care of herself after.

"All right then." Lorelei came up behind her and touched her on the shoulder. "If you need anything or want anything, you can talk to me. Or ask Erik. You can come and stay with us if you want."

Erik, Lorelei's husband, had assumed a sort of elder brother/clan leader role in their lives. It was nice knowing that he'd be there for her, but on the other hand, he'd try to help whether she wanted him to or not. He would want more specialists. More tests.

Meghan held herself still at the thought but it was an effort not to shudder. No more tests, no more false hope.

No. She wouldn't be having a little chat with Erik if she could help it. And she'd spend as little time at their place as possible because the man was damn perceptive.

"I'm fine," Meghan said. "I don't need anything."

Nothing but a miracle, and she was fresh out.

Chapter One

Rom felt the first stirrings of the night with some imperceptible circadian measure. A hint of darkness on the breeze. A smoky flavor of yearning that woke in his blood, sharpening his senses, rousing him.

Night. It moved over and around him, whispering, inciting. He lay quietly and savored it.

The early night hours had a song all their own. A song that drew restless crowds, searching for some nameless fulfillment of an unknown desire, to prowl through night streets and clubs, losing themselves in the urgent rhythms of night music.

Rom knew the crowds, knew their boredom and the glitter of their seeking eyes.

They were all the same. They inhabited the night worlds of a thousand cities and centuries, mimicked each other unknowingly in carefully executed exhibits of individuality, moved to the same restless rhythm. They searched in vain for the nameless desire that called them into the night and sometimes settled for the heat and promise in the eyes of a stranger, only to wake to the cold light of day that held no mysteries.

In the day, there were only gritty eyes, aching temples and mouths dry with the taste of stale cigarettes and vanished wraiths of night promises.

Rom preferred the night. He always had.

He came fully awake and sat up on the hard sofa, smoothing back the once-again fashionable length of dark hair that was not much disturbed by his quiet, motionless sleep.

His heart throbbed with the beat of city traffic and the far-off pulsing of a bass guitar. Night. He smiled, feeling it around him like a living cloak of mystery, shining with the soft fires of distant stars.

Valentine was awake, too. Rom knew it, and thought he could sense the disturbance in the air currents signaling his approach long before he heard the soft sound of feet on carpet, then the rustle and muttered curse as body and unexpected object collided.

"Careful," Rom murmured, too late to be any help. "You'll step in the pizza."

Val responded with a low growl and a sharp curse. When he spoke, his tone made the words sound like more curses. "Pizza. You got garlic."

"It amused me."

"It's disgusting. Get it out of here."

"It's part of our cover," Rom said in a mild tone that nevertheless held a thread of something that hinted at granite. "Nobody raises a brow over two wealthy young men who only work at night if they're software designers. Youth is the byword of the industry. So is eccentricity. So is pizza."

"I'm not eating this," Val muttered, not calmed by the speech.

"Of course not. We donate it to the homeless behind the building," Rom said. "Ignore the garlic. It's a standard ingredient."

"You ignore it."

"I have been."

This was the undeniable truth and it silenced Val's grumblings. He continued to brood, however, as he prowled the office. Passing the desk chair, he hooked one leg around it to draw it up, sat in one fluid motion and tapped at the computer keyboard, disturbing the fractal pattern laboriously arranged by the screen saver.

"Get any further with this?" Val asked. It was the closest he came to apology.

Rom accepted it. "Not really."

Val tapped some more, symbols dancing across the screen at his command. "Huh. I'll work on it awhile." He continued, the silence broken by the swift, steady tap of keystrokes.

"Do that," Rom agreed as he stood and stretched to his full height. "I'll take this down." He reached for the cardboard pizza box, delivered hours earlier. "Hungry?"

Val shook his head. "Not yet. You?"

Night sang, hummed, buzzed in his senses. Sharp. Urgent. Dark. "Yes."

"You're going to go watch her again. You're obsessed with that woman." Val came straight to the point, laying open the real source of the tension that had been growing steadily between them.

"I like her music," Rom answered in neutral tones.

"You liked Mozart's music, too, but you didn't follow him around."

"I went to his performances."

"You didn't want to convert him. You want her, though." Val tapped furiously at the keyboard. "I know what's coming. Girl stuff everywhere. Girl things hanging in the bathroom. Waiting for you to get on with it is worse than living with it will be. I wish you'd just do it."

Rom paused, wondering how much he should say in answer to that. Women were something of a sore point with Valentine. Over two hundred years of grief and celibacy would do that. "She's sick," he said finally. "You wouldn't know it to look at her, but I can smell it on her skin. I didn't want to take any of the time she had left, but now her time is running out."

Rom had been watching her for years. He'd waited, giving her the chance to find a mortal love, a family, all the things he couldn't offer her, things he couldn't bear to deny her. Now he would offer her the only ever after possible for her, before the hidden killer that ate away at her took even that option away.

"Get on with it, then. Don't let her die. It's a real bitch waiting centuries for the woman you love to be reincarnated."

Val was a mass of tension. Inevitable, given that he'd spent centuries waiting for his lost love to be returned to him and had decided after the early decades of grief-imposed celibacy to just keep on waiting. He had so much tension bottled up that the others had taken to avoiding him and his hair-trigger temper at all costs about a hundred and fifty years ago.

"Has it crossed your mind that the gypsy might have been wrong?" Rom asked, not unkindly. Since the topic was open, it was a good time to discuss it without fear of it leading to mortal combat.

"It crossed my mind about a thousand times in the first year. Everybody needs something to believe in. I believe in gypsy prophecy."

"Has it occurred to you that if she does come back, she won't remember you, she won't recognize you, and you'll have centuries of pent-up sexual frustration driving you that no human woman could withstand?"

Val stopped dead. He whipped around to look at Rom, and the motion tossed his long blond hair streaked with white, gold and amber around his shoulders. The expression on his face was frightening.

Finally he said, "If she remained human, it might be a problem. But I will teach her to love me again, she will accept my kiss, she will transform, and she will survive being the recipient of my pent-up sexual frustration, thank you very much. Now go do something about yours."

Val resumed his furious typing, leaning in towards the computer and shutting out everything else but the programming problem to be solved.

Work didn't entirely drown out the pain, but it helped. For Val's sake, Rom hoped the gypsy's long-ago prediction proved true, that love would return to him in the Emerald City, and his decades of waiting weren't in vain.

Rom's waiting, at least, was at an end.

The distant, driving bass deepened. "I will," he answered.

Anticipation. Promise. The night pulsed with it. Out in the city, the night was alive with the restless hungers of thousands, following the beacons of brightly lit neon stars to the clubs and corners and coffeehouses. Rom could feel them, calling him to come and feed.

Now the night was warm and clear. Later, a sylvan fog would rise only to clear again with a five minute rain. It rained a great deal in Seattle. Rom wasn't entirely certain he liked it. He did, however, like the glitter of reflected starlight on scattered water droplets that clung to each vein of leaf and petal on the abundant flora. Seattle was a gardener's paradise with the mild climate and frequent rains.

He remembered nights in barren deserts, nights on cool, high mountains with stunted trees. Dry nights. Rain and mist made for variety. So did the lush growth, deep and verdant, soft and inviting like the night.

Mysterious, like a woman's embrace. Like the one he hoped to know this night, before dawn came and the world was lost to him for another day. It was All Hallow's Eve and tomorrow marked Samhain, the night when the world turned a corner, a time of endings and beginnings.

His hunger rose.

Maybe this night, all hungers would be satisfied at last.

Chapter Two

Rom prowled through the crowds of night revelers, merging but not blending unless he chose, moving among them but remaining apart. Yet wasn't he one of them? Didn't the same dark, nameless craving drive him into the same crowded clubs? Didn't his eyes sweep the same faces, searching for the same unrealized fulfillment?

Maybe he wasn't so different. Maybe he wasn't so very changed, after all.

But something tangible called him to this place and to this woman, and his craving had a name. Meghan Davies, Siren. Rom found the band's name appropriate. She didn't lure him to shipwreck and disaster, but the pull was undeniable. Maybe spending more than two hundred years in the company of a man for whom there was only one woman had given him romantic ideas.

The bass coaxed, urged, sang out a challenge in a wickedly sharp and deep, throbbing cant. Rom followed it into the concert and felt hunger sharpen and grow as he made his way through the crowd and came nearer to the stage.

Val was right. He was obsessed with the woman.

She played the bass with eyes closed, fingers gripping and chording, stroking, surging over the strings. She held the solid body of the wooden electric bass in the cradle of her hips and arms, her body moving with soft urgency, keeping time. Auburn hair burned a path to her waist and stood out like a signal fire against the black silk of her short tunic-style dress that left arms and legs and feet bare. The flame color was echoed in her fingernails and the soft, warm curve of her lips. Red, like fire. Like blood.

Heat quickened and deepened in him as he watched her.

Her eyes opened and fixed on his. They were the soft color of smoke. They widened in surprise and recognition, but didn't look away for a long time. When at last they blinked and lowered, they returned quickly.

Rom caught and held her look. She smiled, red lips curving in an inviting shape. She closed her eyes again, losing herself in the dream she created with the other musicians, but now she played to him, a fellow traveler of nightscapes and seeker of dark dreams.

He stayed, listening to the music she summoned up and poured forth. He waited, listening to the building excitement and promise of the night. He watched, the sight of this rock priestess feeding a separate hunger with color and curves and warm-blooded life. If he was successful, he would never see her like this again. It was a sight worth remembering.

He watched, and waited, and he wanted.

When the song was finished she put her bass onto a stand for the band's crew to pack away, and left the stage with the other women who formed the band. Rom watched her go with a surge of anticipation, hunting instincts fully alert and focused on his quarry. It wasn't the first time he'd come to see her perform, or the first time he'd let her see him in the crowd. But tonight he was going to use the backstage pass he'd acquired.

Meghan wasn't surprised to see the orchids waiting for her when the band finished for the night. They were signed with nothing more than the initials R.K., but she knew they came from her mysterious Mr. Tall, Dark and Handsome. He never spoke to her, although she often saw him at their concerts, no matter where in the world they performed.

This was their last live performance of the year, so she would have been amazed if he hadn't sent her flowers, even if she hadn't seen him in the audience.

She was going to miss the flowers. Meghan wondered briefly if he'd send them to her funeral, then dismissed the thought as ghoulish. It might be Halloween tonight, but that was no reason to dwell on the dark future. The present mattered, and in the present she could enjoy the shape and scent of orchids and be happy that somebody had thought of her.

In spite of the increasing incidence of violence from stalkers, Meghan's mystery man didn't worry her. Not just because she was a dead woman anyway, but because Lorelei wasn't worried. And because he fascinated Meghan. She was always a little disappointed when he vanished after a performance.

254

"He sent you flowers again," Lorelei said, appearing beside her as if conjured by the thought of her name.

"You didn't think he'd forget tonight, did you?" Meghan asked.

"No." Lorelei touched one blossom with a fingertip. "Invite him home with you."

"I'd have to talk to him to do that," Meghan pointed out.

Lorelei smiled at her. "He has a backstage pass."

"And you know this because you're psychic?"

"I know this because I gave it to him. I checked him out. Erik checked him out. Erik says he can afford you, by the way."

Erik had high standards when it came to finances. Mystery Man had serious net worth. That might be nice to know if she was contemplating anything long-term, but long-term was not an option.

"I'm not exactly in the market for a relationship," Meghan said. "And you know why." It was unfair and it pissed her off, and anger gave her voice a serrated edge.

Lorelei shrugged. "So don't have a relationship. Have sex. He looks like he'd make it worth your while."

Meghan felt her mouth twitch. "Go out with a bang."

"Well, you can limit yourself to hands if you want to, but I think you'll be missing out." Lorelei gave her a wicked look, then went to join her husband across the room, as if the conversation had given her ideas. Or maybe she just wanted to work off the charge built up from performing. The Sirens played sexually charged music rumored to have a very enjoyable impact on the audience's libido.

It affected Meghan's libido, enough to make her seriously consider taking Mr. Tall, Dark and Handsome home with her.

Go out with a bang. That would be some trick or treat. Well, why not? She wasn't too tired. She'd rested all day and the performance hadn't drained her. At least, if it had she wasn't feeling it yet. This was likely to be her last opportunity, and Lorelei was right, he did look like he'd make it worth her while. He looked predatory and dangerous and not at all gentle.

That suited her mood. Meghan didn't want gentle. She wanted release from the unbearable tension inside her, the anger and want and need abrading her nerves. Angry because she wasn't finished, wasn't ready. She wanted more, needed more, and couldn't find it in herself to accept her fate.

Fate could kiss her ass.

She was going to miss out on plenty. She didn't have to miss out on tonight. If he came backstage. If he gave her an opportunity, Meghan was going to take it.

And then he was there, in front of her. He seemed even more dangerous up close. *Good.*

Meghan gave him a long look. "You didn't disappear this time."

Rom smiled at her, liking her attitude, her straightforward manner. She didn't flirt. She simply stood there and looked at him, an attitude of sexual challenge in the line of her body and her posture and her eyes that said *come and get me if you dare.*

He dared.

"No. I didn't disappear this time."

She smiled then, her red-lipsticked mouth curving in that shape that made him want to take a bite. "I should ask you your name. I should ask you what you do."

"My name is Romney Kearns. I do software."

"Oh." Her soft smoky gaze moved over him in unhurried, lingering exploration. The way her eyes turned darker told him she liked what she saw. "You don't look like a geek. Not skinny enough."

"Too much pizza," Rom explained.

She nodded. "The staple of software wizards. I guess you're safe to leave with, then."

"Not safe," he corrected softly. He smiled into her eyes and gave in to the desire to taste her. One taste, in a room full of people. He could take that much and be certain it wouldn't go too far. His hands spread over her shoulders, drew her close. His head lowered to hers.

Her mouth was soft, sweet, filled with dark mystery and living heat. Hunger grew and licked at them both with fiery tongues. The kiss deepened, turned savage. Rom tasted the bright copper flavor of blood and gentled, kissing it away, savoring each drop and the essence of her.

Hunger thrummed in his veins, and it was an effort not to scrape his teeth over her lower lip and spill more. He wanted to sink his teeth deep into her flesh and drink until his thirst was quenched.

Rom knew his eyes burned when he loosened his hold and set her from him. "I'm not safe at all. You should run away."

She touched the tip of her tongue to the graze in her lower lip. "I'm not much for aerobics. Not much for playing it safe, either."

"No," Rom agreed, still tasting the sweet, reckless flavor of her. She tasted wild, hot, as if the life that was slipping away wanted to use itself up.

He didn't want to take her home with him, to the suite of offices and living space he shared with Val. He didn't want to share her or this night with Val, and not because he wanted to spare the man's feelings. Rom wanted to mark her, to possess her, claim her, and instinct told him to take her far from any potential rivals. He had never wanted another woman the way he wanted this one. He wanted her alone and aware of only him.

"We'll go to your place. Invite me."

Her brows arched at his wording. "You're invited."

"I accept." Rom picked up a blossom in one hand and placed the other on the warm curve of her waist. He tucked the flower behind her ear, in the long fall of her hair.

The flower's exotic perfume mingled with the scent of aroused woman. The change heightened all senses, allowing him to note minute differences in respiration, the rush of blood beneath the skin heralding a blush—the thousand tiny physical signs of human reaction were his to read. Fear, deception, lust, they all marked the body in various ways.

Meghan wasn't hiding anything from him and she didn't fear him. She wanted him. That might change, but for now the pulse beating at her throat meant desire. The musky scent of her heat made the hunger sharpen. He pictured her naked, limbs open and sprawled in invitation, allowing him to taste her everywhere.

The thought alone strained his control. It may have been a mistake to go to her without feeding elsewhere first, but he hadn't wanted to wait. He'd waited long enough already.

"Thank you for the flowers," Meghan said.

"I enjoy sending them."

She touched the blossom in her hair and leaned slightly towards him. Rom tightened his hold on her waist, drawing her into his side. A possessive gesture. One that marked her as his and proclaimed his intention.

She didn't resist or move away.

"You don't seem much like a hearts and flowers kind of guy."

"What kind do I seem?"

"Not like any other kind." She slid her leg against his, a subtle shift that would go unnoticed unless somebody was watching them closely, but a clear signal of her sexual interest in him. "And not safe."

"You don't want safe tonight."

"No."

"Then live dangerously," he suggested. His fingers bit into her flesh, then stroked down her hip, giving her a taste of the way he wanted to touch her.

"I intend to."

They walked out into the night together.

Chapter Three

Meghan leaned into her mystery man and let him lead her to a waiting limo. "You travel in style."

"I appreciate creature comforts." He slanted a look at her, his lips not quite smiling. He had the darkest eyes she'd ever seen, set in sharp features and framed by raven black hair worn long. It suited him. Some men looked too young or just untidy with long hair. Romney looked like a throwback to another century.

It was the cheekbones, Meghan thought. You had to have the right bone structure to carry that look off and have it underscore masculinity instead of seeming effeminate. Then there were the muscles. Romney felt as if he'd been carved from marble. And his attitude, king of the concrete jungle.

Although any man who could kiss the way he did deserved to walk like he owned the city, in Meghan's opinion. Her lips still throbbed and the sting from the graze on her lower lip that had bled from the force of his kiss had an answering throb building between her legs. If he could kiss like that, she might not be able to walk after the full performance.

With a slight shake of her head, she set that thought aside and leaned forward to give the driver directions to the house on Queen Anne Hill. The limo drove off and Romney pressed a button to raise the glass, making the backseat a private enclosure.

"Why tonight?" Meghan asked, settling back into the soft leather cushion.

"It was time."

He didn't pretend not to know what she was talking about, and Meghan appreciated that, even if his answer was cryptic. He'd had countless opportunities to get an introduction before tonight if he'd wanted to meet her. And though he couldn't possibly have known tonight would be her last live performance, the timing made for one hell of a coincidence.

Well, coincidence happened. Some called it synchronicity. Whatever the reason, it meant she wouldn't die without knowing what her mystery man's name was. Already she knew his name, his occupation, the sound of his voice and the taste of his mouth.

Meghan found herself staring at his mouth and blinked, wondering how long she'd been doing that. "Sorry," she said.

"No need." He touched her lower lip with one finger, pressing into the soft flesh. "You looked into my eyes and I took a little of your blood. You are not quite hypnotized but something close to it."

Hypnotized. That was funny, but she didn't feel like laughing. She felt like biting into his finger, not hard, just enough to make him feel it a little, using the sharp edge of her teeth.

"What does your hypnotic spell do?" Meghan asked. "Make me want to take you home and do it until the box springs break?"

"Is that how you feel?"

His finger slid inside her mouth, just the tip, and Meghan closed her lips around it, sucking lightly, then letting her tongue dart over his skin before he withdrew.

"No," Meghan said once her mouth was free to answer. "After the box springs break, we can move to the floor or find another bed."

He laughed and lifted her onto his lap, and that was when Meghan noticed neither of them had fastened their seatbelts. "We're violating the seatbelt law," she pointed out.

"I intend to violate more than that before the sun rises." Romney slid a hand up her leg, under the fabric of her dress until it rested on her thigh.

"You have an accent I can't quite place." She curled into him and rested her head on his shoulder, letting her eyes drift shut as he traced patterns over the sensitive skin of her inner thighs. "Almost Irish but it doesn't sound right."

"Welsh."

"Oh."

His hand moved up higher, his fingers exploring her mound until she spread her legs and gave him better access. He cupped his hand over her sex and let his fingers press into her labia, the layers of pantyhose and a thong providing very little separation between his hand and the flesh growing swollen and slick for him.

"The driver," Meghan said, although she didn't try to close her legs or move away as Romney pulled her skirt up higher.

"I'll make him forget anything he might see."

That made no sense at all, but for some reason she accepted the explanation as adequate and lifted her hips to make it easy for him to peel her out of her hose and underwear, leaving her bare under the black silk dress bunched around her waist.

His hand returned to her sex, now fully exposed, stroking, exploring, circling the swollen nub of her clit and then flicking it hard enough to make her gasp.

"Romney," she said, her voice throaty with desire.

"Rom."

"Rom," Meghan repeated, liking the sound of his nickname and the intimacy of it. Then she laughed. "You must hear a lot of bad jokes about that, given your business."

"Most humans don't find me funny." Rom drew his finger over her clit slowly, then plunged it into her with no warning. The abrupt penetration made her gasp and her hips thrust towards his hand in reflex.

"I'm not laughing at you." There was nothing funny about the way she was sprawling on his lap, half naked, legs open, feeling the heat spread over her skin and the graze on her lower lip burn as he took her with his hand. "Kiss me again, Rom."

"If I kiss you now, it's likely to go too far." He thrust a second finger into her and twisted them both, moving them in and out of her. Meghan groaned.

"You're banging me in the back of a limo, and you're worried about getting too carried away in public?"

"Yes." His voice was hard with a hint of music to it, the accent softening his tone. "I won't take you here, Meghan, but I will make you come for me."

One arm tightened around her, holding her so close against his chest that she couldn't draw a deep breath. He took her with his fingers, flicking them over her clit, driving them into her sex, making her pant and then moan and then finally scream as he drew it out and kept her on the verge of orgasm, almost but not quite able to reach it. Then he plunged three fingers into her

261

and rubbed his thumb over her clit and she felt herself come apart, shattering into a thousand shards and fragments.

When her lips and voice were able to work in unison again, Meghan managed to say, "You're very good at that."

"I've had a great deal of time to practice." He kissed her forehead, a light brush of his mouth, his fingers still buried inside her. For some reason it hurt to think of other women lying naked and open for him to take and the hurt twisted like a knife in her gut.

It shouldn't matter. She didn't know this man, and it was unlikely she'd see him again. So what if he knew his way around the female sex organs as if he'd made a science of the study, it was just sex and what would she prefer, to have a last fling with an expert or a man who didn't believe the G-spot existed?

The hurt coming on the heels of orgasm brought her down more effectively than an ice bath. Suddenly, Meghan was very aware of her position, her state of undress, and the fact that the limo driver was staring at her pussy in the rearview mirror.

"Oh, hell." She tried to move, to dislodge Romney's hand and pull her dress back down, even if the damage was already done and a stranger had gotten a front-row seat to the show. Rom didn't let her.

"Stay where you are." He looked down at her, his eyes burning into hers. "I can't take you yet, but I'm damned if I'll let you hide yourself from me." Then his lips twisted in an almost-smile. "Actually, I'm damned anyway, according to some. But your body is going to belong to me and I am not finished looking at or touching what is mine."

"Yeah, well, you and the city of Seattle," Meghan snapped, waving at the mirror.

"He won't remember a thing."

"Because you'll hypnotize him into forgetting that a world-famous musician lost her panties in his backseat. He's probably taken pictures by now." Meghan glared at Romney but she still reacted with treacherous heat and need that was far from sated when his fingers moved inside her.

"Yes, I will hypnotize him into forgetting. And there is no camera."

"You are the strangest man." Meghan closed her eyes and gasped as his fingers moved in and out of her—slow, sure, making her want more no matter how many people watched.

"What if I told you I'm not a man?"

"What are the alternatives?" Meghan asked. "You have long hair but nobody would mistake you for Bigfoot. I'm not saying aliens don't exist, but if they do they're probably not into sex and hypnosis. Whatever you are, you're definitely male."

She could feel the distinctive proof of that jutting into her hip, the heat of him burning through the layers of clothing.

"And you are definitely female." He slid his fingers out of her and rested his hand on her sex, cupping her as if staking his claim. Possessive. "And so very human. So fragile that I bruised you with a kiss."

"Made my lip bleed, too," Meghan pointed out.

"Yes, I do remember." One finger glided lightly over her labia. "I know the taste of your mouth and your blood and soon I'll know how you taste everywhere."

"You could find out now," Meghan suggested, forgetting their audience of one. She wanted to feel Rom's mouth on her sex, his tongue thrusting into her.

"Not yet." Rom gave her pussy a last petting, then pulled her more upright on his lap, tugging her skirt down at the same time. Meghan didn't know where her underwear had ended up and she didn't care. No point wasting time putting it back on when it'd be coming right off again.

"Why?"

"Why not yet?" Rom gave her an unreadable look. "Because I want you too badly. Because I haven't satisfied my hungers elsewhere. I don't trust my control and I won't take all of you and risk making a choice for you that you might regret afterwards."

"I don't really have time for regrets," Meghan said. Although right now she did regret the fact that his mouth wasn't between her legs. The topic did, unfortunately, remind her just how short time was, how little of it she had to waste.

"Things change." Rom ran a hand along the curve of her thigh, her hip, up until it closed over her breast. The pressure of his hand on her made her arch into him, wanting more.

"Some things can't."

He laughed, a low sound. "There are more things in heaven and earth than are dreamed of in your philosophy."

"Shakespeare," Meghan said. She sighed in pleasure when his fingers closed over her nipple and tugged. "I'd be willing to believe the alien theory, on second thought. You quote the bard, and you really know what to do with your mouth and hands. Although I'd argue that an alien man is still a man."

"I'm not an alien, but I am *other*." Rom traced the outline of her breasts and then slid under the fabric to cup her bare skin, rubbing his thumb over her nipple under the silk. "In the ways that matter right now, I am very much a man, however."

"One of my best friends married a Viking." Meghan made a soft sound of delight when he lowered the straps of her dress down to make it easier to run his hands over her breasts, stroking, cupping and squeezing the sensitive flesh that ached for his touch. "*Other* can work out pretty well in the sexual compatibility department."

"We do have sexual compatibility."

"Any more compatible and the upholstery back here would catch fire."

Meghan's skin already had, her nerve endings were burning, flames licking under the surface, all of her ready to combust.

"Are you ready to burn for me?" His hands moved over her and Meghan couldn't track the question, let alone answer it.

Chapter Four

Meghan didn't realize they'd reached their destination until it finally registered that Rom had stopped and why. The car was no longer moving.

"This is embarrassing," she said. "The driver is looking at my breasts, which is probably not worse than him watching me spread my legs for you, but still, I'm thinking he really doesn't need to see my nipples."

"How could he? My hands are covering them." Rom squeezed the soft curves resting in the palms of his hands and then let her go, restoring her dress and her to some semblance of order.

"You're really going to hypnotize him so he doesn't remember this?" That would be a nice trick, although if it didn't work what was the worst case scenario? Having the story trumpeted in all the tabloids with accompanying grainy photos? It could happen, but she really had bigger things to worry about than PR and her image.

"Yes."

He sounded so confident, but it made no sense to her. Meghan shook her head and felt around for her underwear.

"Looking for these?" Rom pulled a scrap of fabric out of his jacket pocket and Meghan stared.

"Why didn't I notice what you were wearing?" she asked. She took in the suit jacket, the silk dress shirt, the pants. "I saw your eyes, your face, I noticed your hair. I never saw what you were wearing. It didn't register."

"Maybe you were taken with my face."

"Maybe you really did hypnotize me." Meghan slid off his lap, thoroughly unnerved. It was as if part of him had been hidden from her, blocked off, and only now revealed. What else wasn't she seeing?

"I did tell you." Rom gave a graceful shrug and returned her panties to his pocket.

"What exactly are you?"

"I told you I was dangerous." He leaned over and kissed the corner of her mouth, and that was enough to make the pulse leap in her throat. "But you've invited me in and I won't be shut out tonight."

"You make it sound like I'm not allowed to have second thoughts." Meghan swallowed with an effort, her mouth dry, far too affected by this man.

"You're allowed. But you haven't changed your mind. You want me."

She did, and she hated that it was so obvious. Her nipples were hard and distended, clearly visible under the fabric of her dress. Her underwear was in his pocket and her dress probably sported a damp patch.

"Don't let it upset you." Rom touched her cheek, then the scraped spot on her lower lip. "You need me tonight. I'm here."

He retrieved the flower and laid it in her hand. Meghan looked down at the blossom and wondered when it had fallen out of her hair. About the time she'd lost half her clothes and most of her mind? Another detail she hadn't noticed and should have. She sat there, holding the fragile bloom, while Rom got out, went around to the driver's window, spoke in a low voice, then returned to help her out of the car.

"What did you do, bribe him?" Meghan asked.

"I clouded his memory. Even if you didn't object, I have no desire to leave him with a clear image of your naked body. That's mine to remember." Rom's fingers dug into her shoulder, a small hurt but one that helped her focus.

"You sound like a jealous boyfriend." Meghan keyed the code into the security gate. They walked through it and she heard the distinctive sound as it locked in place behind them. Was it a good thing or a bad thing that he was inside it with her?

"Possessive," Rom said. "Not quite the same thing. I won't make irrational accusations about your behavior with other men, but neither do I want to share you. That includes letting other men see you naked."

"I don't make a habit of getting naked in public, so it's not likely to be an issue." It wasn't likely to be an issue anyway, because after tonight she wouldn't see him again, and after that, well, she was going to lose more weight and before long nobody would want to see her naked.

Great, now she was depressed about the future, or her lack of one, and the fact that a man she didn't even know and wasn't sure she should be alone with would never be her boyfriend, even if he wanted to be. Which wasn't likely. If he'd wanted to be her boyfriend, he'd missed plenty of chances.

"You don't want to be my boyfriend, anyway," she burst out, then wanted to groan when she realized what she'd said.

"No, I don't." His hands tightened on her. "I want to be your lover."

"Oh."

There was nothing more to say to that, so Meghan focused on entering the right combination into the keypad by the front door. It opened and they walked through it, then closed it behind them. She automatically hit the setting on the pad inside the door that armed the security system but wouldn't be set off by normal movement indoors. It would take opening a door or window to trigger the alarm.

She turned to face Romney. "About this lover business."

"Not business. Pleasure." His hands traced the edge of her dress, just touching her skin, then fisted in the fabric and tore it. He opened his hands and the remains of the dress fell away. Meghan dropped the orchid and saw the white blossom lying on the black silk and thought, *pretty*. Then Rom kissed her again and she didn't think anything at all.

His mouth devoured hers as he crowded her body against the door, the fabric of his suit jacket abrading her nipples. His body pressed into hers, crushing her breasts into his chest and he rode his knee between her thighs, partially lifting her with her sex grinding into his thigh.

She couldn't breathe and didn't care. She dug her hands in his jacket and yanked, wanting it out of her way and his skin bared to her touch. He let out a soft laugh against her open mouth and shrugged off the jacket, then unbuttoned the shirt and let that fall, too.

"Pants," Meghan said, in case he'd forgotten about them. "Get rid of those, too."

"I'll have to let go of you to do that."

"Damn." She ground her pelvis into him, then bit her lower lip. "Okay, just do it."

Rom released her and left her standing on shaky legs, naked, leaning on the door for support while she watched him undo his pants and slide them off his legs, kicking his shoes free in the process. That made her mind work again.

She wasn't sure when she'd lost her shoes but her feet were bare now. In the limo? They were probably still there. Then he straightened and she saw his cock, full, jutting towards her, and forgot about her shoes again.

She dropped to her knees and leaned forward, taking the head of him into her mouth. He buried his hands in her hair. "Ah. I didn't expect that."

He wasn't objecting, though, so Meghan drew him deeper, taking as much of his length into her mouth as she could, running her tongue over and around him, tasting him. She slid a hand between his thighs to cup his balls and he reacted, thrusting himself between her lips.

She closed her eyes and savored the sensation of his hard cock pushing in and out, fucking her mouth, feeling heat building inside her, her clit throbbing with need, her sex swollen for him. His fingers hadn't given her enough relief. She needed more. Needed him hard and hot between her thighs, driving into her, fucking her.

"Enough." He pulled out of her mouth and took hold of her shoulders, drawing her upright. "I want to taste you. Show me your bedroom."

"This way." Meghan led and he followed, his hand on the small of her back, fingers dipping lower to touch the dimple just above her bare ass. She managed not to stagger or stumble on the way, then collapsed across the bed on her stomach.

"Very nice." Rom ran his hands over her ass, then down, nudging her thighs apart and exposing her sex to him. He thrust a finger into her from behind and Meghan gasped at the abrupt penetration. She was slick and ready, his finger sliding into her easily, and he followed it with a second.

Meghan felt the bed dip as he joined her on the mattress, one hand moving underneath her to stroke her clit while his fingers moved inside her from the other side. "That feels so good," she sighed.

"I'm sure it tastes even better." He slid his hands away, turned her onto her back and lifted her higher on the bed, allowing him to move between her open thighs. "Let's find out."

The first touch of his tongue outlining her labia nearly made her come off the bed. He explored her with his mouth, thrust his tongue into her, then sucked at her clit. She felt the sharp edge of his teeth and the sensation sent her spiraling up.

"Rom. Now," she gasped out.

He drove his fingers into her again while his mouth took her and she splintered.

"You taste delicious." Rom raised his head and licked his lips. Meghan felt her inner muscles clench in reaction. She was throbbing everywhere, nipples, clit, vulva, her pulse pounding in her throat, blood roaring in her ears.

He moved over her, his thighs hard between hers, his cock hot and urgent against her pussy, the wall of his chest crushing her breasts.

"Meghan." He flexed his hips, driving the head of his cock inside her, and Meghan felt herself opening for him, stretching around the width of him.

One bright side to having no future—birth control and disease prevention simply weren't issues. Meghan arched underneath him, straining to take more, loving the feel of him bare and thick inside her. She wanted him all the way inside her, and when he came she wanted to feel the liquid jet pulsing into her depths.

"Rom." She shifted under him, restless, impatient. What was he waiting for?

"I love seeing you under me like this." He smiled at her. "I love the feel of your flesh under mine, your sweet, hot cunt taking my cock. I can feel you opening for me, so wet, so ready for me." Rom rocked into her, giving her another inch.

"Rom. I need you now." She arched up into him.

"Dying for it, are you?" He lowered his head to her neck, kissing the pulse point at her throat.

He had no idea. He couldn't have any idea, the words were coincidence. And she was dying for it, aching for him, on fire for him. "Fuck me."

"Oh, I will." Rom's voice was a dark promise in the night.

She felt his teeth scrape over her skin and then his mouth closed over hers again, hard, hot, taking her breath while he drove inside her and took her body. He was relentless, holding her down while he thrust his length into her again and again, forcing her to take the slow pace he set, not letting her shift to get more pressure where she wanted it, not letting her come.

The need built inside her until she would have screamed with it but his mouth devoured hers, allowing no sound escape.

Now. Now, she urged him with her mind, as if he could hear her. She needed more, needed it now.

Maybe he was psychic as well as a hypnotist because he changed his rhythm and began to slam into her, fast and furious, driving deep into her, taking her. She felt her inner muscles begin to pulse and then spasm in an

269

orgasm that seemed to build and build, stretching out forever as he fucked her, peaking when she felt the burst of liquid heat as he spilled himself inside her.

Her heart felt like it was going to explode inside her chest, beating too hard, too fast, as she lay gasping under him.

Finally, she managed to say through bruised, swollen lips, "So you came to kill me with sex tonight."

"No." His lips moved over hers in a kiss as light as the brush of butterfly wings. "I just came to kill you."

Chapter Five

Meghan went still, wondering just who was on top of her, inside her, and how she could get away from the threat he posed. She wasn't noticing things she should, wasn't seeing everything, and even when she'd realized that earlier, she couldn't seem to care about it.

She'd taken this stranger home with her, invited him in, locked them both in the house together. Her heartbeat accelerated, something she didn't think was possible, hammering in her chest while her breath came in too-fast gulps.

"You're hyperventilating." Rom pulled out of her and rolled off her in one motion, lifted her, drew her forward until her legs hung off the bed and pushed her head down between her knees. "Stay there, don't move."

And she couldn't. Even when he left the room, she was paralyzed, as if her flesh had frozen into a living statue of a woman and not the real thing. She heard the sound of her laboring lungs in the empty room, and then Rom was back, holding a paper bag, forcing her to breathe into it.

So that really does work, she thought when her lungs returned to their normal rhythm and the black dots swimming in her vision began to clear.

"Better?"

Meghan nodded, but didn't try to speak. Rom pulled the bag away and set it aside, then climbed back onto the bed. He wrapped his arms around her and drew her down to lay beside him and she went, unresisting, limp.

"What just happened?" she asked after a few minutes.

"I scared you." Rom's hands moved along the curve of her spine, stroking her, his touch soothing.

"You said you'd come to kill me. You didn't think I'd be scared?" Meghan huddled into him, even though it was stupid and suicidal, because she wanted the press of his flesh against hers, his warmth, his strength. His comfort. Which made no sense, but what about tonight made sense?

She could easily believe the veil between the worlds had grown thin and strange things walked the earth this Halloween.

"I didn't think I'd panic you." His lips brushed her temple. "Are you so afraid of dying?"

"Not afraid, exactly." Meghan spread her hand on his chest, feeling his heart beating under her palm. "The idea pisses me off. I want to kick the Grim Reaper's ass, but I don't think a black belt is much use against the incorporeal."

Rom laughed. "No."

"See, this is what I don't understand." Meghan lifted her head and looked into those dark eyes of his. "You send me flowers for years. My friends approve of you. You finally introduce yourself to me and we have fantastic, amazing sex. Some of which is in front of an audience, and I don't care, which is so not like me. Then, in the afterglow, you tell me you're going to kill me and you don't sound like it's a joke. Even if you did, that's not the kind of thing you joke about unless you're a serial killer. Then when I have a panic attack, you calm me down and now you're laughing and rubbing my back."

She shook her head and felt the slide of her hair against her naked back. "Make me understand, Rom."

"You already do, if you let yourself."

Meghan lowered her head to pillow it on his shoulder, closed her eyes, and rested against him while he held her.

If she let herself. What did that mean? What did she understand? He'd told her he wasn't human. What was he?

Rom did something that affected her mind, like hypnosis. He'd made the driver forget her. He'd kissed her hard enough to draw blood and he'd acted like it was an aphrodisiac instead of a gross-out. He'd told her to invite him into her home.

"Would you have been able to come inside if I hadn't invited you?" Meghan asked.

"No."

That was easier to hear with her eyes shut, for some reason.

"Can you see your reflection in a mirror?"

"Yes. That's just the Hollywood version. The blank mirror is so dramatic. Cue danger music."

"Of course." She nodded, her cheek rubbing against his skin as she did. "I should have realized that Hollywood would screw up the facts about *vampires.*"

"You should." Rom twined his fingers into her hair. "Movies screw up the facts about so many things."

Meghan let out a low groan. "Don't tell me about them. I don't want to know what else exists outside of a movie screen that shouldn't."

"That hurts." Rom rolled onto his back and drew her on top of him. His erection prodded her belly. "Do you really think I shouldn't exist?"

"Well. Vampires. The undead." Meghan shook her head. "Most one-night stands are not this weird."

"If you don't like weird, you shouldn't pick up strange men on Halloween." Rom shifted her, sliding her along his length, settling her legs down on either side of his so that his cock rode against her labia.

"I didn't pick you up, exactly." Meghan rocked her hips into him and felt her clit react as he pressed into her, not quite entering her, but making her want to change her angle and take him all the way inside. It was such a tease and her body hungered for his so sharply. "You picked me up. I think. The details are a little hazy."

"Maybe we picked each other up." Rom gripped her hips and lifted her just a little, adjusted his position and thrust up into her while he pulled her back down onto him at the same time. The abrupt entry made her gasp.

"Maybe we did." Meghan tipped her head back, braced her knees on either side of him and began to raise and lower herself on him, riding him, impaling herself on him.

She started to laugh as the word association registered. "I'm fucking Vlad the Impaler. You're staking me with your inhuman cock."

"There, you are feeling better now."

Rom reached down and rubbed her clit. The direct contact sent so much sensation arcing through her that for a moment she couldn't move. She let out an inarticulate sound, not quite a whimper or a moan but something in the middle or maybe both at the same time.

"Rom." Meghan dropped onto his chest, her hair falling over them both like a cover.

"Too much?" His voice was low, knowing. His finger stroked over her clit again and she trembled, feeling a deep pulsing inside her in response, hot and urgent. Her inner muscles clenched around him, gripping his cock.

"I can take it." Her voice sounded breathy and soft to her own ears. Not exactly convincing.

"I can take you." Rom thrust up into her and kept up the pressure on her clit until she shuddered and groaned, unable to move, paralyzed by pleasure.

"I hope so, because I can't seem to move and I'm so not finished."

"I'll finish you."

"That sounds so final," Meghan said, her voice muffled by his chest. "What are you going to do, suck my blood?"

"If you'll let me." Rom pulled out and rolled with Meghan, coming to rest over her as she lay on her back, their positions reversed. "It's an option. I think it beats the alternative, don't you?"

"So you know about that."

"Yes."

So Rom knew her secret. Considering everything else, that didn't surprise her. It did explain why he'd never approached her before, and why he'd decided it was time now.

She arched up into him, loving the feel of him on top of her, his weight, the brush of his skin against hers, his cock resting against her sex. "Just out of curiosity, are there a lot of bloodsucking fiends in the software industry?"

"Not many, but we do have to adapt to changing times and shifts in the job market. The technology field has a lot of jobs for night workers." Rom smiled at her and moved his hips, making his cock glide along her labia and rub against her clit.

"Seattle must be a big attraction, then. Long, dark days in winter, lots of rain, not too many sunny days."

"It suited us." Rom lowered his head to kiss the base of her throat, then moved down to draw her nipple into his mouth.

"That feels so good." Meghan dug her hands into his hair, holding him to her as if she thought he might try to get away before he finished her as promised.

"It'll feel better when I bite you." Rom released her nipple and turned his attention to its twin, sucking hard. She groaned in reaction and bucked her hips into him, trying to gain more pressure where she wanted it.

"How does that work, anyway?" Meghan asked. "One bite and I become a born-again bloodsucker?"

"Not quite." Rom kissed his way down her belly and nipped at her clit, making her shriek before he moved back up her body, settled between her thighs and thrust into her again, hard and sure, filling her with one stroke. "I drink you dry and then you drink me."

She blinked at him, trying to understand, moving her hips in rhythm with his automatically. "Sounds complicated."

"Not really."

"Would I have to kill people? Because I couldn't do that."

"No. You don't need to take that much, just about the amount a blood donor gives. If it worries you, you can implant a post-hypnotic suggestion to drink juice and eat a cookie." Rom lowered his full weight onto her, pressing her into the bed, driving so far into her that he touched the opening of her womb and she ground her pelvis against him in response.

"So good. So deep. More," she gasped out.

"I'll give you more."

His mouth took hers, hungry and urgent. His body moved on hers, in hers, taking her hard. He drew her lower lip into his mouth and scraped it with his teeth, drawing blood, tasting her while he fucked her.

Need roared through him. The need to extend his fangs, sink them into her soft flesh, drink the hot blood just below the surface of her smooth skin, drink her while he buried his cock deep inside her, swallow the last of her life while he spent himself into her womb.

But not without an invitation. Not without her choosing it. He held himself in check, taking as much of her as she was willing to give him and taking every inch of it.

"I want you," he breathed against her lips. "All of you, every bit, every drop. I want you tonight and tomorrow night and every night. Mine to hold, to look at, to fuck. Mine to keep."

275

Her eyes opened halfway, her lids heavy, her eyes dark. "Not a one-night stand?"

"Not even close." He drove into her again, a deep, hard stroke.

"A package deal, two for one." She moved under him, twining her legs around his waist to open herself more fully to him. "I get you and I get to keep my life. Sort of."

"You do already work at night," Rom pointed out. "Not too much of a change. And if you don't want me, I'd still offer you the option. I would try to change your mind about us, however."

"Forever is a long time to be alone." She opened her eyes all the way, meeting his directly."

"Yes." He quickened his pace, feeling her inner muscles clenching around him, angling to put more pressure on the spot deep inside her where she craved it most.

"Do it," she said, turning her head to expose more of her neck to him. Hunger shot through him, fierce, hot, undeniable.

"Are you sure?" He wanted her, but he wanted her to be certain.

"I'm sure. Take me now, make me come while you do it."

He did. He sank his fangs into her exposed throat, drank her as he drove into her harder, faster, taking all of her. Her pussy clutched at his cock as the orgasm built, her inner muscles gripping and drawing him deeper, triggering his orgasm, milking him dry. He pumped himself into her as he drank the last of her, then raised his head to look into her eyes as she lay beneath him, trembling in the aftershocks.

"What happens now?" Meghan asked.

"Now you die."

Chapter Six

Rom drew the edge of one fang along his wrist and pressed it to Meghan's mouth. "Swallow."

She did, her throat working convulsively.

"More."

He forced her to drink until she turned her head away, eyes shut, body still as if in sleep. He pulled out and rolled off to lay beside Meghan, gathering her into his arms. A shudder rippled through her.

"It hurts," she said in a hoarse whisper.

"Yes."

It hurt to die, it hurt to be reborn. He wouldn't leave her alone and hurt in the dark. Rom held her close, knowing she would be aware of his presence and comforted by it. Tremors wracked her frame for what seemed like hours. Finally she stilled and rested in his arms. A long time later, she moved her head on his shoulder.

"Rom."

"I'm here." He kissed her mouth, a soft brush of lips, a light tracing of his tongue against hers.

"This has been a very strange night." Her voice was a sigh of sound, but it was steady.

"It's not quite over yet." Rom kissed her again, a little harder this time. "Although the dawn isn't too far off. You should come home with me to sleep, it's safer there."

"Right." She yawned. "Because my roommates won't know that sunlight will turn me into a human torch now."

"That's not quite true, but you'll find it very uncomfortable." Rom smiled at her and sat up, lifting her into his lap. "The bigger problem is our vulnerability while asleep. Especially when you're new, you won't wake easily, even if you're in danger. And you should decide what you want to tell them, how you want to answer the inevitable questions."

"Makes sense. Okay." Meghan yawned again and stretched, her body arching. "We'll go to your place. I get to see Dracula's castle. This should be cool."

"It's not a castle. It's the upper floor of a nice, modern building. Office space and apartment combined."

"No dungeon or spooky torches or tormented spirits? I think I'm disappointed."

Rom laughed. "Well, there's Val. He might spook you."

"Val. What's a Val?" She angled her head to look at him as she asked the question.

"Valentine. My roommate and partner." Rom smiled at her. "I should warn you, he doesn't like women."

"Gay." Meghan nodded. "No problem."

"Not gay." Rom felt his lips twitch at the assumption that was, in retrospect, logical of her to make. "Grief-struck. He lost his wife."

"Oh." Her face went serious. "That has to suck. Was it before or after he became one of the legions of the undead?"

"Before."

"And he chose to live forever with his grief?" Her brows shot up in surprise.

"No, he was told he would find her again and he decided to wait."

"What, reincarnation?"

"Is it stranger than vampires?" Rom asked her.

"Well, no." Meghan sat all the way up and hopped off his lap. "So how do we do this, fly?"

"I'll have the limo pick us up at the gate."

Her face fell, disappointment clear in her expression. "Don't tell me, that's another thing Hollywood got wrong. Vampires can't fly."

"Only if we buy a plane ticket."

"Damn." She scowled and scuffed her toe in the carpet. "I can be seen in a mirror, get exposed to sunlight, and I can't fly. But I have to drink blood. None of the cool stuff, all of the gross-out."

"Enhanced senses and strength are pretty cool," Rom said. "And the hypnotic stare comes in handy."

"Well, yeah. And I don't have to worry about dying because I'm already dead."

"Always a bright side." Rom stood and reached for her, drawing her against him, enjoying the feel of her soft breasts touching his chest.

"There's a huge bright side." Meghan touched him, her hands running over him. "I get you. Tonight and tomorrow night and every night. If I hadn't been dying, you never would have approached me, would you?"

"No." His arms closed around her, holding her close. "I wanted you to have a chance at a mortal love, children. I can't give you that, Meghan."

"You can give me more than enough." Her lips brushed the skin at the base of his throat in a soft caress. "You gave me a second chance, and immortal love. You do love me, don't you?"

"Yes. I have for some time."

"It should seem scary that you've been watching me, but it seems comforting." Her arms wound around his waist as she leaned into him. "Like I've had an angel watching over me."

"That's a nice upgrade from bloodsucking fiend." Rom slid a hand under her chin to raise her face to his and gave her a kiss that was long and deep and thorough.

***

The limo driver really didn't remember her, Meghan noted with some amazement. And her shoes were in the backseat, where she must have kicked them off. She picked them up and turned them in her hands. How completely things had changed since she'd last worn them, and how quickly.

"I see you found your shoes." Rom gave her a heated look, as if he was thinking about the way she'd lost them.

"Yes, and quit trying to make me blush."

"He doesn't remember." Rom touched the back of her neck, stroking her skin with a light touch, tempting her.

"You're insatiable." But she climbed into his lap and slid her arms around his neck. "I like that in a man."

"Vampire," he corrected.

"Whatever." Meghan cuddled into him and let out a soft sigh of contentment.

"Do you think you brought everything you need?" Rom angled his head in the direction of the overnight bag she'd packed.

"I have clean undies and my toothbrush. I'll call the house and ask somebody to have the rest packed up and sent over later." Meghan wiggled her ass in his lap, rubbing against him. "Maybe I should have packed more pairs of panties. You ripped off all the clothes I wore earlier. I could run out."

"Then you'll have to stay naked. What a shame." Rom ran his hand under her shirt and followed the curves of her breasts.

She laughed. "Yeah, I can tell you hate the idea. Your roommate probably wouldn't like that, though, and I bet the hypno stare doesn't work on other vampires."

"You'd win that bet." Rom tweaked her nipple through the flimsy fabric of her bra.

"How big is your place, anyway?" Meghan arched into his hand as she spoke.

"I told you, it's the top floor. Big. Plenty of space for privacy." He lowered his head to scrape his teeth over her nipple and she shuddered in reaction.

"That feels so good, Rom." She sighed as he nipped at her breasts, feeling heat rising under her skin, pulsing low between her legs.

"Near dawn," Rom said, kissing the valley between her breasts. "I might have time to get inside you again before we fall asleep."

"Sounds like it'll be a good way to wake up." Meghan smiled at him and moved into his kiss as his mouth came to claim hers.

It was a short ride to Rom's building. He carried her bag over his shoulder and held her around the waist with his other arm, as if he didn't want to let go of her. The apartment seemed empty when they entered it, and Rom guided her to his bedroom, set her bag in a corner and began stripping. "The sun is rising. Get naked."

"The romance is dead." Meghan grinned at him and got out of her clothes at high speed, her fingers flying, fabric slithering to the ground.

"Well, so are we." Rom pulled back the covers on the king-sized bed and climbed in, patting the empty space beside him. "Come here."

She felt her clit swelling and her sex growing slicker. "You didn't tell me turning into a bloodsucking fiend would make me a sex fiend." Meghan joined him on the bed and moved her body against his, rocking into him with urgent motions.

"It doesn't. That's all you and me."

"Nice."

"Very." Rom pulled Meghan on top of him, positioned her, and drove his cock up into her until he was seated fully inside.

"Ahh." Meghan sighed her satisfaction and cuddled into his chest, grinding her pelvis into his as a strange weight settled over her, pressing her down. "Is that dawn?"

"Yes." Rom's lips brushed her forehead. "We'll finish this when you wake up."

"Better than coffee." Meghan tightened her inner muscles around him and then slid into a deep, dreamless sleep.

Hours later, Meghan was spent and smiling as she punched numbers into her cell phone. She was lying on her belly in the bed and Rom was running his hands over the curves of her ass. She wiggled to let him know she appreciated the attention.

"Hi, Lisa," she said when the phone was picked up on the other end. "I wanted to let you know where I am so you won't worry."

"Let me guess," Lisa said. "There's a guy."

"There is." And he was scraping his teeth over her bare ass, making her shudder.

"I knew something was up with you. That's the reason you've been so upset lately, isn't it?"

"Well…" It was a good explanation, and Meghan hated to lie outright.

"And you didn't want anybody to know until you two had worked it out," Lisa went on. "I don't blame you, the press gets a hold of everything and no fledgling relationship needs that kind of pressure."

"Exactly," Meghan said. "So I'll be moving out. Have moved out, actually. I need to arrange to have movers come and pack up my things."

"No problem. Give me your new address and I'll take care of it."

Meghan recited the information and hung up before she started moaning into the receiver. Behind her, Rom lifted her hips and pushed her legs apart.

"Sex fiend," she said, but it sounded like an endearment and not an accusation.

"You want me to stop, then?"

"*No.*" Meghan arched her lower back to angle herself for him and pushed back into him as he pushed into her.

His soft laugh floated over her as he took her again.

She was thoroughly sated when they finally dressed and left the bedroom, just in time to hear the doorbell.

"Expecting somebody?" Meghan asked Rom. "A client? A victim?"

"No."

They walked towards the door, but a tall blond man dressed all in black beat them to it. "I'll get it."

He must be the elusive Valentine, Meghan decided.

After checking the peephole and presumably ensuring that there wasn't a militant brand of Jehovah's Witness on the other side bearing a wooden stake, he opened the door.

"Meghan?" Lisa came through the door and nearly collided with Valentine. "Hello."

Val stared at her for a long moment before he spoke. "Lisette."

"Lisa," she corrected.

He took a step forward, one hand moving up to touch her hair and tuck a strand behind one ear. "You've cut your hair."

"No, I always keep it short. It gets in the way enough as it is."

"Let it grow and I'll braid it for you."

She snorted. "What is that, a pick-up line? I don't date Goths."

"You don't like my clothes?" Valentine leaned towards her and said, "They come off."

"I thought you said he didn't like women," Meghan said, nudging Romney.

"He doesn't. He likes this one, though." Rom shrugged and pulled her closer. "This should be interesting."

"Love is in the air." Meghan grinned at him, letting him see the emotion brimming her eyes.

"Is it." Rom gave her a long look, reading the answer in her face, then bent his head to kiss her. She leaned into it, her lips softening under his, opening for him, giving him her heart with her response. He'd given her so much, and there was so much more ahead, tonight and every night to come. She'd thought she'd reached the end, and it was just beginning.

About the Author

To learn more about Charlene Teglia, please visit www.charleneteglia.com. Send an email to Charlene@charleneteglia.com or join her forum to join in the fun with other readers as well as Charlene Teglia! http://charleneteglia.com/forum/

Look for these titles

Now Available
The Gripping Beast by Charlene Teglia

Coming Soon:
Miss Lonely Hearts by Charlene Teglia

Samhain Publishing, Ltd.

It's all about the story…

Action/Adventure
Fantasy
Historical
Horror
Mainstream
Mystery/Suspense
Non-Fiction
Paranormal
Red Hots!
Romance
Science Fiction
Western
Young Adult

http://www.samhainpublishing.com